MW01147505

Fractured

Battling Demons, Volume 2

Kris Morris

Published by Kris Morris, 2016.

FRACTURED

First edition. August 29, 2016.

Written by Kris Morris.

This is an unauthorised work of fiction based on a television series. All royalties paid to the author will be donated to TheHorseCourse, a children's charity in Dorset, England.

Thank you to my dear husband for believing in me, my sons for inspiration, and my friends Carole, Abby, Janet, and Anneke for ceaseless encouragement and for tolerating my insecurities.

Special thanks to my dear friend Abby Bukofzer and my son Karl for assisting with editing. And to my talented husband, Tim, for designing book covers.

I love you all!

Chapter 1

The gloomy skies and falling mizzle seemed to exacerbate Martin's sense of foreboding as he drove along the A-39 on his way to Truro. His sessions with Dr. Newell had forced him to confront painful childhood memories. The revelation that his parents' failure to feel any love for him was a product of their own inadequacies, initially brought a sense of relief. He had even allowed himself to accept that there was not something inherently wrong with him, an idea which had for years explained his parents' loathing of him. But in doing so, he had permitted what his wife referred to as his demons to shake loose of the emotional restraints he had used to control them for forty-odd years. His ramparts had been breached, leaving him feeling vulnerable.

The wind buffeted the Lexus as he made his way on to the River Camel bridge. He glanced out his side window as a flock of sandpipers mined the mud for invertebrates before sprinting off across the tidal flat, their frenetic movements rousing an egret from it's stiff, unipedal stance. It flew up and Martin's eyes tracked it for a moment. The gracefulness of its wingbeats had a temporary palliative effect on him, easing his tension as the bird crossed the span in front of him. He drew in a deep breath and held it before letting it rush back out in a heavy sigh.

The precipitation was falling in sheets of wind-blown rain by the time he arrived at his therapist's office, and he flipped up his collar before making a dash for the building.

Dr. Newell opened their session by re-addressing Martin's concerns that his own issues could negatively affect his son. "Martin, without getting into the whole nature-nurture debate,

I'd like to stress that I truly believe your struggles stem almost entirely from your abysmal upbringing. I'm sure you came into this world with a sensitive and introverted temperament, and that you would have benefited greatly from having parents who were loving, encouraging, and gentle with their approach to discipline. Unfortunately, that didn't happen for you. Quite the opposite I'm afraid."

"I think I'm beginning to understand that," Martin said, resting his elbows on the armrests of his chair and lacing his fingers together in front of him.

The therapist scanned the folder of patient notes on his desk. "From what you and your wife have told me, your son is also rather sensitive and introverted."

"Yes, but he seems happy."

"Good. You and Louisa are the sort of parents that James needs if he's to grow up confident and comfortable in his own skin."

Martin shook his head. "But I have very little to go on. I don't know the first thing about raising a child."

"You may be lacking in experience, Martin, but you have the benefit of hindsight. You'll be able to appreciate your son's emotional needs as he grows, because you learned first-hand how *not* to parent a sensitive and introverted child.

"You'll also have a much better understanding of how James will react to any disciplinary measures that you and Louisa will need to take.

"Louisa will need your guidance, in fact. She'll likely struggle to be able to relate to your son the way that you will. I can assure you, Martin, that your presence in James's life can only be beneficial."

Martin eyed the man dubiously. "I'm not so sure. I don't even know how to play with my son. Louisa thrusts plastic giraffes and stuffed bears at me ... tells me I need to play with him. I'm at a loss. I feel ridiculous trying to entertain him with those sorts of things."

"There are other things a boy needs from his father. I suspect you'll excel in many of those areas. You must have been a fine teacher or you never would have been appointed a team of registrars. And you're knowledgeable about many things. You and James may share a hobby at some point—astronomy, model building, or repairing old clocks," he said, waving a hand in the air. "It's really hard to predict how much any of us will have in common with our children."

"James appears to enjoy watching surgical videos with me, but Louisa disapproves. She worries that they'll make a lasting impression. I personally, don't see the problem. She doesn't think twice about allowing him to watch videos of talking, impertinent train engines."

"Perhaps that's a topic that needs to be addressed at an upcoming couple's session." Dr. Newell leaned back in his chair and steepled his fingers. "Now, as to your concerns about becoming like your father ... Have you struggled with staying in control of your anger when dealing with James?"

"Up to this point, no. I find James calms me. I'm concerned about the future ... if I may become short-tempered when he tries my patience. I worry about what will happen to our relationship when he becomes aware of my—my issues. That he'll be embarrassed by me ... wish he had a different father."

The psychiatrist came around to sit on his usual perch at the end of the desk. "I hate to have to tell you this, but most children do have times when they wish for different parents. We can't always make our children happy. I'm sure you've had children in your surgery whose parents have tried to do just that. And those children have probably left a trail of destruction in their wake."

Air hissed from Martin's nose as he shifted in his chair. "I understand all of that, but I don't want to make life more difficult for my son by being who I am … by his being associated with me. Right now, James enjoys my company, but I'm afraid that when he gets older … when he discovers my … idiosyncrasies …"

"That he won't want you any more? That you'll be rejected?"

Martin rubbed his sweaty palms on his thighs. "James is the first person who's accepted me the way I am, who doesn't seem to object to my … *unusual* qualities, as Louisa would say. I know there'll come a time when he'll wish I wasn't … me."

"Martin, you will understand and accept James for who he is, and there's every chance that James will feel the same way about you. I think that's the most likely scenario, in fact."

Martin swallowed back the lump in his throat as he considered the therapist's words.

Dr. Newell returned to his chair, pulling himself up to his desk. "I asked you last week to make several lists of adjectives. How did that go?"

"Fine. It didn't seem terribly complicated." Martin pulled a piece of paper from his breast pocket and handed it to the man.

After scanning the lists, the psychiatrist looked up at him. "Which of the items you have listed here would you say is the most important to you?"

"Social confidence. I think that if I felt more confident in social situations it would make it easier for me to be polite. And perhaps, if I were more confident in social situations, I could better tolerate people. Louisa would like to get out more than we do. I want her to be happy."

The doctor nodded. "I find it very interesting that you have *liking people* on the list describing the man that *you'd* like to be, but that you think James and Louisa want you to be well-liked. That suggests to me that how you see *yourself* is what's important to you, but you think that how others see you is what's important to your wife and son. That you aren't as concerned with how others see you as you think your wife and son are."

Martin shook his head. "I don't understand where you're going with this."

The doctor picked up his pen, clicking it in and out. "What I'm suggesting is that maybe we need to discuss where your motivation for making changes is coming from. It's fine to want your family to be happy with the man you are, but it's more important that *you* are happy with the man you are."

Martin left Dr. Newell's office mulling over what he had said, thinking about the conversation he would need to have with Louisa when he arrived home that night.

Chapter 2

The rain had stopped, but the wind had turned colder as Martin walked from his psychiatrist's building to the hospital next door. He found Chris in his office going over statistics and operating costs for the Cornwall ambulance system.

"Mart, good to see you!"

Martin laid his binder down on Chris's desk and took a seat. "Mm, yes. How have you been keeping?"

"Quite well," Chris replied as he set his biro down and eyed his friend. "You've lost a bit of weight, mate. All okay?"

"I've just been preoccupied with some personal issues," Martin said, shrugging his shoulders. "Not much appetite ... you know."

Chris cocked his head at him. "No, I don't know. Is there trouble over there in Paradise?"

Martin gave a derisive snort. "No. I've, ah ... I've been seeing a therapist ... trying to work through some things from my past."

"Oh, about your parents?" Chris asked as he tried to conceal his surprise at his friend's openness.

"Mm."

"How's it going?"

Martin rubbed at a fingernail. "It's been difficult. There have been some memories that resurfaced that I'd rather not think about. But I need to deal with things if I want Louisa to stay with me."

"Well, I admire you. You know, Mart, you really did get stuck with some crap parents."

"Mm, I'm aware of that." Martin cleared his throat and got up from his chair. "How do you think we'll fare with this NHS committee tonight?"

"I just really can't say. Money's tight, and they have to make cuts somewhere. I just hope it doesn't have to be at the expense of the citizens of Cornwall. I need you to make a pretty convincing argument that the air ambulance is absolutely vital to the coastal communities, Martin. That any cuts right now could put lives at risk."

"I'll do my best."

Chris got up and walked towards the door. "Come on, let's go see if they have anything decent to eat in the canteen."

The committee meeting started promptly at half six. Martin glanced around the room, noting what he deemed to be the usual assortment of pencil pushing bureaucrats and puffed-up time wasters.

He had presented his arguments, stressing his point the best he could. But he was getting the feeling that the committee members did not appreciate the patient transport problems that were unique to Cornwall, the isolated moors and coastal areas in particular.

The meeting dragged on, and Martin was getting anxious to get on the road and home to his family. After all the other presenters had pleaded their cases, Chris led everyone out to the hall where a Royal Cornwall spokesperson was waiting to begin a tour of the hospital, focusing on the services they provided.

The group was just beginning to move down the hall when Chris pulled Martin aside. "Why don't you slip out and head on home, mate. It'll be late by the time you get back, even if you leave now.

"Are you sure? You may need someone to back you up later."

"Nope, I'll be fine. This thing could go on for a while. You've done what I needed you to do."

"I'm not sure I helped our case tonight. Sorry about that."

"You did all you could." Chris shrugged his shoulders. "I'm not sure anyone could persuade this lot any differently. I think they came into it with their minds made up. You get on home to that lovely wife of yours, and I'll give you a call as soon as I hear of a decision on this."

"Good luck." Martin turned to make his way towards the hospital entrance. He groaned when he slipped behind the wheel of the Lexus and looked at the clock. *Eight-twenty already. No time with James and Louisa tonight.*

Traffic was light, and Martin made good time. James would be sound asleep in bed by now, and Louisa, once the activity at the school had wrapped up, would come home and curl up under a blanket on the sofa with whatever book she happened to be reading at the moment. The corners of his mouth tugged up as he remembered her promise of the proper kiss that would be awaiting him when he got home.

He was coming up on Wadebridge and would be back in Portwenn in another ten minutes. As he approached the bridge over the River Camel, headlights from a vehicle coming around the curve on the other side of the span shone in his face, blinding him momentarily. As his eyes readjusted to the darkness, the outline of a large oncoming transport lorry loomed in front of him. He hit the brake and tried to veer, but the guardrail prevented him from avoiding a collision.

The fear that he may be leaving his wife a widow and his son fatherless swept through him in an instant, before a tremendous jolt of energy coursed through his body.

The tour back at the Royal Cornwall was concluding with a stop at the Emergency Department. The group's arrival was timely. They were able to observe as a call came in requesting an air ambulance. A lorry had collided with an automobile near Wadebridge, resulting in two casualties, one critical.

Chris leaned back against the ED check-in desk, his arms crossed in front of him. "The transit time to the Royal Cornwall by Wadebridge's ground ambulance will be a minimum of forty-five minutes," Chris explained. "With critical cases such as this, it's not likely the patient would survive without helicopter transport. Our air ambulance cuts twenty-five minutes or more off that transit time, so I'm sure you can see just how vital the service is for the people of Cornwall."

The group waited, listening in on the conversation between the ground unit on scene and the dispatch unit at Newquay where the air ambulance was based.

Dispatch: "The air crew's been made aware of the situation and should arrive at your location in approximately twelve minutes. Do you have vitals for us at this time?"

Wadebridge Paramedic: "We have one male victim with minor cuts to the face and hands ... normal vital signs. He's being transported to Newquay by ground. We're working on extricating the second male victim from the vehicle. He's haemorrhaging from both an injury to the upper left thigh and the lower right arm. His arm is pinned between the door of the vehicle and the door frame. We suspect a fractured right femur as well as fractures to the lower legs. We'll get his vitals to you as soon as we have them."

Dispatch: "Okay, keep us informed of any further information or any changes to the situation. They'll be expecting you at RCH. in about thirty minutes."

Awareness began to return to Martin. He could hear voices. And there were lights ... lights shining on him, in his face. He squinted and tried to raise his hand to shade his eyes, but he couldn't move it. He pulled harder, and searing pain shot up his arm and through his shoulder. He heard the voices again, this time louder and clearer.

"Try to stay still, mate! We're going to get you out, but you need to stay still! You need to stop moving!"

Martin was confused. He didn't recognise the voice, and he was wracked with pain.

A shadowy figure moved to the left of him. "Sir, you've been in an accident. Try not to move. We're going to take care of you."

Martin attempted to respond, but he found himself gasping for air. The light was getting brighter and the images clearer. He could now make out the face of a man beside him, illuminated by a pulsating light.

"Sir, I'm a paramedic. I'm here to help you. Can you hear me?"

Martin tried to nod his head, but his thoughts and movements were now dulled by an excruciating pain rippling through his body.

He could hear more voices now ... conversation. The paramedic's voice echoed behind the ringing in his ears. "Sir, are you Martin Ellingham? The police officer ran the tags on your vehicle, and it's registered to Martin Ellingham. Is that your name?"

Martin forced his head up and down. He tried to look at the man beside him, but his eyes wouldn't focus; the image was blurred by tears.

The committee back at Royal Cornwall waited to hear further word of the patient being prepared for transfer. The hospital spokesperson explained that, once the victim was on board the air ambulance, a prehospital evaluation would be conducted, and Royal Cornwall would get more complete information, which would be needed to prepare for the incoming patient.

Wadebridge Paramedic: Dispatch, we have some preliminary vitals for you."

Dispatch: "Go ahead Wadebridge."

Wadebridge Paramedic: "BP is 100/75 ... heart rate is 95. The patient is cool and clammy and in severe pain. We're getting a drip going now and will administer fentanyl."

Dispatch: "Thank you Wadebridge. Let us know when the transfer to the heli has been made."

Wadebridge Paramedic: "Righto. Dispatch, I've just been informed that the critical victim has been identified as Martin Ellingham, the GP over in Portwenn. Thought you might want a heads-up on that."

Dispatch: "Thank you Wadebridge. We'll pass that information on to RCH."

Chris felt the blood rush from his head when he heard the paramedic's words. He immediately began to run through the likely scenario when Martin was brought in. The arm injury sounded severe, and they would be needing a vascular specialist on hand. Royal Cornwall's man was good, but not a surgeon with the experience or skills that Martin would likely be needing.

He put in a call to Robert Dashwood, a colleague and former tutor of Martin's, now at Imperial Hospital in London. Robert and an orthopaedic specialist would be flying down and planned to arrive in approximately four hours.

Chris then called the police constable in Portwenn to inform him of what had transpired, asking that he find someone to drive Martin's wife to Truro. The next call he would need to make would be to Louisa, and Chris was dreading that task.

"Dr. Ellingham, I'm Andy Foster, one of the paramedics out of Wadebridge. The air ambulance should be here in a few minutes. We're going to get a drip started ... give you something for the pain. You're pretty tangled up in the wreckage, so we're going to need to cut the vehicle apart. There'll be some noise, but we're going to get you out, Doc."

Martin found the light growing dimmer again and sounds becoming muffled. There was a smell though ... a familiar smell. He could feel his trousers growing wet. He couldn't make sense of what was happening. It was dark and cramped. He couldn't move his legs, and his right arm was fixed in an excruciating position. Warmth spread across his thighs, and a feeling of fear and humiliation overcame him. The sensation returned him to consciousness. The familiar smell filled the air again, triggering an intense wave of nausea. He couldn't control the urge to vomit any longer.

He began to cough, choking on his own vomited matter, and he struggled to breathe, as his surroundings became fuzzy once again before turning to inky blackness.

He was back in theatre, a body laid out and prepped in front of him. The whine of the bone saw pierced his ears. The smell of blood permeated his senses. The smell of blood ... that was the smell!

Martin was brought back to the light and the present by the sound of Andy Foster's voice. "Doc, I'm going to cover you with a blanket now while we cut you out of here. How's the pain ... any better?"

Martin tried to shake his head in answer to him, but he was trapped in agony.

The paramedics worked frantically to get him out of the vehicle. He was haemorrhaging from both his right arm and left leg, and they could get to neither injury to stanch the flow of blood.

He listened to the paramedics shouting directives over the din of breaking glass, the hum of motors, and the metallic creaks and pops generated by the equipment being used to free him. He fought to stay awake, but he could feel life slipping away from him.

Chapter 3

Martin was on the verge of losing consciousness as the rescue crew worked to free him from the Lexus. They broke out the windows and pried off the roof before folding back the dashboard.

The release of the components which had pinned his legs in the vehicle caused a sudden intensification of the pain he was in, and he screamed involuntarily, the sound muffled by the blood and regurgitated material in his mouth.

Another metallic screech preceded an agonising jolt that shot through his arm and shoulder, sucking the breath from his lungs.

"Okay, he's free!" shouted one of the ground medics.

"Someone watch his arm ... we'll take him out on this side!"

Martin cried out again as his body was lifted from of the wreckage and placed on a gurney. The pain was excruciating. He wanted it to stop; he wanted to die.

The incessant flashing of emergency vehicle lights dimmed as he was quickly loaded on to the helicopter. He tried to listen to the voices around him, but the ringing in his ears was growing louder. He caught enough to know, though, that it was a desperate situation.

A female member of the crew spoke to him reassuringly as she caressed his uninjured arm. "We're going to have you to hospital very soon, Dr. Ellingham."

Martin stared up at the woman with unseeing eyes as tears rolled down his cheeks.

"We're on our way to hospital now. Your family will be there for you," she continued. "Hang on, we're almost there now. Your family will be waiting for you, so you need to hang on."

He listened to the female voice. It was lilting, like Louisa's. It was comforting, like the voice she used to console their son.

She was kneeling over him with James in her arms. She was emotional, hysterical. "Come back here, Martin!" she cried out. "You cannot just leave us! Don't—you—dare!" His eyes blinked involuntarily with each enunciated word. "Don't you <u>*dare*</u> *walk away!"*

He didn't want to leave them, to walk away ... to, yet again, be cheated out of being loved. His parents had cheated him out of the love that he'd longed for his first four decades on Earth, but he had James and Louisa's love now. They didn't want him to leave. They wanted him, and that was his reason for living.

After getting the answer phone message at the surgery, Chris scrolled through his contacts and rang the number Martin had given him for his aunt in case of an emergency.

Though he didn't give a reason for his need to reach Louisa, the abruptness of Chris's words and the seriousness of his tone caused Ruth to worry.

Louisa was on stage, introducing the Portwenn Primary teachers, when Pippa Woodley hurried over to tell her that she needed to take a call in her office.

She glanced between Pippa and the rest of the staff. "We're not quite done, yet."

"Just go, Louisa. It sounds important. I'll finish up here."

Louisa's thoughts turned to James, and she rushed down the hallway, anxiety about her son building. She pulled her mobile from her pocket and turned it on. There was only one missed call from a number she didn't recognise. Fingers fumbling with her keys, she unlocked her office door, trying not to fear the worst. "Hello, this is Louisa," she said breathlessly after grabbing the phone from her desk.

"Louisa, it's Chris Parsons. I'm afraid I'm calling with some bad news."

Her breath caught in her throat. "What is it, Chris?"

"Martin was in an accident on his way back to Portwenn tonight. I've asked—"

"An accident? A car accident?"

"Yes. I've called your consta—"

"Was he hurt? He wasn't hurt, was he?"

"Yes, he did sustain injuries. They haven't brought him into the Trauma Centre yet, but you should be here. I've spoken with your constable. He's going to see to transportation for you."

Louisa leaned forward on her desk as her head began to spin.

"What do you mean, the Trauma Centre? Is it bad, Chris? He'll be all right, won't he?"

"He hasn't come in yet. The air ambulance is on its way. I was assuming you'd be at home so there may be someone waiting for you at the surgery. Stay there in your office, and I'll see if I can get hold of your constable again ... have someone come and pick you up. I don't want you walking home."

Louisa was trying to absorb what Chris was telling her while at the same time mentally making arrangements for James's care.

"But Chris, is he all right? Is Martin all right?"

"We'll know more when they bring him in. Right now, it's important that you get here. I have your mobile number. I'll call you the minute I know more."

She rang off, and sitting back on her desk, she began to cry.

"Louisa?" A soft voice said. Joe Penhale stood in the doorway. Her face, drained of colour, told the constable that she had received the news.

"I'm going to run you over to Truro," he said. "I picked Ruth up and took her to your place. She sent Poppy on home and said you shouldn't worry about James; she'll stay with him. We should go though." Joe came over and took Louisa by the arm, leading her down the hallway.

"Joe, did Chris tell you anything?" Louisa asked as they sped down the road out of the village.

"Just that the doc was in an accident. We'll find out more when we get there." Joe reached out and squeezed her hand.

When they approached the River Camel bridge, the flashing lights of the remaining emergency vehicles illuminated the Land Rover. A policeman waved traffic through in the oncoming lane. Joe glanced over at Louisa, but it didn't seem to have registered with her that this was where her husband's accident had occurred.

Martin could just make out the movements of people around him. The roar of the helicopter's engine became a muffled hum in his ears. The medics on board scrambled to try to slow the bleeding from his wounds, applying pressure to a severe laceration on his inner thigh and to the brachial artery in his upper arm. A third IV was started in an effort to keep up with the body fluids he was rapidly losing. Splints were affixed to both legs and his right arm.

He drifted in and out of consciousness. The periods of awareness brought excruciating pain. The periods of darkness sank him into mental misery, bringing back memories from his childhood—sitting on the floor in his father's study, blood pooling on the wood under him and soaking into his clothing; his father grasping and pulling on his arm, causing horrendous pain; being shoved into the cupboard under the stairs.

He was laying on his injured arm with no room to move. He tried not to cry, but the pain was excruciating. A warm wetness spread across his lap and with it came the surety that he had yet again lost control of himself.

The smell of the blood on his trousers nauseated him, and he could no longer keep his stomach contents from being expelled. Pain, smells, and the fear he was feeling made it difficult to breathe. He swallowed back a sob; he had been told to be quiet.

Chris stood by the Emergency Department desk, waiting for further word about his friend. The committee members were transfixed by the drama unfolding before them.

While concerned for Martin, Chris still had a job to do, and he forced his attention back to the NHS committee he had been charged with influencing. "Now that everything has been turned over to the air ambulance medics, the transmissions will be between the staff here at Royal Cornwall and the air medics on board the helicopt—" Chris was interrupted by the voice of one of the ambulance team.

Air medic crew leader: We have the patient on board and are now in transit. We've been able to slow the haemorrhaging but the patient's BP is still falling. I suggest you notify the blood bank to be ready for us.

Royal Cornwall: We're already on top of it.

Air medic: Brilliant. We have the latest vitals for you.

Royal Cornwall: Go ahead.

Air medic: BP is 85/68. Heart rate is 105. And we now have a body temperature—96.3. We've wrapped the patient in a warming blanket and would like permission to start a dopamine drip.

Royal Cornwall: That's an affirmative on the dopamine. We'll be ready for you when you arrive.

Air medic: Jolly good. We're about five minutes out.

Martin's vital signs indicated that he was going into hypovolaemic shock, a life-threatening condition that often develops in polytrauma patients who have suffered massive blood loss. Though Chris had told his friend's wife he would call her with any news, this was news he thought would be best delivered in person.

Louisa sat quietly next to Joe Penhale, thinking about the phone call she had received less than an hour before. She bit at her lip as Chris's words now began to penetrate more clearly. She looked over at the constable.

"Joe, would Chris have told me that I needed to come right away if Martin hadn't been seriously injured? Would they have needed the air ambulance?"

The constable hadn't shared all of the information passed on to him by Chris. He had been on scene after autos were hit by lorries before, and he knew that the occupants in the car usually did not fare well. "I don't think we should try to make guesses about what's happened, Louisa. We'll find out more when we get there. Should only be another fifteen minutes or so," he said, trying to give her a reassuring smile.

Chapter 4

As soon as the air ambulance landed on the helipad, the air ambulance crew rushed an unconscious Martin to the hospital Emergency Department. The ED team was waiting for them, and the transfer of the patient was made to the Royal Cornwall's specialised Trauma Centre.

Chris quickly excused himself from the NHS group when he heard the announcement of Martin's arrival. "I hope you'll forgive me, but that's my mate in there," he said, waving a hand. "I need to go. I'm sure you'll keep me informed of your decision," he added, as he backed through the automatic doors.

He pressed himself against the tiled wall, out of the way of the men and women of the trauma crew as he watched their heroic efforts to save his friend. Martin was unrecognisable to him, his face pale and bloodied. He looked lifeless on the table, and his wounds were severe. Bones were visible, protruding from his right forearm and lower left leg.

The Trauma Centre team went to work assessing his injuries as blood trickled steadily from several wounds, even as hospital staff tried to slow it. A team member held down a pressure dressing which had been placed over the laceration on his thigh, adding additional dressings, one on top of the other, as the last one became blood-soaked. Another team member inserted a Foley catheter equipped with a temperature sensor to monitor both urine output and core body temperature, both important indicators when assessing the severity of shock.

"Get another warmed Hartmann's solution going in him," ordered Ed Christianson, the consultant in charge of the trauma team. We need to get his core temp up. What about haematocrit?"

"Twenty-three percent," replied a team nurse.

Ed waved a hand at a male nurse. "Okay ... Flannery, get a jugular IV going and get packed cells started."

The young man gave Mr. Christianson a nod before pulling a plastic pouch from a cart.

Chris glanced at his watch, realising Louisa would be arriving shortly. He pulled Ed Christianson aside and asked him for a brief rundown so that he would have some information to pass on to Louisa.

"He's very critical. We've slowed the bleeding from the external wounds and have been pushing the warmed Hartmann's to get his core temperature up ... given him colloids to replace the lost fluids, but the vitals continue to deteriorate.

"We're going to take him into CT next. No doubt we'll have internal injuries to deal with. Most likely the spleen or a renal artery has been compromised ... could be the liver, too. I'll know more after we get some pictures. We'll get him stabilised as best we can ... take him into theatre and patch him up for now. Then we'll let the guys from Imperial clean up after us when they get here. We'll start there, but as you know, like most polytrauma cases, we'll have to play catch-up for a while."

"Thanks, Ed. I know he's in good hands."

Ed patted Chris's shoulder. "I don't envy you having to explain all this to his wife."

"Yeah, well ..." Chris said. The surgeon turned and started towards his patient before Chris called to him. "Ed ..."

Mr. Christianson took a step back and raised an eyebrow at him. "Yeah?"

"Do everything you can with that arm. I keep hoping he'll get back to doing surgery again."

The man gave him a nod. "Yep, I'll do my very best."

Chris walked down the hallway to the lavatory, ducking in long enough to collect his thoughts before going to find his friend's wife.

Joe and Louisa had arrived at the Emergency Department waiting area a half hour after the air ambulance arrived. Having been instructed to wait until Chris came to talk to her, Louisa now grew increasingly anxious about Martin, hoping that her worst fears would not be realised.

Her breath caught in her throat when she looked up and saw her husband's friend walking towards her. She didn't need to ask; the strain showing on his face told her the news was not good.

He led her to a nearby break room and sat her down, pulling up a chair next to her. "It was a bad accident, Louisa. Martin's struggling right now, but our Emergency Department people are very good. He's still in the Trauma Centre at the moment."

Tears welled in her eyes as Chris began to detail the situation. "He's lost a considerable amount of blood, but they've slowed the haemorrhaging. However, deteriorating vital signs suggest that he's bleeding internally. He'll be going to CT next. Once we have those images, we'll have a better idea as to what's going on."

Louisa listened, unable to respond. The fear and worry that she had kept under control up to this point was now overtaking her. She had been plunged into a horrible nightmare.

Chris continued. "He has several fractures—both lower legs and the right femur, as well as his right radius and ulna," he said drawing a line across his forearm with his finger. "The left lower leg fractures and the right forearm fractures are open, meaning the bones have come through the skin. He also has a severe laceration to his left thigh."

Unable to contain her emotions any longer, Louisa began to sob quietly. Chris got up to get a box of tissues before sitting back down beside her. He slid over and put an arm around her trembling shoulders. "He has an excellent team working on him," he said. "And I called Robert Dashwood as soon as I heard about the accident. He'll be arriving in about three hours. There's no better vascular specialist in the country." He gave her a small smile. "Well, not for the last five years or so anyway."

She took in a slow ragged breath and nodded her head.

"And Robert's bringing Imperial's top orthopaedic surgeon with him to handle the fracture reductions. Martin really couldn't be in better hands."

"Thank you for calling them, Chris. I appreciate it and I'm sure Martin does as—" Louisa glanced up at her husband's friend. "Does Martin know they're coming?"

Chris shook his head. "He's not been conscious."

She squeezed her eyes shut. "Is he going to be all right? I just want to know he'll be all right."

Martin was a straight shooter, but Chris wasn't sure if he would want him to be completely honest with Louisa. "It's a precarious situation. He's in what we call hypovolaemic shock ... shock caused by massive blood loss. His condition is critical at the moment. The first priority is to figure out where he's losing blood, and get that taken care of."

Louisa straightened up in her chair. "I want to see him, Chris."

"I don't think that'd be a good idea. They need room to work in there."

"But if ... if something should happen ... I have to see him, Chris." She watched him, her eyes pleading.

"I'll see what they say, Louisa. But we need to do what's in Martin's best interests ... right?"

"Yes, yes. You're right. But if I can ... will you let me know?"

"Certainly," Chris said, patting her hand before getting to his feet. "I'll take you back to the waiting area, then I better get back down there."

Martin had regained consciousness by the time Chris returned. As he approached the Trauma Centre doors, he could hear his friend moaning in pain.

"Hey, Mart, it's going to be okay," he said, hurrying over to take hold of his uninjured hand. "You have a great team working on you. You're going to be okay."

Martin grabbed on to Chris's sleeve. "I want ... to see Louisa! I need my ... wife!" he said, his voice weak and hoarse.

"You don't want her to see you like this, Martin. Let them get you into theatre ... get you stabilised and cleaned up a bit. Then you can see Louisa."

"Chris ... please! I ... need her!"

Chris's gaze flitted between the blue illuminated numbers on the patient monitor, warning of the patient's deteriorating vital signs, to the surgeon in charge. "Ed ...?"

The surgeon gave him a nod of his head. "Make it quick; they'll be ready for us in theatre soon."

Louisa rushed over when she saw her husband's friend appear at the E.D. doors.

"He's asking for you. They're almost ready to take him to surgery, so this'll have to be brief," Chris said, moving her towards the Trauma Centre. "And Louisa, Martin's very anxious and distressed right now. Do what you can to ease his fears ... encourage him."

Chris tried to prepare Louisa for what to expect, but he could see the shock on her face when she walked up to the table that her husband was lying on. His face was swollen and spattered with now dried-on blood, his skin pale and bluish in colour. They had covered his body with a warming blanket, but his limbs were exposed as the team continued to work to slow the haemorrhaging.

"Focus on his eyes, Louisa. This will be easier for you if you focus on his eyes," Chris said softly.

Instruments and metal trays clattered, plastic wrappers rattled as they were peeled away from equipment, and the voices of the doctors and nurses in the room hummed in her ears. She could hear her husband's breathing—rapid and shallow—as she approached, and the fear in his eyes was obvious.

Martin turned his head when he saw her movement at his side. He attempted to reach for her, but his arm fell limply, dangling over the side of the table.

She picked up his hand and held it to her face. "I'm here, Martin."

A team member's movements drew her gaze involuntarily to his fractured legs. She wanted to be strong for him, but the tears began to flow when her eyes settled on his mangled arm.

She leaned over, placing a gentle kiss on his forehead, and he let out a moan as another jolt of pain coursed through him. Pulling back, she caressed his cheek. "Shh, Martin. I'm here ... right here."

"Louisa ... I don't *want* to leave you!" he said, his voice raspy and whispered as he began to cry.

"You're not going to leave me; you're going to be *just—fine*. You have all the best people helping you."

Martin nodded his head at her "Love ... you and ... and James. Always."

"I love you too, Martin. They're going to take you to theatre now, but I'll be with you when you wake up. I'll be right next to you, holding your hand." She forced a reassuring smile.

Ed Christianson gave a jerk of his head.

"Louisa, they're ready for him now," Chris said.

She nodded back. Then, leaning over she touched her lips to his before talking softly into his ear. "I'm not going anywhere,

Martin. I *promise*. I'll be right here with you when you wake up."

Chris laid a hand on his friend's arm for a moment before taking hold of Louisa's shoulders and steering her towards the doors. Martin's breathing became more rapid, and panic entered his eyes again as he watched her move away.

"I'll be waiting when you wake up, Martin," she said, giving him another encouraging nod.

He started to call out to her, but a nurse shifted his arm to prepare him to be moved, and his words were garbled in a loud groan.

Chris took Louisa back to the still empty break room, sitting her down at the table.

"Louisa, I'm going to go get you something hot to drink. Would you prefer tea or coffee?"

She shook her head. "I don't care."

Chris returned a short time later with two cups in his hands. Louisa had her head resting on her arms on the table top.

"How are you doing?" he asked.

"I feel a bit nauseous."

"That's understandable. It's been an emotional shock." Chris slid a cup over in front of her. "He's in excellent hands, Louisa. The next few hours will be critical, though. They'll get the internal bleeding under control, then hopefully we'll see some improvement."

"How long will it take them? How long before I can see him?"

Chris sighed. "It depends on what kind of damage has been done, but I would guess one to two hours."

Louisa rested her elbows on the table to steady her cup of tea.

"Erm, Louisa, I hope you don't mind, but I called my wife. She's going to be here in a few minutes to keep you company. I know that you two have never met, but I thought you might benefit from having someone to talk to about all of this."

Louisa looked at him with red-rimmed eyes. "That's very kind of you, Chris ... and kind of your wife."

"Carole's known Martin almost as long as I have. I thought ... well, I hope it helps."

Louisa sipped at her hot tea. "Chris, could you go and let Joe Penhale know the latest on Martin? Tell him thank you for me? I just can't talk to anyone right now ... answer questions."

"Sure. You sit tight. I'll be right back."

Chapter 5

Chris re-entered the break room a short time later. "Louisa, this is Carole," he said as he held the door for his wife.

"Oh, Louisa," she said stepping forward and embracing her. "I am so sorry. I was shocked when Chris called me with the news."

Louisa fought to keep her composure as she wiped at her cheeks. "It's very nice of you to come."

"Well, I'm sure we would have met eventually, but I wish it was under different circumstances." Carole took a step back and pulled her purse strap over her shoulder.

"Louisa, I thought maybe we could wait in my office," Chris said. "I think we'd be a lot more comfortable, and there's a sofa if you'd like to have a lie down. It's just a few minutes' walk from here."

Her gaze darted towards the surgical theatre. "Thank you, Chris. But I want to stay close to Martin. I don't want him to be off on his own here. And someone might need to talk to me ... have some news," she said, wrapping her arms around herself.

Noticing blood on Louisa's clothing and a smear of blood on her cheek, Carole turned to her husband. "Chris, why don't you stay here with Martin, and I'll go with Louisa to your office. You can ring me if you need us or have news."

Chris shoved his hands into his pockets and nodded his head. "That'd be fine. I'll give you a call the moment there's anything to report, Louisa"

"Thank you, Chris," she said as she and Carole made their way towards the hall.

They stopped first at the lavatory. Carole used a wet paper towel to wipe the blood from Louisa's face before dabbing what she could from her skirt and the sleeve of her jumper.

"There, that's better," she said, giving her a smile. "Now, let's go see if we can find the stash of biscuits I know my husband is hiding in his office."

The CT scans had confirmed Mr. Christianson's suspicions. Martin's liver had been lacerated and his spleen had ruptured. Both were bleeding into his abdominal cavity.

Chris sat in the theatre gallery, looking on as Mr. Christianson made a midline incision to gain access to his patient's internal organs. He packed off all four quadrants of his liver with laparotomy pads before manually compressing the haemorrhaging area until the anaesthetist restored his fluid level. The laceration was then sutured and the packing material removed.

The surgeon then turned his attention to the removal of the spleen. After cutting through the ligaments supporting the organ, he tied off the splenic artery before completely freeing the organ and removing it.

The blood which had haemorrhaged into the abdominal cavity was suctioned out, and clean-up was done by flushing the area with saline solution. Ed thoroughly inspected the other organs, assuring himself before he closed that there were no further injuries.

He then went to work on the open fractures in Martin's leg and forearm, placing temporary shunts into injured blood vessels to restore adequate blood flow to his damaged limbs. The wounds were then left open, but bandaged, to be properly repaired by Mr. Dashwood and the orthopaedist from Imperial when they arrived later. The laceration to his thigh was packed off and bandaged, as well. That, too, would require the skills of the visiting surgeons.

Chris left the gallery and hurried down to get a report from Mr. Christianson.

"Well, do you have good news for me to pass on to Martin's wife?" Chris asked as the man scrubbed the blood from his arms.

The surgeon's face was drawn. It was almost one o'clock in the morning, and being charged with the care of a critically injured Martin Ellingham was an onerous responsibility.

"Well, his vitals look a lot more favourable now than they did before we went into theatre." He sighed heavily. "I don't mind telling you, Chris, I'll be happy to pass this case on to the chaps from Imperial. I'm glad you called them."

"That's a relief. I was afraid I might be stepping on toes. But it's what Martin would have done. When can his wife see him?"

"I'd say give them another fifteen minutes to get him settled in CCU, then bring her down. It'll be a while before he comes around, but she probably just wants to be close to him."

He pulled several sheets of paper towelling from the dispenser and wiped his hands dry. "You should, er ... make sure she knows he's going to be a hurtin' unit when he wakes up."

"Yep, I know. Thanks a lot, Ed. You've done outstanding work tonight," Chris said before exiting the room.

Louisa had dozed off before Chris returned to his office. Carole put her finger to her lips as she got up and stepped into the hall with her husband.

"How is he, Chris?"

Chris blew out a breath of air. "He's out of surgery and his vital signs have improved. I really should discuss this with Louisa first, though. Sorry 'bout that—proper protocol," he said before giving her a kiss.

"No need to explain. Maybe we should let her sleep, though. She was so exhausted, and she'll need her energy later, I'm sure."

"Yeah, well ... I told her I'd let her know as soon as I had any information."

They returned to the room, and Chris jostled Louisa awake before relaying the details passed on by Mr. Christianson. "You can go and see him now if you like," Chris said. "He won't be awake for a while yet, so if you'd like to slee—"

Louisa was on her feet and halfway to the door before Chris could get the words out. "No, I told him I'd be there when he woke up."

"Is Ruth staying with James tonight?" Chris asked as they walked through the hospital corridors.

"Yes, she—" Louisa stopped in her tracks. "Oh no! I haven't even thought to call her. Chris, would you mind? She's probably out of her mind with worry."

"Certainly. We'll give you some time alone with Martin, and then Carole and I'll stop in after I make the call," he said as they arrived at the Critical Care Unit.

Chris stopped with his hand on the door handle. "Louisa, I should prepare you ... Martin's going to be in a lot of pain when he wakes up. They'll get analgesics into him as quickly as possible, but it can sometimes take a little while to get things under control ... figure out what'll work for a patient. So be prepared for that. I'll get in touch with Ruth and try to be back before he comes around."

Pushing the sliding glass door of the unit aside, Chris gestured for Louisa to go through.

Martin was still asleep, but his colour was much better, and the blood had been washed from his face. Though still very tenuous, the situation didn't look as grave now as it had in the Trauma Centre.

A nurse was in the room, changing out the bottle on the IV stand. Chris spoke softly to her before picking up the chart at the end of the bed and flipping through the already lengthy patient notes.

Louisa stood at her husband's side, her hand reaching out tentatively, before pulling back. "Where can I touch him?"

Chris slipped the notes back over the hanger on the end of the bed and walked to her side.

"His left arm and hand and his head are fine. He has some nasty bruising to his chest from the seat belt ... you can touch him, just be gentle. There's an incision extending from the lower end of his sternum to below his belly button, so avoid that area."

Chris pointed to the bottles, suspended over the bed and explained, "Martin's lost a lot of blood. They're still replacing what he's lost with colloids— erm, a blood volume expander—and packed red cells. The other bottle is Hartmann's solution—fluid replacement with mineral salts. It helps to prevent acid from building up in his system."

Louisa shook her head. "Packed red cells?"

"Mm, packed red blood cells. It's the oxygen-carrying red cells that have been separated out from blood plasma. If we just gave him fluids and colloids, his blood would become too dilute—not enough red cells. It says in his notes that he's had eleven units of whole blood already, but the haemorrhaging is under control now. They need to get his platelet count and red blood cell count straightened out though."

"Eleven units ... is that a lot?"

"It's considered massive blood loss, so yes ... it's a lot."

Louisa's hand trembled as she placed it on her husband's arm and bent down to press her lips to his forehead.

Chris moved a chair over next to the bed. "Have a seat, Louisa."

The nurse put a hand on her back. "He's not awake, but go ahead and talk to him. Hearing is the first of the senses to respond."

Chris moved towards the door. "I'll go call Ruth, okay?"

"Mm, yes. Thank you, Chris."

The door rumbled shut behind him, and Louisa was left alone with her husband. She sat down in the chair and worked her hand under the blanket to where she could make contact with his skin. His fingers were limp and cold, and when she leaned over to kiss him, he smelled of antiseptic—the same smell she had become used to in their own home. She smiled, thinking back a few months to when Martin had her disinfecting fruit, because Joan's little white terrier had been on the kitchen table. It had annoyed her at the time. Now she wanted nothing more than to have him healthy and obsessing about germs again.

She stared at his face, bruised and swollen, cuts on his forehead and right cheek. *From shattered window glass?* she thought.

With her free hand, she brushed her fingers through his hair. "I love you so very much, Martin. You have to be all right, you know. You have a little boy at home who needs you. And I need you. So, you need to keep fighting. You've been through so much already in your life. You can do this. You're strong; I know you can do this."

She laid her head down on the mattress, and, holding his hand against her face, she drifted off to sleep.

Martin's trembling roused her a short time later. His eyes barely open, he stared at the ceiling as beads of perspiration formed on his face, and he gave a soft groan with every short, rapid breath.

"Martin, I'm right here," Louisa said as she got to her feet.

She glanced up as the door slid open and Chris stepped into the room.

"He's waking up, and I think he's in pain. Can you do something?" She pressed her hand over her mouth and blinked back tears.

"Hey, Martin," Chris said as he pressed the call button on the wall. "Can you open your eyes for me? Come on, mate. I need you to wake up so we can figure out how to help you." Martin's breaths came in stuttered gasps. Louisa stepped back as she quieted a sob.

Taking hold of his friend's good hand, Chris squeezed it gently. "You need to look at me, Mart."

Martin blinked several times before squinting his eyes against the bright lights in the room. Chris walked over to the switch and dimmed them before returning to his friend's side.

"It ... hurts," Martin forced out, his voice barely audible.

"Yeah, I know. It must hurt like hell," Chris said. "Help's coming. Ed's on his way."

By the time the surgeon reached the CCU, Martin's body was trembling from the pain he was in, and his groans could be heard down the corridor.

He looked frantically around for his wife. When he spotted her standing off out of the way, he reached his hand out to her.

She hurried to him and put her cheek against his. "It's all right, Martin. They're going to help you."

Ed Christianson came through the door and immediately adjusted the morphine drip. "Hang in there, Martin. We're going to make you more comfortable."

It took several excruciatingly long minutes before the drug began to work its magic, and the patient's body began to relax.

"Where's your pain at, Martin? On a scale of one to ten, where's your pain?"

"Seven," he answered, his face still taut as he released an occasional moan.

"Okay, let's bump it up a bit more then. I want to see you no higher than a three."

Mr. Christianson continued to increase the morphine until his patient's breathing had slowed and a bit of colour had returned to his cheeks. "What's your pain level now?"

Martin's eyes drifted shut momentarily before he answered sluggishly, "I'm ... nod sure."

"Okay, let's see how you do there." Ed went to the foot of the bed and picked up the chart, making a note of the new morphine dose.

The door slid open and Robert Dashwood and the other consultant from Imperial stepped into the room.

Chapter 6

Ed moved aside as the two surgeons came through the door. "I'm Robert Dashwood, the taller of the two men said, extending a hand to him.

"Ed Christianson," the surgeon replied, returning the gesture. "Thanks for coming down to help out."

Robert gave Ed a sombre nod. "It was a shock to get the news. How's our patient?" he asked, glancing over at Martin.

"He's pretty heavily medicated, but his pain seems to be under control. We've been struggling with hypovolaemia, but that appears to be in hand now."

"Internal injuries?"

"Yep. Judging from the abdominal rigidity and tenderness, I was pretty certain of it. The CT showed bleeding from the liver and spleen. He wasn't going to make it until you fellas got here so we took him into theatre. I've done a laparotomy ... fixed both issues."

Ed walked back to the bed and pulled the patient notes from the hanger, handing them to Robert. "I've put in temporary shunts in both the arm and the leg and packed off the laceration in his thigh. The full trauma series will have to wait until he's stable."

"Hello, Robert," Chris said as he shook the silver-haired man's hand. "It's good to see you again. Although not under these circumstances."

"Yes. It wasn't news I was happy to hear—my star pupil." He glanced over at the short, distinguished looking man next to him. "Forgive my manners," he said. "This is Will Simpson, our top ortho man at Imperial."

"Pleased to meet you. I'll do my very best for him," Mr. Simpson said, giving a nod towards Martin as he exchanged handshakes with Chris and Ed.

Chris introduced the surgeons to Louisa, before Robert walked over to the patient's bedside.

"Martin ..." he said, squeezing his hand.

Martin's eyelids fluttered before he looked up at Mr. Dashwood, glassy-eyed.

"Hey, Martin. I hear you had a rough trip home tonight."

Martin blinked as he struggled to place the man's face.

"Martin, it's Robert ... Robert Dashwood, from Imperial. Do you remember me?"

"Yess ... Roger," he answered, struggling to clear the narcotic fog.

"*Robert*. Your old tutor, from Imperial ... in London."

"Mmm. Whad are you ... you doing 'ere?"

"Parsons called me. We're here to get you put back together, my friend."

Robert moved to the foot of the bed. "Can we take a look at what you've done to yourself?"

Martin closed his eyes, nodding his head sluggishly.

The surgeon moved the blankets away from his patient's legs before pulling on a pair of exam gloves. Will Simpson joined him as the first bandage was removed. The steady beeps of the heart monitor jumped before accelerating as Robert lifted Martin's leg slightly so that they could get a look at the posterior side. The patient released a slurred expletive while tremors rippled through him.

"Sorry, Martin. We're almost done here," Robert said, his brow wrinkling.

Louisa sat in a chair in the corner of the room, biting at her cheek as she averted her eyes.

"We need to get some pictures. But hopefully the damage is limited to the obvious mid-shaft fractures," Mr. Simpson said as he straightened himself back up and crossed his arms in front of him. "We'll need to address the nerve and vascular damage, obviously."

He gently palpated Martin's right leg. "We're looking at surgery here as well. We're going to need to prioritise these repairs, but we'll want to get the fractures taken care of today."

"Well, this one doesn't look too terrible, Martin," Robert said after pushing the blankets aside and uncovering the laceration in his thigh. "Some debridement and vascular repair, then I think we should be able to stitch that one up."

The surgeon tucked the blankets back around his patient's legs before going to the other side of the bed to examine his arm.

Martin cried out in pain as Robert unwrapped the bandage that was covering the injury. "I feel ... s-sick," he forced out through ragged breaths.

Mr. Simpson grabbed a basin, and Martin vomited into it before a nurse came over with a wet cloth to wipe his face.

"Martin, are you nauseated when you're *not* having as much pain? Is it the pain or the morphine that's making you feel ill?" Robert asked.

Martin closed his eyes and shook his head. "It ... hurss. I'm di-ssy."

Robert noted the beads of perspiration that had formed on his patient's face as well as the increasing pallor to his skin.

"Martin, I want you sedated before they start messing around with you down in radiology. We'll cut back on the morphine and up the amount of midazolam that you're getting. Hopefully, we can take the edge off your pain and help you with the nausea as well. Will and I'll take a look at that arm and leg of yours while you're out, too." He turned to Ed. "Can you get a central line in him before he goes down to radiology?"

"Yep," the surgeon said before stepping aside to talk to the nurse.

"What's a central line?" Louisa asked.

"A catheter ... a tube that will be fed through Martin's subclavian vein," Robert said, pressing his fingers to his chest. It will help us monitor his condition during surgeries, and it can also be used to administer medications, fluids, parenteral, or IV, nutrition ..."

Will leaned over the bed, resting his arms on the rail. "Martin, Mr. Christianson's going to get a central line going, then we'll get some pictures of your injuries. After that, we'll have some decisions to make. But considering what you've been through already tonight, we're going to use external fixation on those fractures for now. We'll go back in on Sunday or Monday ... see how things look and decide how to proceed from there. How does that sound?"

Martin lay, staring through hooded eyes.

"Do you understand what we're saying, Martin?" Robert asked.

He turned a bleary gaze towards his old tutor. "Where iss Lou ... Louissa? I wan my wive."

Louisa pushed past Will and took her husband's hand. "I'm right here, Martin. I'm right here."

"Louissa, I don' like ... don' like all these ... people."

"I know it's overwhelming, Martin. But they need to be here ... they're all here to help you. You've been in an accident, and they're all here to take care of you," she said. "You've been hurt, and you have some broken bones. But Will and Robert are going to fix everything."

He watched her intently. "Like Shtan n' Lollie fiss effrything?"

Louisa cocked her head at him and furrowed her brow. A smile slowly spread across her face. "Stan and Ollie? Like Laurel and Hardy you mean?"

"Mmm." His eyes crinkled as he looked back at her.

"You made a *joke*, Martin," she giggled as she wiped tears from her cheeks. "Now of all times!"

"You looked ... ub-sed. I wan-ned to see ..." His eyes drifted shut for a moment. "I wan-ned to see your ssmile."

Louisa leaned down and gave him a gentle, lingering kiss.

Chris stood watching the tender scene play out then took in a deep breath and turned to Robert. "Well, what do you think?" he asked.

Will took Louisa by the arm. "Let's go and have a chat in the hall, shall we? Let Martin sleep."

She shook her head and pulled her husband's hand to her lips.

Chris came around the bed and put his arm around her shoulders. "Come on, Louisa. We need to clear out for a bit anyway while Ed puts in the central line."

Louisa pulled away reluctantly. "I'll be back in just a few minutes, Martin."

Carole was waiting in the hall when they left the room, and she walked with the group to an isolated waiting area at the end of the corridor.

Robert gestured to Louisa to take a seat.

"I want to be sure that you feel you're being included in all of this, Louisa. Do you have any questions?"

"Is Martin's going to be all right. He *is* going to be all right, isn't he?"

Will Simpson cleared his throat. "I think it might be helpful for you to understand our concerns about your husband's condition, and then we'll address how we plan to deal with those concerns," he said, dropping into a chair opposite her.

"You may have heard us use the term polytrauma," he continued. "That simply means that Martin has sustained multiple serious injuries. On their own, none of these injuries pose a terribly difficult treatment challenge. However, when a person sustains several major traumas, the body's natural healing processes become compromised. There are metabolic changes, changes in the cardiopulmonary system, and the immune system is weakened. Martin has a lot more than the observable injuries to deal with right now."

Robert moved over to take a seat next to her. "Bear in mind, Louisa, that Martin's spleen had ruptured. The spleen's main function is to clean dead blood cells as well as bacteria from the body, so all that bacteria spilled into his system.

"Therefore, infection is a very real concern right now. This is why we don't want to start repairing fractures with plates and screws that can add to the risk of infection.

"Our plan is to go in today and debride ... erm, clean out any nonviable tissue. Then we'll irrigate, or wash out, the wounds and repair any vascular and nerve damage. And, of course, we'll reduce the fractures. In other words, we'll get the bones and bone fragments put back where they belong.

"We'll use what we call external fixators to hold things in the proper position. The wounds will be left open until the risk of infection is lower."

Louisa rubbed at her temples and shook her head. "What are fixators?"

"With external fixation, metal pins are inserted through the skin and soft tissue, into the bone. The pins are held in place by an external metal frame," Mr. Simpson explained. "It looks a bit gruesome, but it's the best approach for Martin."

Louisa pulled her hands over her face as the enormity of the situation overwhelmed her.

Robert put his arm around her as she began to shiver. "I know this must be very frightening," he said, "but I can assure you that both Will and I have had patients with similar injuries before, and we've had good outcomes. We just want you to be aware of the risks, and also to understand why we aren't going in today, fixing everything at once."

"I just—want—someone ..." Louisa broke down. "Will someone *please* tell me that Martin's going to be all right!" she said, her voice tight with grief and fear.

Carole took a seat on the other side of her and wrapped her arms around her, holding her until her crying quieted.

Will cleared his throat. "Louisa, Martin has a team of surgeons, doctors, and hospital staff worthy of the Queen. He has a very long road ahead of him, but I'm cautiously optimistic."

Louisa tried to absorb it all. *Cautiously optimistic. Is that the best they can give me?*

Robert leaned his forearms on his thighs and folded his hands. "We have a good bit of work to do, but first we need to get Martin down to radiology. We'll be sedating him before we do any more messing around though." The surgeon rested a hand on Louisa's and gave her a firm nod. "We're going to take good care of him."

Louisa sniffled and forced a smile to her face.

"Do you mind if I see Martin, Louisa?" Carole asked. "Just to give him my best. I haven't seen him in quite a while."

"That'd be fine, nice really."

Louisa rested her head in her hands, taking in a deep breath before getting to her feet.

Robert waited until Carole and Louisa had walked away before turning back to Chris. "We'll have to see what the CT images and x-rays show, but it's possible some hard decisions may have to be made."

Chris drew down his brow and cocked his head. "What? You're not suggesting amputa— No. *No.*"

Robert put his hand up. "It's just something that we need to keep on our list of options. I'm very concerned about the high risk of infection that we're dealing with right now. And there's been a lot of damage done to that arm. It's something that may have to be consid—"

"No!" Chris said, shaking his head vigorously as he took a step back. "I can't believe it's even on the table at this point!"

"Keep your voice down ... *please,*" Robert admonished.

Chris took in a deep breath before blowing it out. "Martin's going to fight to keep those limbs ... you know that, Robert."

"Yes, I do know that. And Will and I will be as well. I promise you that, Chris. I'm just wanting to give you some time to get your head around the possibility is all. It might be a good idea to broach the subject with Louisa. It's not the kind of thing you want to have to make a split-second decision about. That's all I'm saying."

Chris gazed down the hall towards his friend's room, shaking his head. "Not now. I think it's more than she can handle right now. I'll broach the subject with her later if needs be." He tucked his hands under his arms. "Will you take care of the right leg tonight?" he asked, leaning heavily against the wall.

"I spoke with Will about that. He feels we should play it by ear ... see how Martin's vitals look by the time we finish up with the left leg and the arm. The two open fractures are going to take a bit of work, Chris. He's going to be on the table quite a while for those two problems alone."

"Yes, I understand." Chris closed his eyes and shook his head. "I'm sorry. It's just that Martin and I have been friends since med school and ... well, life hasn't been very easy for him. Just do everything you can."

"We will, Chris."

Carole and Louisa returned to the CCU room, and Ed left to go talk with Robert and Will.

"I brought someone to see you, Martin," Louisa said as they approached his bed.

Carole walked over and put a hand on his shoulder. "I won't stay, Martin. I wanted to say hello and to tell you that I'll look after Louisa. Don't worry about her. Just work on getting well."

"Mmm," Martin replied groggily.

"I'll stop in again when you're feeling better." Carole leaned down and brushed a kiss against his cheek before moving towards the door. "Louisa, I'll wait down the hall for you," she said, giving Martin an anxious glance before stepping out of the room.

Louisa pulled a chair up to the bed and sat down, taking her husband's hand.

His hazy gaze settled on her. "You're ssso beaudi ... ful."

Louisa pulled his hand to her lips, and he brushed his thumb against her cheek. "Please don' worry ... 'bout me."

"I'm your wife; it's my job to worry about you." She stood up and touched her head to his.

"I'll be in thea ... I'll be in there a long ... long time. Go ged some sleep so I don' ... so I don' worry."

Louisa smiled down at him. "*You* are worried about *me*?"

"Mmm." His eyes softened, and he gave her hand an anaemic squeeze.

The two London surgeons came back into the room. "Martin, we're going to let you get some sleep now. Once you're sedated, Mr. Christianson will get a central line into you. Then we'll take you down to radiology. When you wake up we'll have a talk about what the pictures tell us," Will explained.

"Mm." Martin's eyes shifted back to his wife. "I love you, Louissa."

Louisa leaned over and pressed her lips gently to his "I love you too, Martin."

Robert injected more midazolam into Martin's arterial line. "We'll talk in another hour or so, Martin."

A hospital aide came in and wheeled him down the hall. "He'll be back in about a half hour, Louisa," Will said as he and Robert headed out the door.

A little over an hour later, Robert Dashwood, Will Simpson, Ed Christianson, and Chris Parsons stood around Martin's bed.

Robert explained their plan for surgery. "Martin, the pictures showed what we were expecting them to, but we were pleased that there seems to be less nerve involvement in the arm than we had feared.

"So tonight, we'll debride and clean up the soft tissue, irrigate, then repair the nerve and vascular damage. After that we'll take care of the fractures ... secure everything with the external fixators. If your vital signs look good after we finish with the two open fractures, we'll work on that right leg and the laceration to your thigh. Are you good with the plan?"

"Mmm. But don' ... bollocks this'sup," he said as the corners of his mouth edged up.

"Must be the pain meds," Robert said, giving the trio of physicians a smile. "Don't worry, Martin. It'll be a proper job."

Chapter 7

Louisa followed Martin and the surgical team as far as they would allow, before she said goodbye. "You're going to be fine, Martin. Will Simpson says you have a team of surgeons and doctors worthy of the Queen."

"Mm. Louissa, I leff something for James ... in my desk drawer. Juss if something happens."

"Nothing's going to happen. I'm going to go get some sleep at Chris and Carole's, and I'll be back here when you wake up. *Hmm?*"

"Yess. I love you."

"I love you too."

Louisa kissed him and then watched as he disappeared through the theatre doors.

When she returned to the waiting area, Chris and Carole were there.

"Mart's in theatre now?" Chris said as he got to his feet.

"Mm-hmm. Do you think we could go now?" Louisa asked.

"Of course. We'll get some warm food into you, then you need to get some sleep," Carole said, putting an arm around her shoulders.

After a meal of bean and lentil soup with a side of crusty bread, Carole showed Louisa to their spare bedroom. Finally alone with her thoughts, Louisa let all her emotions flood out. When she was too exhausted to cry any longer, she closed her eyes and drifted off to sleep.

While Louisa slept, Martin's surgical team worked to save the life and limbs of a respected colleague and friend.

They debrided the wounds to his fractured arm and left leg, removing all tissue that was too damaged to recover. Then, using saline, they flushed the wounds thoroughly to remove any remaining bone fragments and dirt.

Robert took over with vascular repairs as Will managed the repair of severed nerves.

Then came the meticulous task of fitting the bones back into their proper places. They were held in place with long, metal, threaded pins, first screwed into the bones before being secured with metal bars on both sides of Martin's leg and forearm.

Passing an ultrasound transducer over his patient's leg and foot, Robert checked for adequate blood flow.

"It looks good," he said, glancing up at Will. "Nice strong pulse."

"All right, let's finish up. Then we'll see where we're at with his vitals." Will extended his hand and a technician slapped a pouch filled with antibiotic beads into it. The orthopaedist packed it into a wound before the support team took over with bandaging.

Robert stretched as he looked over at the anaesthetist. "How's he doing? Should we keep going or call it quits for now?"

"I think you could get that right leg stabilised. His vitals are holding okay," the younger man replied as he adjusted the tube in Martin's throat. "His BP is 105/78 though, so be prepared to scrub it if his pulse pressure narrows much more."

The fractures in Martin's right leg were reduced, and the external fixators were attached to hold the bones in place.

"His core temp's dropped to 98.2 and the BP is now 102/80," the anaesthetist cautioned.

"All right, we better call it quits for today," Robert said as he reached over to check Martin's fingers for the warmth that would be expected with adequate circulation. "Will, can you check his toes?"

The surgeon gave him a satisfied grin. "Nice and toasty."

"Brilliant." Robert stretched and yawned. "Okay, Martin, my friend, let's take you back to that lovely wife of yours."

Seven hours had passed since Louisa had watched Martin disappear through the theatre doors. It was now mid-morning and the daylight had roused her. She scrambled out of bed and slipped into the bathroom, splashing cold water on her red and swollen eyes before showering quickly.

By the time she had dressed, Chris and Carole were up. They had a hot breakfast waiting for her when she came out to the kitchen.

"Good morning! How did you sleep?" Carole asked as she put a plate of fried eggs and sausage on the table in front of her guest.

"It was hard to *get* to sleep ... a lot running through my head. But I slept quite well actually."

"That's good. You needed the rest. Hopefully this will be an easier day," Chris said as he took a seat.

"God, I can't imagine it could be any more difficult. Have you heard anything, Chris?" Louisa asked as she reached for a slice of toast.

"Not yet, but they had a lot of work to do. I'll get you over to the hospital as soon as we finish eating. I'm assuming you're rather anxious to get back?"

Louisa gave her husband's friend a tepid smile, "Yes, I just hope things look better today."

A still sleeping Martin had been returned to the Critical Care Unit shortly before Chris and Louisa arrived back at his room. His face was covered by an oxygen mask, and he was buried in thick layers of heated blankets.

Chris went directly to the chart hanging on the end of the bed and flipped through the most recent notes. He returned it to its hanger and began to pull at the blankets.

"Let me show you what they've done here, Louisa. It can be rather unsettling to see these contraptions for the first time, and it'll be helpful to Martin if he doesn't see your initial reaction to all of this."

Louisa moved hesitantly to Chris's side as he folded the blankets back to expose Martin's legs which were elevated on foam blocks. She tried to remain in control, but she couldn't hold back the tears when she saw the cold mechanical frames penetrating her husband's flesh.

"I'm sorry, Chris. That just looks so ... awful. Are those things painful?"

"Yes, it's not comfortable. It will of course get less painful with time." He waved a finger at Martin's left leg. "The tibial fractures ... erm, the large bones in the lower leg ... can be quite painful. He's going to hurt, but we'll do our best to make him comfortable."

Louisa's eyes scanned over her husband's legs, her gaze coming to rest on the gaping lacerations.

"The wounds are being left open for now due to the risk of infection," Chris explained. "They've been packed with beads that release antibiotics into the damaged soft tissue. They then bandaged the wounds with a clear plastic vacuum dressing that keeps everything sealed. This keeps the tissue moist. If soft tissue dries out it becomes nonviable."

Chris pulled a chair up for Louisa when he noticed her face blanching.

"I'm sorry, more information than you wanted?"

Louisa wiped the moisture from her palms. "No ... no. I need to know all of this, it's just ..."

"Hard to see, isn't it?"

"Mm-hmm." she took in a deep breath and blew it out. "Okay, I think I'm ready to see his arm now, Chris."

Chris tucked the blankets back in around Martin's feet before going to the side of the bed.

Martin's arm was being held at a ninety-degree angle in a foam sling suspended from a rod over his head. Chris opened the Velcro closures on the top side of the sling. His arm looked much the same as his left leg, having received the same surgical treatment.

"According to the operative notes, they didn't get to the repair of the laceration to Martin's thigh. They'll have to get that on his next trip to theatre."

"Why? Did something happen during surgery?" Louisa asked, anxiously.

"No. There was concern about his narrowing pulse pressure, or the difference between the upper and lower blood pressure numbers. That difference is used to calculate how effectively his heart is pumping blood. A narrowed, or smaller, pulse pressure number isn't a good sign. Martin's body had had all it could take."

Louisa swallowed hard and nodded her head. "He's so terribly swollen and bruised, Chris. Is that normal?"

"Exactly what we'd expect. It could take weeks for all the swelling and bruising to clear ... months more likely. Martin's going to have a very long recovery, Louisa. We both need to be making some plans for the next six months or so."

Chris refastened the Velcro on his friend's sling before turning to her. "Erm, Carole and I were talking before you got up this morning; we'd like to offer you a place to stay for as long as you need it. You could even have James join you over here. Carole said she'd be happy to help out with his care when you want to be here with Martin."

Louisa reached out to embrace him. "You and Carole ... this has been a nightmare. I really needed help ... Martin needed help, and you were both there for us. I appreciate your kindness so much."

Noticing movement to her side, Louisa looked over to see Martin trying to raise his arm. She hurried to the other side of the bed and took hold of his hand. He moaned softly before she saw his eyes open slightly, and she reached out to stroke his face. He mumbled unintelligibly.

"Martin, I'm right here."

His eyelids fluttered slightly before opening a bit more, and he turned his head towards the sound of her voice. He watched her, his gaze unfocused. "Is'sit over?"

"Yes, Martin, it's over. It went very well."

He stared back at her. "Did they cud id off?" he asked, his voice soft and breathy.

Louisa leaned in closer. "I'm sorry, Martin, I couldn't hear you."

He turned his head and pulled his hand free from hers before grabbing at the blankets, trying to pull them back.

He reached across his chest to his side and his breathing quickened.

"What do you need, Mart?" Chris asked as his friend groped frantically.

His chin began to tremble. "Oh, God! They cud id off! They cud ... id off, Chris!" he cried out hoarsely.

It suddenly registered with Chris what Martin had been searching for.

"No, Mart. They didn't cut it off. Your arm's up here, mate," Chris said, guiding his friend's head so that he could see the sling, positioned out of his previous line of sight.

Martin's breathing slowed, and tears of relief began to flow.

Louisa leaned down and pressed her cheek to his. "Oh, Martin," she whispered.

She pulled several tissues from the box beside the bed, and Chris pulled the oxygen mask from his face so that she could wipe it dry.

She dabbed gently at his cheeks. "Everything's fine; you still have two arms and two legs."

He let his head settle back into the pillow as his eyes drifted shut again.

Chris left a short time later to get some work done in his office. Louisa sat in the chair by her husband's bed, holding his hand and brushing her fingers through his hair.

How quickly their lives had changed. Yesterday at this time, Martin was talking to her in the school gymnasium. He had gone out of his way to stop to say he loved her. Yesterday life seemed challenging enough, with school term having just started for Louisa and Martin trying to work through all the difficulties created by his horrible upbringing. Today, she found herself wishing those were the only challenges facing them.

Chapter 8

Louisa had fallen asleep with her head lying on the mattress, nestled against her husband's hand. She was awakened by Carole's voice.

"Louisa, the surgeons are here to check on Martin," she said as she rubbed her hand on her back.

Sitting up abruptly, Louisa tried to get her bearings. She had been dreaming—dreaming that she and Martin were walking along the coastal path. It was a beautiful day, and the warm sun was comforting as it hit their backs. Then, the ocean water, which had been gently lapping at the shoreline, began to roil as the sky turned black and a torrent of rain began to fall.

They turned to run for home, the dirt under their feet turning to mud as they made their way forward. Suddenly, Martin's feet slipped out from under him, and he began to slide down the hill towards the cliff's edge. He grabbed frantically for something to stop his skid—rocks, branches, tufts of grass. She screamed his name as his body disappeared over the rocky ledge, his fingers gripping tenuously to the edge. She ran to him and grabbed on to his wrists as he struggled to overcome gravity. Feeling him slip from her wet and muddied hands, she watched in horror as he fell towards the rocks below. But his descent downward slowed until he was floating in the air, just out of reach of her fingertips.

She was calling to him in her sleep when Carole came to wake her. She grasped on to Martin's hand, breathing a sigh of relief when she felt the warmth of life in him. Turning to Carole and embracing her, she broke down in tears.

"Louisa, what's wrong?"

Louisa's sobs slowed, and she took in several ragged breaths. "It was a bad dream, that's all. I'm sorry."

Carole held her close until she regained her composure, and then she turned to the surgeons waiting in the doorway. "We're going to go down the hall for a cup of coffee. We'll be right back."

"Sure, take your time," Robert said.

When the two women returned a short time later, Louisa stood inside the door with her arms crossed in front of her and her head tipped down. "I'm sorry about that. This is all beginning to take a toll, I suppose."

"It's quite all right. It's to be expected actually," said Mr. Simpson. "We just stopped by to check up on your husband. Has he been awake at all?"

"He woke up shortly after I got here this morning, but he fell back to sleep pretty quickly. He's been asleep since. That's normal, isn't it? He's all right, isn't he?"

"Yep. It's perfectly normal. The anaesthesia is still affecting him, and his body's just worn out." Will pointed to the IV bottles suspended over the bed. "It doesn't help that we have a very potent cocktail of medications that we've been pumping into him— antibiotics, anti-inflammatories, analgesics, and a number of other drugs to keep him stable. It's all exhausting."

Robert finished writing in Martin's medical chart and looked up at Louisa. "I think Mr. Simpson and I are both reasonably happy with how things went in theatre. We have a lot of work to do yet, but I feel much better knowing that those limbs are stabilised."

Louisa dropped heavily into the chair next to the bed. "Do you know when you'll do the final work on his fractures?"

If all looks good on Monday, we'll take him back in to remove any nonviable soft tissue and drain off fluid accumulations. We *may* close the wounds at that time. It's more likely, however, that we'll need to repeat the procedure at least one more time. We'll also need to do some additional work down the road—skin grafts for sure, probably some reconstruction."

Louisa sat quietly, her bottom lip clenched in her teeth. "I didn't realise this would be such a process. It's a bit frightening to think about all that Martin still has to endure."

Robert gave her an understanding nod. "I'm sure it is. My advice would be to take it one procedure at a time. Try not to think too far ahead. I probably don't need to tell you, Martin will *not* be a patient patient. This is going to be a long and frustrating ordeal for him. He'll need all the encouragement you can give him."

Robert reached in front of Louisa and put his hand on his patient's arm. "Martin ... Martin, can you wake up so we can talk?"

Louisa stood up and stroked her husband's face. "Martin, Robert and Will are here. Can you wake up so they can talk to you?"

He moaned softly before squeezing his eyes shut and pressing his hand to the side of his head.

"Martin, are you having pain?" Robert asked.

"My head ... hurds."

"Will, can you dim the lights?" Robert pulled out his pocket torch and checked his patient's pupillary reflexes.

"Martin, the trauma series showed a slight cerebral contusion, which would, of course, contribute to the headache. We'll need to keep an eye on this. As you know, this will worsen some before we see improvement. Let us know if the headache gets any worse, all right?"

"Mmm." His arm flopped back over his eyes.

Louisa shook her head as her brows knit together. "I'm sorry. Can you explain that to me?"

"Certainly," Robert said. "Martin has some bruising on his brain. This is quite common in high speed traffic accidents. We found bruising on his lungs as well. He leaned back in his chair and pulled a hand up to stifle a yawn. "Has anyone explained the effects that the shear forces had on your husband's body?"

Louisa furrowed her brow and shook her head. "I'm sorry, what do you mean by shear forces?"

"The organs in the body have different densities, and therefore they accelerate and decelerate at different rates. When your husband's body was subjected to the rapid deceleration which he experienced in his accident, his lung and brain tissue travelled faster than the denser tissues surrounding them. This results in the lungs and the brain pulling away from the other tissues, resulting in contusions—bruising.

"We'll monitor this closely. It will almost certainly worsen before we begin to see improvement."

Louisa closed her eyes, sighing heavily. "What exactly does this mean for Martin?" she asked, as she glanced up at her husband who had once again drifted off to sleep. "How will it affect him? I mean, is it serious?"

Robert pulled up a chair and sat down. "It means that he could develop some difficulty breathing. If he does, we can give him supplemental oxygen. Or, in a worst-case scenario, put him on a ventilator temporarily."

"But his lungs will heal?" Louisa asked as she caressed her husband's hand.

"Yes. We should see improvement by the end of the week. So, I think this will be manageable, Louisa. But I wanted you to be aware of some potential problems ahead."

It was half three by the time the surgeons left Martin's room. Carole returned with two cups of tea and sat down next to Louisa.

"I really need to get back to Portwenn— pick up some clothes, toothbrush and toothpaste ... that kind of thing. Could you stay with Martin while I do that?" Louisa asked.

"I could drive you. It's expensive to take a taxi, and you must be exhausted. It'd be easier on you if I drove you." Carole urged. "Chris could probably stay with Martin."

Louisa cupped her hand against her husband's cheek. "I would feel much better about leaving if Chris could stay with him."

Carole got to her feet and set her cup on the tray table. "I'll go and call him right now."

Louisa stood up and kissed her husband's forehead. "Martin, can you wake up so that I can talk to you?" she said softly in his ear.

A scowl crept on to his face, and he pulled his head away from her as his eyes opened into slits.

"I need to leave for a while ... to go home and pick up James. And I need some clothes and things."

His eyes opened wider, and he turned to look at her. "James is here?"

"No, Martin. I'm going to make a trip back to Portwenn. I'll bring him back with me, and we'll stay with Chris and Carole."

"I wanna see 'im ... see James. Can you bring 'im?" he slurred.

"I'll ask Chris, but I really don't think they'll let him in to see you. Too many germs you know."

"Mmm." He watched her for a moment before averting his eyes. "Louissa ... pleasse ..." Pulling in a breath, he whispered stridently, "Please—don'—leaf me!"

Louisa pressed her fingertips to her eyes and swallowed hard. "I promise ... I will *not* leave you." She brushed her hand over his head one last time before going to find Carole.

The drive to Portwenn seemed interminably long. Louisa was anxious to both see her son and Ruth, as well as to get back to her husband.

Ruth met them on the surgery terrace with James perched on her hip. The baby reached his arms out to his mum.

"James, I missed you!" she said as she took him from the elderly woman. She turned and smiled proudly at Carole. "*This*—is James Henry."

"What a handsome young man you are, James Henry," Carole said, her flattery earning her a wonky smile from the boy.

Ruth eyed Carole. "I'm Martin's aunt, Ruth Ellingham."

"Oh, sorry," Louisa said as James reached for the brightly coloured beaded necklace around Carole's neck. "Ruth, this is Martin's friend Chris's wife, Carole Parsons. Carole and Chris have been of immeasurable help, Ruth. In fact, Chris is sitting with Martin while I'm gone."

"How is he?" Ruth asked, worry etched on her face.

Louisa's shoulders slumped. "Could we go in and discuss it over a cuppa? I'm absolutely shattered."

Carole took James upstairs to change his nappy while Louisa apprised Ruth of the situation. They went into the kitchen and Louisa set about heating water and putting out cups, milk, and sugar.

"Martin's better than last night, Ruth. But it was a bad accident. He's..." Louisa stepped to the counter, picking up a box of tissues before joining her husband's aunt at the table.

She took in a deep breath before continuing, "You know most of the details, but Martin was back in surgery around two o'clock this morning and they didn't finish with him until after ten. They set his fractures ... or whatever they call it. They used external fixators to hold everything in place."

"But he handled surgery all right? No complications?"

"No complications, but they weren't able to take care of the laceration he has in his thigh. Chris said something about his blood pressure and how it indicated his heart wasn't pumping effectively any more. So, they stopped for today, and they'll fix that injury the next time they have him in theatre."

"No head or spinal cord injuries, though?"

"Well, I guess the latest news is that the x-rays and CT pictures that they got in the middle of the night showed bruising to both his brain and his lungs. One of the surgeons told me that he could develop breathing problems."

Ruth toyed nervously with the handle of her teacup. "The cerebral contusion ... how bad is it?"

"Robert Dashwood, the vascular surgeon that came down from London, described it as slight."

The old woman blew out a breath. "Well, that's a bit of good news, I suppose."

"This is all so terrifying, Ruth." Louisa pulled a tissue from the box. "Martin's in so much pain. The few times that I've seen him hurt he's been so stoic. He groans from the pain he's in now, sometimes actually scre—" Louisa broke down, putting her hands over her face and sobbing.

Ruth fidgeted uncomfortably until her nephew's wife had composed herself, and then gave her a piercing stare. "This is your chance to prove to Martin that he *can* trust you to be there for him, Louisa. That you won't take off on him when you hit a difficult patch. You *are* being tested, no doubt about it. But if you can stay by his side through this ... Well then, I think you'll have gone a long way in earning back that trust that you say you so dearly want from him."

Resting her folded hands on the table, Louisa nodded her head. "I *will* be there for him, Ruth."

"*Good*. I fully expect that from you."

Louisa tapped her fingers against her teacup and turned her head away. "Well, I better go pack some things and get back to the hospital." She hurried off under the stairs.

Before they headed back to Truro, Louisa wrote a note to Poppy, explaining that they would not be needing her services until further notice, but that she would still receive her wages as usual. Louisa didn't want to be worrying about losing their childminder in addition to all the other worries she had. She charged Ruth with getting the message to the girl.

She also needed to make a call to Dr. Newell. He would want to know about Martin's accident, and she also needed to cancel their upcoming appointments. She went to the consulting room, looking for the therapist's phone number. Pulling open Martin's top desk drawer, where she knew he kept his appointment calendar and contact list, she noticed a sheet of stationery paper. It was a letter, written in her husband's familiar script. She picked it up and sat down in his chair to read it.

Dear James,

One beautiful summer day, you came into the world and changed my life. You gave it direction— focus—purpose. When your mum handed you to me, I held you up at arm's length to examine you with the eyes of a medical professional.

What an odd looking little creature you were, definitely human and yet so alien to the world that I had existed in all my life. You were so small that I could encircle your body with my hands.

You stared back at me as I studied your features, seemingly as curious about me as I about you. You had no preconceived notions about me. To you, I was a blank slate on which I was free to write my own story, not the story dictated to me by my parents, my teachers at boarding school, nor society in general. No one had yet informed you that my cerebral nature, social awkwardness, and introverted personality would prevent me from ever fitting into the mould that society had created for the ideal human being. Yes, you were so alien to the world I had known.

You were born in a modest little pub in the middle of the Cornish moorland. And like that little pub in the middle of a rather bleak landscape, you became a little haven for me in an otherwise rather bleak life. Your mum can share with you sometime why I describe my life in this way, but suffice it to say, you and your mother were my salvation from a rather lonely and miserable existence.

As I knelt by that disgusting old pub sofa, watching you in your mother's arms, I realised my life would never be the same. You had changed me in an instant.

It's an overwhelming responsibility to be a father, especially the father of a son. I know that you will look to me for guidance. I also know that I'm responsible for being an example of what it means to be a good man. I fear that I will often fall short in that regard, and I hope that you will forgive me my many shortcomings.

But I will strive to be the father you deserve, and of this you can be sure—you will never question my love for you, James Henry. I wish for you a most happy and fulfilling life, my dear boy.

I will always cherish you,

Dad

Louisa leaned back in her husband's chair, and closed her eyes. *Martin, you just have to be all right.*

Chapter 9

It was past James's bedtime by the time Carole and Louisa arrived back at the Parsons', and despite the fact that he was in a strange place, the baby went off to sleep very quickly.

Chris picked Louisa up and drove her back to the hospital so that she could see Martin again before visiting hours were over. He was awake but groggy when she walked into his room.

"How's James?" he asked as she settled into the chair next to him.

"He's just fine. He went right to sleep at the Parsons'. It makes me wonder if he had Ruth up half the night last night."

"Mmm, iss possible."

"How's the pain now ... any better than it was?"

"Maybe."

Louisa slipped her coat from her shoulders and flipped it over the back of her chair. "Ruth says to say hello. She's planning to drive over tomorrow." She reached up and brushed her fingers through his hair. "She's quite worried about you."

Martin furrowed his brow. "Iss'a long drive ... for someone ... her age."

Louisa stroked his cheek. "You're going to get yourself into trouble with her talking like that, Martin Ellingham."

"Mmm ... yes."

Two male nurses stepped into the room. "We need to shift you just a bit, Dr. Ellingham. Mr. Simpson wants us to give you a little extra analgesia before we do that though," said the taller of the two men as he adjusted Martin's morphine drip.

They waited a few minutes for the medication to take effect, recording vital signs and dosage alterations in the patient notes while watching Martin for signs that he was responding to the additional medication.

"How are you feeling now, Dr. Ellingham?"

Martin's response was too garbled to be understood, and he stared, glassy-eyed, at the men.

"You must be Dr. Ellingham's wife," said the second man.

"Yes, I'm Louisa." She stood off to the side with her arms clutched around her.

"It's nice to meet you. We need to roll your husband over a bit. He's going to be in this bed a while, and we don't want him developing pressure sores, so we'll be trying to shift him every two hours or so."

The men worked together to move the sling holding Martin's arm above his head.

"Okay, Dr. Ellingham, we're going to turn you towards your wife. We'll be as gentle as we can."

One of the men rolled Martin's upper body while the other swung his right leg over his left so that he was lying on his side. Martin grimaced and let out a long, groan. A rattling sound could be heard in his chest as he gasped for air and began to cough.

He began to retch, and one of the men hurried over with a basin while the other grabbed a small pillow, holding it firmly against the surgical wound in his abdomen. Even with the added support of the pillow against his belly, the contractions of his abdominal muscles were agonising, and it caused Martin to gasp for air, triggering a coughing fit that brought up phlegm mixed with blood.

Louisa hurried over, reaching for her husband's hand. Fine tremors coursed through him as he attempted to regain control of his breathing. His face began to look more relaxed, but Louisa could see that the ordeal had exhausted him.

"Should I go and find Chris?" she asked him.

He shook his head. "No … I'll be … fine," he said, his breathing shallow and rapid. "I'm tired." Maybe you should go. Gessum sleep an' …"

His eyes drifted shut and his breathing slowed. She kissed him goodnight before slipping out quietly.

Louisa was awakened Sunday by the typical morning sounds of the Parsons family. She was feeling much more refreshed, having had a good night's sleep.

After grabbing a quick breakfast and going over James's usual routine with Carole, Chris drove her to the hospital. It was a bright and sunny late summer morning, and the air had a softness to it more typical of spring. It bolstered her spirits, and she hurried towards the building, hopeful for a better day.

Louisa had noticed Chris's deepening brow when she had related the details of Martin's coughing episode the night before. It only added to her uneasiness when he went immediately to Martin's side, foregoing his usual perusal of the notes hanging on the end of the bed.

He pulled a stethoscope from his suit pocket and placed it on his sleeping friend's chest. His face tightened.

"What's the matter, Chris?" she asked, her anxiety growing as the doctor's head tipped to the side and his lips pulled into a tight line.

Chris held up a hand to quiet her as he worked his way up Martin's chest with the stethoscope, finally holding it to his neck.

"I may be hearing some abnormal breath sounds. I'm going to step out and give Robert and Ed a call—just to be on the safe side. I'll be right back," he said, giving her a tense smile.

He returned shortly. "Robert should be here in just a minute. He's just down the hall."

Louisa heard footsteps rapidly approaching in the corridor before the surgeon came through the door. Chris passed him his stethoscope.

The man's bushy eyebrows pulled down. "Yep. I hear it, too. Let's get him down to CT," he said.

Chris left the room abruptly, and Louisa looked apprehensively at Robert. "What's going on. Is something wrong?"

"We're hearing something called Hamman's sign. It's a crackling noise that corresponds with his heartbeat.

"For some reason, air bubbles have formed in your husband's chest. When his heart beats, it pushes against those air bubbles. It's the sound of the bubbles popping that makes the crackling noise. We'll get a CT scan, and hopefully that'll tell us what's going on in there."

Robert gestured to Louisa. "Come over here, you can hear it for yourself." Louisa listened through the stethoscope.

"Do you hear the crackling sounds?" he asked.

Louisa refocused her attention. "Yes, I think so."

"Lay your hand on his chest, you can feel the vibrations," Robert said, adjusting the placement of her hand.

Martin began to stir and opened his eyes. He looked at Louisa, half awake and bewildered.

She caressed his chest gently and leaned over to place a kiss on his cheek. "Sorry to disturb you."

"Martin, we're going to take you back down to CT. Chris noticed crackles in your chest this morning, and we want to check it out."

There was a delay in his response as his slowed brain processed the information. "Hamman's sign?"

"Yep, we need to rule out a tracheal tear."

Martin squeezed his eyes shut. A tracheal tear would in all likelihood mean more surgery.

Thirty minutes later, Chris and Robert stood analysing the pictures from the scan.

Chris walked to the bed and put a hand on his friend's shoulder. "Martin, you do have a tracheal tear ... posterior mediastinal. It's not severe but it's large enough that it needs repair. We looked at your previous scan and it wasn't visible then. It was there, but it was too small to show up on the CT. You probably enlarged it when you had the coughing fit yesterday."

"Mm."

"We'll do a posterolateral thoracotomy, fix the tear and get out of there," Robert said.

Chris patted Martin's shoulder. "Ed Christianson will do the repair, Mart. I don't have to tell you; the guy does excellent thoracic work."

"Martin, I'm going to go and start scrubbing up. I'll be assisting on this one. We'll take good care of you, Ace," Robert said before turning to leave.

Chris smiled at the surgeon's use of the moniker which had been bestowed on his friend during medical school, and then moved towards the door. "I'll, er ... step out of the room. Give you two some time alone."

"Thank you, Chris." Louisa stroked her hand over her husband's head. "You're just keeping me on the edge of my seat you know."

Martin rubbed his hand over his eyes, turning his head away. At a loss for any words of encouragement that she hadn't already worn out, Louisa pressed her cheek to his. "I love you, Martin."

Louisa had been dozing in the chair while Martin was in theatre, and was awakened by the sound of approaching voices and the rumble of the sliding door. She stood and hugged herself as they wheeled her husband's bed back into the room. He had a mask over his face, providing him with humidified air to breathe. One of the nurses explained that it was important to keep the airway moist to facilitate healing.

Chris entered the room a short while later. "Everything went very smoothly, Louisa ... no nasty surprises."

She blew out a long breath. "Do you think this will take care of the problem?"

"It should. They made an incision from just under his right nipple on around to his back. Then they cut through one of his ribs to get to the tracheal tear. The repair looks excellent though."

"That's a relief." Louisa sat back heavily into the chair. "Chris, Martin looked absolutely defeated after you told him he'd be going back to theatre, and I didn't have a clue as to how to help him."

"It's been a nightmarish couple of days, and Martin's no dummy; he knows what he has ahead of him. It's has to be daunting."

"Do you think this is it now ... for any new problems to crop up?"

"All I can tell you is that once we get past the first forty-eight hours, the odds of things really going south begin to decrease."

Chris moved over to Martin's bedside and pulled the blankets back. "They put in a couple of drains to keep fluid from accumulating in his chest. This should make it much easier for him to breathe. And thoracotomies are inherently painful procedures so he has a thoracic epidural which should make him much more comfortable."

He pulled up his arm and glanced at his watch. "I have a business lunch in a few minutes, but then I could relieve you for a while if you'd like to run down to the canteen."

"That'd be good, Chris. I don't want to leave until after Martin wakes up anyway."

Shortly after Chris stepped out, there was a soft knock on the door and Ruth stuck her head in. "Everybody decent in here?"

"Yes, Ruth. Come on in." Louisa got up from her chair and gave the woman a hug. "It is *so* good to see you." She waved a hand at the bed. "It's been a bad morning. They discovered a tracheal tear, and he's just come back from theatre."

"Oh dear, that's not good. Thoracotomy?"

"Mm-hmm."

Ruth walked to the bed and leaned over slightly to scrutinise her nephew. "Not too bad as far as the facial wounds go." She hesitated, and then pulled back the covers at the foot end of the bed. "Oh, dear lord, Martin!" she exclaimed softly, shaking her head. "Well, my nephew never has been one to do things halfway."

She went to the head of the bed and pulled open the Velcro closures on the sling supporting his arm. The look on her face conveyed her distress.

"That bad?" Louisa asked.

Ruth shook her head. "It's a severe injury—yes." She pulled up a chair next to Louisa and took a seat. "Have they said what their expectations are? Will he have full use of the arm?"

"I don't know, Ruth. I've been afraid to ask. Robert said that he was pleased with how things had gone with the surgery, so I'm hopeful."

Ruth stared at her nephew for a few moments, her eyes tearing, before abruptly changing the subject. "How's my great nephew doing in his new quarters?"

"He went right to sleep last night. Martin and I wondered if he'd been up a lot for you the night before."

"Yes." Ruth sighed. "It seems I misplaced his purple dinosaur, and he wouldn't go to sleep without it." She fixed her gaze on the monitor next to the bed, watching the fluctuating numbers. "I discovered it in the refrigerator this morning, next to his bottles of formula," she said, reaching into her purse and retrieving the plush reptile.

"Oh, I'm so glad you brought it with you. It should make him feel more at home while we're here."

Martin began to stir, groaning softly as he lifted his arm in an attempt to reach the most recent violation. Louisa got up and hurried to his side grasping his wrist to hold his arm back. He lashed out at her with a feeble swing.

Ruth hurried over to the other side of the bed. "Martin, you need to lie still. It will only hurt more if you thrash about." She looked up at her nephew's wife. "Louisa, go and get either a consultant or one of the nursing staff."

Louisa returned promptly with Ed Christianson. "Hey, Martin," the surgeon said. "Try to lie still, and we'll get this epidural going for you." He toyed with the catheter snaking out from under his patient.

Martin stared at Louisa, wild-eyed.

"It won't hurt so much in just a little bit," she said, giving a nod of her head.

"Are you getting any relief from the pain, Martin?" Ed asked some seconds later.

Martin nodded his head, his eyes softening.

"Good. We're all done in theatre, and the repair looks excellent. One more hurdle cleared, eh?"

"Mmm."

Martin turned his head, and his eyes connected with Ruth's, tears welling in them as he reached his hand out to her.

A very surprised Ruth walked over and took hold of his hand. She leaned over and gave him a spontaneous kiss on the forehead before her impassive self took over again and she straightened herself.

"I'm ... gla' zure ... here," he said softly.

"I'm glad *you're* here. You have a rough road ahead of you, Martin. But you're very lucky to be alive." The old woman reached a hand out reflexively and caressed his cheek.

Chapter 10

Chris stayed with Martin while Ruth and Louisa went to the canteen to get lunch.

"Is that all you're going to eat, Louisa?" Ruth asked, looking at the small salad on her tray.

"I'm really not hungry, Ruth. I'm sure my appetite will come back once I know that Martin will be all right."

She poked abstractedly at the chunks of lettuce on her plate. "Ruth, what was Martin like when he was young?"

"Well, much of what I know about ... Little Marty ... is second hand information passed on by Joan and Phil. I'm afraid I didn't spend the time with him that they did. I regret that now, but it's water under the bridge, as they say." Ruth peered up from her lasagne. "I *can* tell you this much; he could just about drive Joan crazy with his incessant questions. Very, *very* curious child."

"But would you have guessed he'd grow into the man he is today, or did you picture him becoming someone different?"

"I guess I might have been less surprised if he'd become a research scientist tucked away in the back of a lab somewhere, or even a farmer in the back of beyond somewhere."

Louise stopped chasing her salad and stared at her husband's aunt. "Martin? A *farmer*?"

"Yes. Joan said he loved it at the farm when he was young—the animals, working with her in the garden, tinkering with Phil on the machinery. And I think he liked the quiet. Joan said he would disappear, and she'd finally find him lying in the long grass, watching the clouds overhead."

"What happened along the way ... to *that* Martin?"

"I don't know, dear. It seemed like something changed in him between the time I saw him at age four and when I returned to London two years later. He was always a shy boy, even as a baby. I rarely got a chance to hold him because he would cling to his nannies." The elderly woman gazed out the wall of windows on the far side of the room. "When I saw him at the age of four, he was very sensitive. I would imagine that made him vulnerable to Christopher and Margaret's belittling and coldness. When I saw him next, after my father's funeral, he had become withdrawn. He seemed to have shut down." Ruth pointed her fork at Louisa. "*I* credit his lovely parents. But I don't know," she said shrugging her shoulders. Why all the questions?"

"Hmm, I guess he seems like such a mystery sometimes. I know some of what his childhood was like, but it all seems so strange. It's hard to imagine how someone who'd been so unfortunate as to have been a child of Margaret and Christopher Ellinghams' could develop into the sort of father he is to James Henry. Where did he learn that? Certainly not from *his* parents, and certainly not at that boarding school where he spent most of his childhood."

Ruth laid her fork down and dabbed at her mouth with her napkin. "Well, I suspect his time with Joan and Phil, fleeting as it was, influenced him to a degree. But I think Martin did also learn many of his parenting skills from Margaret and Christopher. Many children of less than ideal parents grow into less than ideal parents themselves. They become bitter and take it out on their own offspring. Or they just imitate the same flawed parenting strategies that were used with them when they were children. Martin, on the other hand, learned from his parents' mistakes—what the negative effects were on him—what he needed and didn't receive. And Martin has a tender heart. He would never do anything to hurt his son. That tender heart, though, made him quite susceptible to his sterile upbringing and the harsh disciplinary tactics, both at home and at school."

Louisa pushed her half-eaten salad to the centre of the table. "An accident like this can certainly put life in perspective. I just want him well again, Ruth."

"You and me both. We should get back to that man of ours," Ruth said as she stood to leave, putting her hand on the younger woman's shoulder. "Martin will need every ounce of help and encouragement that you have to give him to get through this ordeal, Louisa."

"He has whatever he needs from me, Ruth."

Chris was reading a medical journal when the two women returned to the CCU. Martin had been sleeping but woke when they came into the room.

"Martin, you're awake," Louisa said, giving him a broad smile.

"Mm ... yes," he said sluggishly.

Louisa went over and took his hand before pressing her lips to his forehead. She noted the heat emanating from his body and pulled back. "Martin, do you feel all right?"

He turned his head and stared at her, blinking slowly before his mouth curled into a knowing smile. "You were making ... a joke."

"No, I'm serious this time, Martin." Louisa's head whipped around. "Chris?"

"Yes, Louisa. His temperature *is* elevated, but we're staying ahead of it. We were anticipating this, and it'll be very closely monitored."

She looked dubiously at her husband.

Martin looked past his wife to his friend. "I tol' ... you," he said before closing his eyes and drifting back off to sleep.

"Chris, you *will* tell me if there's anything to be concerned about, won't you?"

"Yes, I promise I will. And I was going to tell you about this, but you noticed he was febrile before I had a chance.

"This is something we need to stay on top of, and certainly, if he weren't in a hospital situation, this infection could have dire consequences. But we're hitting him hard with broad spectrum antibiotics that will help him to fight this off."

Louisa looked nervously back at her husband.

Chris leaned forward, resting his arms on his thighs. "I'm not trying to change the subject but, Ruth, Carole was wondering if you might like to have dinner and spend the night with us. It would save you a drive back in the dark."

The elderly woman gave him a crooked smile. "I do appreciate the offer, but I didn't come prepared for an overnight."

"I can get a toothbrush from the nurses station if that's all you need," Chris said.

Louisa put her hand on Ruth's shoulder. "I would feel better knowing you're not on the road after dark."

"Now you sound like my nephew," she replied, narrowing her eyes at the younger woman before turning to her nephew's friend. "That would actually be quite nice, Chris. That's very kind of you and your wife."

"Good, that's that settled. I'll call Carole and let her know," he said as he moved towards the door.

Louisa pulled the chair back up beside Martin's bed and took his hand in hers before looking up at her husband's aunt. "Ruth, you're a doctor ..."

"Yes, I believe I have a piece of paper that says something to that effect."

"I'm worried about Martin's fever. Chris made it sound like it's nothing to be concerned about, but... Well, are you worried?"

"I can't say that it doesn't concern me. However, Chris is quite correct in saying that infection is to be expected with

Martin's kind of injuries, especially with the hypovolaemia and the splenectomy. They have him stabilised, but the effects on his immune system, metabolism ... just what do you know about hypovolaemia?"

"I know that it's caused by blood loss."

"Yes, and there are other causes. But in Martin's case, it was massive blood loss. This condition affects just about every system in the body— respiratory, metabolic, endocrine, vascular. And these effects aren't immediately rectified when the fluids are replaced. It will take Martin time to recover, and until he has, things will be rather precarious. For one thing, he'll be more prone to infections."

"Does that mean that this infection he has will be harder for him to fight off?"

"Yes, but as Chris said, they've started him on some powerful antibiotics."

"I see."

Ruth and Louisa continued their vigil by Martin's bedside. Ruth had dozed off in her chair, and Louisa was resting her head on the bed next to her husband's hand when he began to mumble something in his sleep. She raised her head, trying to make out what he was saying. Most of it was so slurred and garbled that it was unintelligible.

She cupped his cheek in her hand. "I'm here, Martin," she said softly.

"Iss nod ... don' ... *don'*. His mumblings were getting louder, and he was becoming agitated.

Louisa turned as Ruth approached.

"I wan' ... out!"

Louisa reached her hand out to wake him, but Ruth grasped her arm.

"Just let him be for a bit," Ruth said, giving her a confident nod.

"Please don' ... nod in there. I din know whad to... *No, Mum!*" Martin's mumbles turned to whimpers and he began to flail his free arm about.

"Okay, maybe you should wake him, dear," Ruth said.

"Martin, wake up. You're dreaming." Louisa ran her palm across his head, and he cringed, turning his head quickly away from her, bringing his arm up to cover his face.

Louisa took his hand, holding it against her cheek, and she leaned over, whispering in his ear. "Martin, you need to wake up. You're having a dream—a nightmare."

Martin blinked rapidly and then stared at his wife, wild-eyed and disoriented.

His eyes focused in on his aunt before he turned his head away in embarrassment.

"Maybe I'll just step out for a bit ... give you two some time," Ruth said before slipping out the door.

His ragged breaths began to ease, and he turned his head back to look at the ceiling. Louisa studied his face, noting the darkening circles under his eyes. His lids became heavy, and he dropped back off to sleep.

In light of the infection that had developed, the decision was made to postpone Monday's scheduled surgery until Wednesday. Robert and Will had gone back to London to tend to their duties there. They would drive back down late on Tuesday and planned to be in theatre with Martin early the next morning.

Chris came to Martin's room in the evening to collect Ruth and Louisa. As they sat around the Parsons table that night, Ruth described in great detail and with great enthusiasm, the plans that she and Al had for Joan's property.

"I'm sure she never dreamed that her little farm would turn into such an enterprise," Carole remarked. "I'm really impressed with all that you and Al have accomplished already."

"Well, it's mostly on paper at this point. Now if we can just make it happen."

Turning to Louisa, Ruth added, "I suppose technically this is Martin's enterprise. Al and I have just been playing with it."

Louisa looked at the old woman, her head cocked. "I don't know what you mean, Ruth. Martin's had no involvement in this whatsoever."

"Well, maybe not directly. But I do consider him the chief financial officer."

Louisa laid down her fork. "Ruth, I'm not following you at all. What are you talking about? Joan left you the farm in her will."

Ruth shifted in her chair and screwed up her face. "I think I may have said too much already."

"Ruth, if you don't tell me, this will be eating at me. And I really don't need that right now."

The elderly woman slowly folded her napkin and laid it next to her plate. "Several years ago, my brother decided to renege on an agreement that he had made with Joan and Phil. When Uncle Dick died, he left the farm to both Joan and Christopher. Christopher had no use for it and told Joan and Phil as much. He said that they could have it, that he didn't want it. Forty years later, Christopher and Margaret came to *visit* Martin. When Martin took them out to see Joan, Christopher announced that he wanted his half of the value of the farm—three hundred thousand pounds. Of course, Joan didn't have that kind of money.

"She was furious. She thought that Martin was complicit. She was very hurt. Not by our brother—that came as no surprise. But she was devastated, thinking that Martin had turned on her that way. She really loved him," Ruth said, fondling her teacup.

"She told all three of them to get out. They left, and she avoided Martin—wouldn't return his calls. As it turned out,

Martin had sold his flat in London to pay off his father. He didn't want Joan to know, but of course Christopher would never think to honour his son's wishes."

Louisa sat, dumbfounded. "Why didn't Martin ever tell me about this?"

"I wouldn't have known either if Joan hadn't let it slip, much as I did just now. I think that your husband, because of his past experiences, has become a master at hiding any affection that he feels for people."

Louisa folded her napkin and laid it down before glancing up at Carole.

"Come on, let's clear these dishes," Carole said as she got up from the table and patted Louisa on the shoulder.

Louisa went to bed that night thinking about how painful it must have been for Martin as a child, to have had his affections constantly rebuffed. And how reticent he had been about expressing his affection for her. She was beginning to see life through her husband's eyes.

Chapter 11

Chris left early the following morning, and when Ruth and Louisa arrived at Martin's room he was already there, looking through the recent additions to Martin's patient notes. Louisa could see, as she walked towards her husband's bed, that his condition had not improved overnight. Air wheezed and rattled through his respiratory tract as he laboured to breathe, and a clear mask covered his face.

"Good morning," she said with faux cheerfulness as her hands latched on to the bed rail, her knuckles whitening.

Martin nodded lethargically, looking up at her through red, heavily hooded eyes.

The overnight hospital staff had started him on humidified oxygen in an attempt to raise his blood oxygen level and to thin the secretions in both his lungs and his airways.

Louisa wrapped her arms around herself and moved towards the foot of the bed. "What's wrong, Chris?" she asked softly, alarmed by both her husband's pale colour and the obvious difficulty he was having moving air.

Chris raised a hand up to silence her momentarily as he finished reading through Martin's chart.

"Okay, here's what's going on," he said as he hung the chart back up on the end of the bed. "Fluid has collected in Martin's lungs—a result of the pulmonary contusions. He's also dealing with a bacterial infection in his trachea and bronchial tubes.

"They came in and took x-rays of his lungs, and the bruising has worsened, as we expected it would. Seventy-two hours is when the severity of the bruising usually peaks, after which time we typically see fairly rapid improvement."

He rubbed a hand across the back of his neck. "So, in other words, if we can get him through the day without a ventilator, chances are good that we can avoid using one. The bacterial infection is still a concern, but the hope is that once the bruising begins to recede and breathing gets easier for him, his immune system will be able to fight the infection more effectively."

"He seems to be really struggling. Why not a ventilator, Chris?"

"A ventilator would put pressure on the lungs and could potentially do more damage to the already compromised membranes, so we'll hold off with that unless we think it's absolutely necessary. Ed Christianson's on his way in. When he gets here we'll go over our options with you and Martin."

Louisa turned her back to her husband, trying to stay in control of her emotions. She wiped the tears that were forming in her eyes and took in a deep breath before turning back to him. He looked at her, his gaze unfocused. "I'm sorry, I didn't give you a proper greeting, did I?" The heat radiating from his body was warm against her face, even before her skin touched his.

Ed Christianson entered the room a short time later, walking directly to Martin's bedside as he pulled out his stethoscope.

"Good morning, Martin. Not feeling so great today, eh?" he said.

Martin's head wobbled slowly side-to-side as the surgeon listened to his chest. Worry lines etched his forehead. "Has Dr. Ellingham been coughing?" he asked the nurse who had been in the room for the last several hours.

"Some, but he doesn't seem to have enough air to bring anything up."

Ed twisted the stethoscope around his hand. "Chris, I'm thinking we should get a respiratory therapist in here to suction out his lungs and airways, then try some heliox. Any thoughts?"

"Those are my thoughts, actually. I'll get it lined up," Chris said before leaving the room.

Mr. Christianson turned to Louisa. "Why don't we step out for just a minute to talk, let Martin rest."

Louisa glanced over at Ruth, noticing the strain on the elderly woman's face as she watched her nephew labouring for every breath. She took hold of her arm and led her out to the corridor.

Mr. Christianson unwound his stethoscope and flipped it around the back of his neck. "Martin's really having to work against both his compromised lung walls and the mucous that's built up in both his lungs and airways. We'll get a respiratory therapist to suction out those secretions, then we'll switch him from oxygen to heliox."

Louisa tipped her head. "What's heliox?"

"It's a blend of oxygen and helium. Helium's lighter than oxygen so it'll be easier for Martin to move than oxygen alone. It'll also create less turbulence in the airways. It's in Martin's best interests to try to get him through the day without a ventilator, so hopefully this will buy us a bit of time," Ed explained.

"Is he getting enough oxygen? He looks very pale," said Louisa.

"His blood oxygen is quite low right now— eighty-eight percent. Not dangerous, but definitely not high enough. We'd like to see that number above ninety-five percent, so we have a bit of work to do."

Louisa worried her bottom lip as she glanced through the glass door at her husband.

"We'll keep at this a while longer, but we're not going to take any chances, Mrs. Ellingham. We'll have him on a ventilator the minute we see a potential danger."

Ruth crossed her arms in front of her, tapping a finger against her elbow. "He seems to be struggling terribly."

"Yes, he is. I know it's hard to see him like this. Watching someone fight for air is gut wrenching. But try to be encouraging. Right now, the goal is to get him through the day. Then hopefully we'll see some improvement with the contusions," Ed said.

Two respiratory therapists had arrived while Mr. Christianson was talking with them, so Ruth and Louisa waited in the corridor until they had finished their work before returning to the room.

Chris came in a short time later. "Well, that's a bit of an improvement," he said as he wagged a finger at the patient monitor. "His blood oxygen level's up to ninety-one percent, so I'm sure he's more comfortable now." He pulled up his wrist and adjusted his watch. "There'll be a nurse in here with him constantly, so if you'd like to get a bite to eat this would be a good time."

"Mm, I don't want to leave him," Louisa said, clasping her husband's hand in her own.

"Louisa, you need to take care of yourself," Ruth said as she patted her shoulder. "You'll be of no use to Martin if you're home sick in bed."

Chris jerked his head towards the door. "Come on, doctor's orders. He probably feels like he's run a marathon or two, so I'd imagine he'll be asleep for a while."

Louisa reluctantly left with Ruth. They ate a quick lunch together, before the elderly woman headed back to Portwenn for a business meeting with a contractor. When Louisa returned to the CCU, Martin was still sleeping.

The respiratory therapist came by again late in the afternoon and suctioned out his lungs and airways again. When Chris came down early that evening to collect Louisa, he was all smiles.

"I just spoke with Ed Christianson. Mart's latest x-rays look clearer and his bloodwork shows improvement as well."

He wagged a finger at the monitor. "His O2 level's up to ninety-eight percent, too. The infection's still a bit of a concern, but we both feel pretty confident that Martin will shake it now that the other problems are clearing up. So ... I think we should go and celebrate. We'll take you out for dinner tonight."

Louisa dropped into the chair by the bed and exhaled slowly. "This is the first bit of good news in three days. And the first time I've felt myself relax in as much time. Could I have a few minutes with Martin before we go ... if you don't mind."

"Certainly. I need to collect some papers from my office. I'll be back for you in a little while."

A little more than an hour later, the Parsons sat with Louisa at a table in the restaurant where she and Martin had eaten not so long ago. Fragrant lilies were again ornamenting the tables.

James watched from his high chair as Chris tapped his fingers against the edge of the table before picking up his spoon and joining in, smacking it against his metal tray.

Louisa looked around at the disapproving looks from the diners around them before quickly dumping bits of dry cereal out in front of the boy and prying the spoon from his hand.

"Sorry about that, Louisa. I'm afraid I got that started," Chris said before hesitating. "Erm, Martin mentioned that he'd been seeing a therapist, someone to help him sort out some childhood issues. How's it going for him?"

She looked at him uncertainly, remembering her husband's reaction to her previous discussion with his boss. "I think it's helped him to remember some things that he might have preferred to keep locked away in that emotional vault of his, but it's been ... Well, let's just say that he looks at some things through different eyes now, maybe admitting some things to himself."

She paused as their waitress arrived with their meals.

Chris reached into the basket of bread on the table and tore a piece off before slathering it with butter. His wife gave him a deprecating glare.

"It's the piece de resistance!" he said defensively. "They have the best bread in Cornwall."

Carole shook her head and rolled her eyes before directing her attention to Louisa. "What were you saying about Martin and remembering things?"

"Well, he'd spent his entire life thinking that there was something wrong with him, and that he deserved the treatment he received as a child," she said as she added more spaghetti to her son's bowl. "Either he deserved it, or there was nothing out of the ordinary about it. It's going to take some time for him to accept this altered view of history. I'm surprised he discussed it with you, Chris."

"Probably not half as surprised as I was when he brought it up the other day."

"Hmm, he's a very private man. Even *I'm* having to come to terms with the fact that there are many things about Martin that I'll never be privy to. I tend to want to know every little detail and ... well, like you said Chris, Martin tends not to dwell on things. Maybe if we're blessed with enough years together, I'll be able to tease half of what I want to know out of him," she said, a pensive expression settling on her face.

"You'll get those years, Louisa." Chris gave her a nod of his head before reaching for another piece of bread.

Tuesday was a blissfully uneventful day at the Royal Cornwall. Martin was sleeping when Louisa arrived that morning, and he didn't wake until after noon. The mask over his face had been replaced by a simple nasal cannula and his breathing had returned to normal but for a few rattly coughs.

Louisa was reading a book in the chair by his bed when he woke up. "G'morning," he slurred.

She looked up in surprise. "Good morning to you as well. Except it isn't morning any more," she said looking at her watch. "You look like you're feeling much better today."

"Mm, iss much easier to breathe."

Though his body continued to fight the infection, Martin's temperature was slightly lower, and his blood work continued to show signs of improvement as well.

Louisa entertained him for a while, telling him about James and Chris's spontaneous concert the previous evening. There was the merest hint of a sparkle in his eyes before his lids drifted shut and he fell back to sleep.

Her appetite having returned, Louisa slipped out to get lunch. When she returned to the room, she settled back into her now familiar position at her husband's bedside, waiting for him to wake again.

Late in the afternoon, he began to stir in his sleep. When Louisa looked up at him he was sweating profusely. His hair was damp and sweat trickled down his temples.

She reached out to take his hand, but he pulled back quickly when she made contact with him. His breathing became rapid, and he began to moan as his mumbled, disjointed babblings began again.

He began to writhe in the bed. "I'm sorry ... don' Mum."

"Martin, it's okay," Louisa said as she tried again to take his hand. He pushed it away and bolted upright in the bed, crying out as the involuntary movement triggered pain in his abdomen and arm.

Louisa put her hands on his cheeks and talked to him until she could see he was aware of his surroundings. "Martin, I'm going to get a nurse to check that everything's okay. Just stay still. *Stay—still.*"

As she hurried towards the nurses station, Chris came around the corner, nearly colliding with her. "Chris, I think

Martin may have hurt himself," she said as she raced back to the room.

"What's happened?"

Louisa moved back to her husband's side and put her hand on his sweat-soaked back. She leaned forward, attempting to make eye contact. "He was dreaming, and he sat up suddenly in the bed. I think he twisted his arm in the sling. I'm not sure."

Tremors rippled through his body. "Where does it hurt, Mart?" Chris asked.

His face contorted in pain. "My arm ... an' belly!" he rasped.

Chris went to the doorway and yelled out to the nurses' station, "I need a hand in here ... *now*!"

He returned and dropped the side rail down on the bed. "Let's lay you back down, Mart," he said as a male nurse moved in to take Louisa's place.

Chris adjusted the morphine drip. He waited a few minutes before removing the bandage from Martin's laparotomy incision, handing it to the nurse. "Call Mr. Christianson. Tell him he's needed here A.S.A.P."

"Yes, sir," the young man said as he moved towards the door.

The doctor gave the wound a quick inspection and then reached for the sling. "Okay Mart, let's take a look at that arm."

Martin shook his head and slapped at his friend's hand. "Don' ... touch it! It hurds!"

Chris ignored the defensive behaviour and pulled open the closures on the sling. "I'll let Ed check you over, but I think the arm's okay, Mart."

The bandage covering Martin's thoracotomy incision was peeled away and the long line of sutures, running from his chest and around his side, was revealed to Louisa for the first time. She grimaced before averting her eyes.

"The thoracotomy incision looks okay, but you've torn a couple of your abdominal sutures," Chris said. "Ed's on his way down to check you out ... make sure that arm's all right, but my guess is he'll just butterfly the sutures in your belly. I don't think you've done any serious damage, mate."

Martin blinked back tears as the intense pain he had been in began to ease.

Mr. Christianson arrived shortly and conducted his own examination.

"Well, the good news is that your fever has broken, Martin. We'll draw some more blood and get some more pictures of your lungs, but I think you've conquered the infection my friend," Ed said, laying his hand on Martin's head. "Put dry sheets on the bed and get Dr. Ellingham a clean gown, please," he told the nurse.

The surgeon butterflied the torn incision before leaving his patient in the hands of the nursing staff.

Martin lay on his back on clean bedding, staring at the ceiling.

"Are you all right?" asked Louisa.

"Mm."

She brushed his hair back with her fingertips and he turned to look at her. "It wass ... it wass blood," he said before he fell back to sleep again."

Chapter 12

Louisa sensed her husband's gaze on her and looked up from the book she had picked up in the gift shop. "Sorry, I didn't mean to ignore you; I didn't realise you were awake," she said, getting to her feet.

"Mm," he grunted softly.

"You look so, so tired, Martin." She rested her hand on his cheek and pressed her lips to his forehead. "I love you," she whispered.

When she pulled back, his eyes were tearing, and his chin trembled as he watched her.

"Oh, Martin. It's going to be all right. You have a lot of healing to do, but you won't be alone with this. Ruth and the Parsons are here to help you, and I'm not going anywhere ... right?"

He shook his head. "No."

"Martin, I'm staying right here with you," she said giving him a strained smile. "I promise ... I'm not going anywhere."

Tears rolled down his cheeks, and he gave a another weak shake of his head.

Louisa's brow furrowed as she cocked her head at him. "Is there something else the matter, Martin?"

"The blood ... there was so mush," he slurred.

"I know. It was a horrible thing that happened." Her fingers brushed through his hair, hanging up on a matted area where blood had dried hard.

She went to her handbag, pulling out the ever-present package of moist towelettes before returning to her husband's side.

Martin forced the sanguineous images from his head. He needed to focus on staying in control. The intense ache in his body was constant, interrupted only by the sharp, searing pain that raced through his limbs several times a minute. The drugs in his system had dulled his senses and alleviated some of the pain, but they, along with his injuries, had also left him feeling vulnerable. He couldn't think about the blood any more. He had to stay focused ... stay in control.

"Whad time iss id?" he asked his wife, his voice thready.

Louisa pulled up her arm and glanced at her wrist. "Almost six o'clock."

His eyes drifted shut for several minutes before he opened them again. "Iss'it morning?"

"No, it's evening. Chris will be coming to pick me up soon."

"Whad time is'sit?"

Louisa picked up his hand and pressed it to her lips. "Almost six. You just asked me that, you know."

"Mm. Time ... goes sslow." He closed his eyes and drifted off again, only to be jarred awake by disturbing images and sensations.

"Louissa, I think ... I think I have blood on my trousers."

"Martin, you don't have any trousers on, just a hospital gown."

"*Noo.* I can ... feel id ... on my lap." He blinked tears from his eyes as he became more agitated. "She'll be angry. I need to ged them off."

He raised his head and began to pull at the blankets, trying to uncover his legs.

"What is it, Martin? What do you need?"

"Don' led her see!" he pleaded. "She'll be angry. Help me ged them off."

"Martin, you're not thinking straight. You're not wearing any trousers. Remember, you're in hospital."

His eyes darted around the room before he relaxed into his pillow again and allowed himself to fall back to sleep.

The door rumbled open and a nurse came in to change out the IV bottles. "I'm going to be in here for a while if you'd like to stretch your legs ... maybe run and get a cuppa," she undertoned.

Louisa yawned and got up from her chair, pulling her arms up over her head. "I *could* use a bit of a break ... if you're sure you'll be in here with him."

The middle-aged nurse smiled and nodded her salt-and-pepper head. "You go on. I have paperwork to do. I'll bring it in here and work on it."

"Thank you." Louisa took another glance at her sleeping husband and slipped out the door.

Even though she was still inside the confines of the hospital walls, it was liberating to be out in the busy corridors, filled with people going about their normal everyday activities. She entered the brightly lit canteen, with its windowed walls that allowed the outdoors in, and she took a deep breath.

A young man, clad in a white coat, passed her. "Mrs. Ellingham ..." he said, giving her a nod. "Is your husband doing any better?"

"Yes ... yes, he *is* a bit better," she said, knitting her brow as she turned to watch his retreating form.

She pulled a bottle of milk from the refrigerator and handed two pounds to the woman on the opposite side of the counter.

"Get used to that, dear," the woman said as the till drawer popped open. "Those young interns are going to bend over backwards to make a good impression on Mr. Ellingham's wife."

Louisa gave the woman a smile and corrected her. "It's *Dr.* Ellingham now; he's no longer a surgeon."

"Oh, he'll *always* be a surgeon in the eyes of the medical students who emulate him."

"Hmm. Well, thank you," Louisa said, holding her purchase up in front of her.

Her husband was still sleeping when she returned to his room. She slipped in quietly and took up her position at his bedside.

"Just use the call button if you need anything, Mrs. Ellingham," the nurse said softly before she headed out the door.

Martin began to stir a short while later, his occasional soft groans, mingled with unintelligible mumblings.

Louisa looked up from her book when she noticed his attempt to reach out to her.

"Hello," she said as she stood and took his hand in hers.

He stared at her, glassy-eyed. "Louissa ... there was so mush blood."

She breathed out a soft sigh. "I know, Martin. It was a horrible accident."

"It got on my ... on my trousers."

"That's okay; we can get you new trousers."

"An' on the floor."

Louisa cocked her head at him. "On the floor? In the car you mean?"

Martin moved his head side-to-side. "It was blood," he said, his face crumpling as he began to cry.

"Shh, shh, shh. It's going to be all right." Louisa had never felt so useless. She had no words that seemed sufficient to console him. So, she lowered the rail and carefully squeezed herself on to the edge of the bed, lying on her side against him. Then, putting her arm between them and holding his hand, she nestled her face into his neck.

Chris came by a short time later to pick her up to go home for the night. When he stuck his head in the door he saw his friend asleep with his wife next to him in the bed. He slid the door closed quietly and went to the canteen to get something to eat.

Louisa woke with a start. She hadn't intended to nod off, but Martin's warmth and the comfort of his closeness had been sedating. She slipped off the bed, trying not to wake him, but her movements roused him from his slumber.

"I'm sorry, I didn't want to disturb you," she said as she leaned over to kiss him.

"Mm."

"I'll need to leave in a little while."

Martin reached his hand out to her. "Jus' ... come back."

"I'll be back first thing in the morning. I promise."

Louisa heard approaching footsteps and turned to look as Chris, Robert, and Will Simpson came through the door.

The surgeons greeted Martin and Louisa before turning their attention to the patient notes hanging at the foot end of the bed.

"Hmm, it looks like it's been a rough couple of days, Martin. Doing better now?" Robert asked as Will began pulling the blankets back so they could assess their patient's wounds.

"Yess."

"Good. I think we can proceed as scheduled then. Do you have any questions for us? Or I guess in your case, advice?"

Martin's eyes drifted shut for a moment before he looked back up at his former tutor. "Don' ... pick ... pickle your neural pathways ... tonight," he said, echoing an admonition Robert himself always gave his registrars the night before a surgical day.

"Good advice. Total abstinence for you, my friend." Robert laid his hand on Martin's arm while giving Will an amused grin.

"We'll be on deck bright and early tomorrow morning. You're scheduled for surgery at half seven," Will said as his fingers tapped against the bed rail.

Louisa rubbed her hands up and down her arms and worried her lip. "How long will Martin be in theatre?"

"It's hard to be real precise, but I would estimate four to six hours. We'll remove any additional nonviable tissue and clean things out again. We also need to take care of the laceration to his thigh. Then we'll repack everything and bandage him up."

Louisa looked at Will, confused. "What do you mean, repack?"

"Well, we discussed this the other day, but you had a lot of information being thrown at you. It's likely we won't close the wounds tomorrow. They'll probably get repacked with the bead pouches that we used before and then vacuum bandaged. We'll take him back into surgery in a couple of days and remove any additional tissue that doesn't look healthy. If all goes well, we'll close the wounds at that point in time. Some reconstruction down the road is likely as well. We'll have to take it a step at a time, though."

"Yeah ... yeah, I remember now." She dropped into the chair in the corner of the room and pressed her hands to her face.

Robert looked at her sympathetically. "I know that it's difficult to see that any progress has been made, but think back a few days. Martin's much more stable now, and we're halfway home on the trips to theatre."

"Is this surgery going to set Martin back at all?" Louisa asked apprehensively.

"Martin's much less likely to develop an infection now than he was two days ago. And the contusions on his lungs won't be a factor this time around," Robert said before hanging the patient notes on the end of the bed. "We'll see you in the morning, then."

"Yes, thank you both ... for all that you've done for Martin." Louisa returned to her husband's side, taking his hand.

"I should get you home to that son of yours Louisa," Chris said. "And, Martin, you need to get some rest. Hopefully, you can manage that on your own tonight." He gave his friend a knowing smile before moving towards the door.

"Mm." Chris's good-natured chaff was lost on Martin. He stared blindly before turning his gaze to his wife.

"I'll be right with you, Chris," Louisa said.

She leaned over and pressed her lips to his. "I've been missing you in my bed you know."

"Mm."

"You go to sleep, and I'll see you in the morning," she said, kissing him on the forehead. "I love you."

"Mm, love you, too."

Chapter 13

Carole and James accompanied Chris and Louisa to the hospital the following day. She had only a short amount of time with her husband before they came to take him to surgery.

Martin's friend had been indispensable to her in so many ways throughout the ordeal, and today was no exception. Chris had managed to bend the rules about children outside the CCU waiting area, and he stood in the corridor holding James so that Martin could see him before going to theatre.

Louisa saw him approaching with her son in his arms and a smile on his face. "Well, we sent your husband off to surgery a happy man, I think. James threw a bit of a wobbler when they wheeled Martin off though." He gave the baby a gentle poke in the stomach. "You almost gave us away, mate."

Louisa walked over, and Chris passed the boy to her. "Did you get to see your daddy?" she asked as she rubbed noses with a sniffly James.

She wiped the tears from her son's cheeks, and then smiled up at her husband's friend. "Thank you so much for doing that, Chris. Martin has been missing him." Louisa settled into the chair next to Carole.

"Well, you two might want to think about doing something fun today. There's nothing that you can do to help Martin right now, Louisa, and it would be good for you to get away from this place. Go shopping or whatever it is women do when they go off together."

He leaned over and kissed his wife. "I'm afraid I have a job to get to, but I'll let you know the minute I hear anything from

Will and Robert," Chris said before heading down the hallway towards his office.

Louisa and Carole spent the morning shopping for clothes for James. Then they returned to the house for lunch, and Louisa put the baby down for a nap.

She rested while James slept, but she kept thinking about Martin on the operating table yet again. She hoped that the assurances she had received that this procedure would be easier than the others would not turn out to be false promises.

She began to hear the soft coos and gurgles of baby chatter, and she knew they would soon turn into howls of protest if she didn't get James up for his afternoon snack. It seemed that lately he was either eating or sleeping every moment of the day.

Carole was putting a pot roast in the oven for dinner as Louisa set James in the high chair with his bottle of formula and a bowl of dry cereal.

"Martin should be getting back to his room soon," she said absently.

Carole glanced over at her friend. "Yep. You're probably anxious to get back to the hospital."

"I am. After the way the last few days have gone ... I'm so nervous that my stomach is churning. I hope that Will and Robert are right about things being easier for Martin this time around."

Carole set two glasses of water on the table and sat down across from her. "Robert and Will are very seasoned surgeons. I don't think they would have told you that if they had any misgivings whatsoever."

Carole scrutinised her friend's face. "Is there something else you're worried about?"

Louisa hesitated. "It's just that ... well, Martin kept talking about all the blood yesterday. He was upset that it had gotten on his trousers. He thought he needed to get his trousers off ... I'm not sure. He wasn't make a lot of sense. But he was so distressed ... I'm really worried about him, Carole. And not just his physical injuries."

Her ponytail whipped side-to-side. "Although, God knows, that's a worry. But it's more than that. He's trying to deal with so much right now—emotionally. I just don't know how much he can handle. He kept talking about the blood. I hope this isn't going to cause more serious problems in the future ... psychologically."

Carole ran her fingertip around the rim of her glass. "I can certainly understand why you'd be worried. The strain that you've been under for the last five days would be tough enough to deal with, but if you have these other concerns in addition, I would imagine you're feeling pretty overwhelmed.

Louisa held her thumb and index finger up in front of her face. "Just a bit."

"The parents that he had and the whole awful boarding school experience must have made for a very lonely and miserable little boy. But Chris has described his parents to me and ... well, maybe being shipped off to boarding school was better than the alternative."

Louisa added some bits of cereal to James's bowl. "I've wondered the same thing, but he's had some nightmares about boarding school as well."

"You know, it's unfortunate that Martin comes across as such an abrasive, unfeeling man," Carole said. "I'm sure it affects how people treat him. In reality, you and I know he's really a very sensitive, shy, and soft-hearted fellow."

James gave Louisa a broad grin as he bounced in the high chair seat. She stood up and placed a kiss on his head before turning to Carole. "How long have you known Martin?"

"He and Chris were roommates when Chris and I started dating. Hmm, must be at least twenty years ago, now." She screwed up her face. "Wouldn't have thought it could have been that long ... makes me feel old."

Louisa took their empty water glasses over and put them in the dishwasher. "You probably know him better than I do after all that time."

"Oh, I don't know about that. Chris maybe. Martin has been a really good friend to him; he taught him some self-discipline. I'm not sure Chris would have stuck it out through medical school if Martin hadn't pushed him. Chris owes him a lot."

"Well, I think Chris has repaid him in full and then some. I hate to think how much worse the last days would have been for Martin and me if we hadn't had you and Chris by our side every step of the way. We'll be forever grateful."

"We're happy that we've been in a position to help." Carole glanced up at the clock on the wall. "Well, I know that you're anxious, so let's go see that man of yours."

Chris called Louisa shortly before they left the house to tell her that Martin was out of surgery and would be returned to the CCU shortly. Louisa hadn't been back at the hospital for more than a few minutes before she heard the door slide open, and they pushed Martin's bed into the room. It took the nursing staff a while to get him settled. They had to get his legs positioned properly, his arm back into the sling that kept it elevated, and ice packed around his injured limbs. Finally, the IVs needed to be adjusted. The epidural catheter had been removed when they were prepping him for surgery, as it was felt to be no longer necessary.

Once he was situated, Louisa approached the bed and pressed her cheek to his before whispering into his ear, "I love you Martin."

Martin tried to shake the medically induced fog from his brain as he listened to the muffled voices around him. His limbs began to ache as he felt them being shifted, and he couldn't make sense of where he was. He tried to open his eyes, but his lids were too heavy.

*He strained to hear what was being said by the people in the room, but their voices were being gradually drowned out by the harsh and belittling voice of his father. "***You'd*** *have to drug 'em to keep 'em. You never did have any financial nous! Grow a backbone, boy! What are you going to do, let people bully you all your life?"*

Martin tried to wake himself, to erase his father's sneering face and mocking laugh from his consciousness. "You want to know why this happened? Because I have a son who lacks even an ounce of sense, that's why!"

Louisa sat down by the bed to begin another anxious waiting game. There was a soft tap on the door before it rolled open and Chris walked in.

"Well, I guess I'm not going to get a look at how things came out today," he said pointing to the packing of ice and bandage material around Martin's arm and legs. "Any sign he could be coming around?"

"No, nothing at all yet. Chris, will he be in pain again when he wakes up this time?"

Chris glanced down at Louisa's hands as they twisted the strap on her handbag. "I would imagine he will be. They've done a lot of manipulating of those limbs and performed very invasive surgery. We'll try to get on top of it right away though. Pain has an adverse effect on a patient's recovery, so we want to make him as comfortable as possible."

Martin had to get away from his father. He tried desperately to run, but his legs wouldn't move. They felt heavy, as if someone was holding them down.

His father's derisive remarks continued as the man gripped him by the hand, pulling him towards him. "Fine, don't enlist! You'll be doing the Navy a favour. They need men made of sterner stuff than you are, boy. You'd never be able to cut it!" Martin tried to pull his hand away.

Louisa felt her husband's fingers twitch in her hand as he mumbled incoherently. "I think he's waking up now, Chris."

His father gripped his hand tighter as he looked him up and down. The old man's eyes filled with disgust as he watched his son squeeze drops of urine from an eyedropper on to a pregnancy test strip. "Look at you! Putting piss on to pieces of paper ... playing at doctors in Portwenn!" Martin jerked his arm back, lashing out forcefully at the man.

Louisa rubbed Martin's hand as he began to rouse. He pulled away from her, flinging his arm out wildly, ripping out the catheter in his wrist.

"Whoa, Mart. You're going to hurt yourself, mate," Chris said as he reached across the bed to grasp the bleeding wound in his friend's arm. "Louisa, please call for a nurse."

Chris pushed a now struggling Martin back down on to the bed. "Martin, you need to open your eyes. Come on. Wake up, Mart!"

The insistent voice of his friend broke through the fog, and Martin opened his eyes.

"Are you with me now, Mart?"

Martin pushed his head back into the pillow as pain shot through his left leg. A nurse hurried in and slid gauze pads under Chris's hand, pressing down on her patient's wrist until the bleeding stopped.

Martin groaned loudly as the pain in his arm and legs intensified.

"Martin, we need to get a new IV going. Then we can get some morphine into you. Hang in there."

Chris looked up as another nurse entered the room. "Page Mr. Dashwood and Mr. Simpson, please."

Louisa slipped back in next to her husband as soon as the nurse had finished inserting the new IV She took his hand in hers. "Martin, you need to lie still."

Robert arrived first and got the morphine drip going again before adjusting it so that Martin was receiving a higher dose.

"Hey, Martin. Chris tells me there was some unruly behaviour ... that you pulled out your other IV. How are you doing now?"

He grimaced and released a slow groan. "Mmrrr! It hurds!"

"Okay, where are you on the scale? Can you tell me that?"

"Eight-aaaaw."

Martin grabbed for his injured arm, desperate to relieve himself of the pain. Robert pulled him back and held him down on the bed.

"That sounds like more than an eight," Robert said as he allowed more medication through the line.

Martin's struggle with his surgeon slowed as the additional morphine began to suppress his central nervous system.

"Can I trust you to lie still, Martin? Can I let go of you now?"

Martin squeezed his eyes shut as he nodded his head. "Where's my ... wive?"

"She's right here," Robert said, giving her a wave of his hand.

Louisa wiped the tears from her face as she came to her husband's side.

"Are you doing better now?" she asked.

Martin closed his eyes and nodded. "I'm ssorry. I upsed you."

She shook her head. "It's all right. I'm better if you're better," she said as she sat down beside him.

Martin looked at her, bleary-eyed, his forehead etched with worry. "This should be the worss' of id. Id should get bedder now."

The guilt he felt for the burden this was putting on her suddenly overwhelmed him, and he swallowed back a sob. "I'm so ... so sorry," he whispered.

He wanted the ordeal to be over—the pain, the fear, the stress. Seeing Louisa so upset sank his spirits. Martin longed for home.

Chapter 14

Louisa slipped out of the room once Martin had fallen back to sleep. She needed to give Carole an update, and she felt an overwhelming need to hold her son.

James was beginning to tire of the games that Carole had been entertaining him with and began to kick his legs and squeal when he saw his mother approaching.

"Hello, James!" Louisa said, reaching out for him.

Carole handed the boy to his mum. "He's really needing some freedom to move, but I haven't wanted to let him down on the hospital floor."

"Martin would thank you for that."

"How's he doing?"

"Louisa dropped down next to her friend. "Is there anywhere private in this bloody building where I can go to have a good cry?"

"Not so great then?"

"He's sleeping right now, but when he first woke up he managed to pull his IV out, which of course bled like crazy. Then he was in a lot of pain. He was grabbing at his injured arm and ..." She took in a deep breath. "Robert tried to pull his hand back but eventually had to hold him down until the morphine took effect."

"Oh, Louisa." Carole fished in her purse for a tissue.

"Martin saw how upset I was, and I think that upset *him*. I feel so absolutely useless right now. I couldn't be of any help to him today, and I couldn't think of a single thing to say that would make him feel any better yesterday."

"Is that why you crawled into bed with him?"

Louisa shot her a quick glance.

"Sorry, Chris saw you." She shrugged her shoulders and passed her the tissue.

"Mm, that's okay. It explains Chris's remark to Martin yesterday afternoon."

"Maybe if I talked to Martin ... assured him that you're doing okay?"

"That'd be nice, Carole. He's probably sleeping right now, though."

"I won't wake him if he is. I'll be back in a tick," she said before heading down the corridor.

Martin had his eyes closed and appeared to be asleep when Carole slid the door open and stepped into the room. She was turning to leave when she heard his voice, gravelly and weak.

"Carole, don' go."

"Sorry, I didn't want to wake you."

"Thass okay."

"Not such a great afternoon I hear," she said, walking over to his bed.

"No ... I upsed Louisa."

Carole straightened out the covers and pulled them up under his chin. "Martin, you need to focus on getting well. Try not to worry about Louisa. Chris and I are taking good care of her. We're making sure she's getting three meals a day—optimally nutritious, of course. And we're reminding her to get enough rest. We're both happy to listen if she needs to talk, as well. And she *has* been talking."

Martin turned his head away and pulled his arm over his face. "She's unhappy," he said, swallowing back the emotions that were threatening to reveal themselves.

"Well, of course she is; she loves you very much. She's afraid for you and it hurts her terribly to see you in pain."

"I'm trying nod to ..." he pulled in a ragged breath, "... to led her see, but iss so hard."

"You mean you're trying not to let her see that you're in pain?" Carole asked incredulously.

"Mmm."

"Oh, Martin. You can't hide *that!* For once in your life, will you please allow yourself to be cared for? Watching you go through this is going to be tough for her, but I'm afraid there's no getting around it ... for either of you. You can help her most by making her feel as if she's of use to you in some way. And I *know* that you need her. Let her know that, too."

She rested her hand on his head. "Well, I wanted to come in and say hello. I'll go now ... let you get some sleep." Leaning over, she kissed him on the cheek before walking towards the door.

"Oh, one more thing." Returning to his bedside, she whispered in his ear. "Be nice to the nurses!"

"Yess."

Carole picked James up in the waiting room to take him home with her, and Louisa stayed at the hospital.

Martin was asleep when she returned to his room, and he didn't wake until almost six that evening.

He turned his head towards the door as it rumbled open.

Chris stepped into the room. "Hey, Mart. I'm surprised to see you awake. How are you doing ... pain any better?"

"Maybe a bit."

"Well, don't lay there suffering. Tell someone if you're topping three on the pain scale, and we'll get you what you need to be comfortable."

Martin gave his friend an incredulous look before glancing down at his battered body. "Ah, thad ... was a joke."

Chris gave a soft chuckle. "It wasn't meant to be, but I see your point."

"I have some news that I think you'll be happy to hear," Chris said as he tapped out a rhythm on the bed rail. "The investigatory committee decided to continue the funding for our air ambulance."

The corners of Martin's mouth turned up slightly. "Thass fery good news."

"You can take full credit, Martin. That damn committee stood in the ED Friday night, listening to the whole rescue operation play out over the dispatch radio. Most of the committee members had made up their minds before they left Royal Cornwall that night."

Chris picked up the patient notes and flipped back the cover. "I should have known better than to tell my literal friend here that I needed him to make a convincing argument to that committee," he said, giving Louisa a smile.

She returned a feeble grin. "Well, I suppose if we were looking for a silver lining in all of this, securing the air ambulance funding would be it."

Chris snapped the cover shut on the notes and slipped it back over its hanger. "The other bit of news I have is that the preliminary investigation of your accident points to driver error as the cause."

Martin's memory of the accident had been sketchy, and he groaned softly. "Oh, God. Was it my ... fauld?"

"No, no, no! The report said that the lorry driver hadn't slept in more than thirty-six hours. He fell asleep at the wheel and drifted into your lane, Mart. There were two witnesses to the accident, and the tire tracks, measurements ... everything corroborated what the witnesses said happened."

Martin closed his eyes and released a soft sigh.

"Well, Mart, are you ready to give your wife back to Carole and me for the night?"

"I need to talk with 'er ... firss."

"Of course. Louisa, I'll be outside. Mart, try to get some sleep. I'll see you in the morning."

Martin waited until the door had closed behind his friend before reaching his hand out to his wife.

"Louisa ... I'm sorry for all this."

"Martin, don't you *dare* apologise for being hurt. None of this is your fault."

"You're unhappy."

"Neither of us is very happy right now, Martin. So, I guess we'll muddle through together, right?" She took his face in her hands and stroked his cheeks with her thumbs.

"Mm. How's James?"

"He's just fine. He really seems to like Carole, and I think the feeling is mutual."

Martin toyed with the edge of the blanket. "Chris wouldn't led me touch him."

"You mean in the corridor ... before your surgery?"

"Mm. He wouldn't come fery close."

Louisa gave her husband a small smile. "He was already breaking the rules, you know ... bringing James down there. Children aren't supposed to go beyond the waiting area ... all the illnesses they can carry."

"Iss James ssick?"

"No, he's perfectly healthy. There *are* rules though."

"But, if—"

Louisa placed her index finger against his lips. "Shh. You're just going to have to follow some rules while you're here."

"Mm." He gazed at her, his eyes tearing. "I tol' you 'bout the blood."

"I understand, Martin. It must have been horrible for you."

He grimaced and shook his head. "No. Not thad. I 'membered something. It wasn't paint ... id wass ... blood wass on the floor."

"At your parents' ... when you were young, you mean?"

"Mm. There was so mush. An' id was on my trou ... ssers."

Louisa brushed her thumb across his forehead. "I'm not sure you're thinking clearly right now. You've been through a lot in the last few days, and you're very heavily medicated. Maybe you—"

"You don' believe me?"

"I believe you're remembering things this way at the moment, but I think once the medication has worn off—"

"No!" he whispered. "I 'membered ... when I wass ... when I was'sin the car."

"Driving home the other day you mean?"

Martin shook his head slowly, closing his eyes for a moment. "In the car ... Louissa. When I couldn't ... I wass trabbed in the car."

Louisa held his hand, caressing it gently. "After the accident, you mean?"

"Mm." He breathed out a soft moan and nodded once. "I wass trabbed ... my arm hurd ... an' I ... I couldn't move. I smelled zumthing." His eyes drifted shut again. "I 'membered the smell. I could fee'lit ... warm an' wet. An' it spread across my ... my lap. An' in the study thad day ..." Martin tried to swallow back the lump that had formed in his throat.

"Martin, we could talk about this later, maybe when you're stronger," Louisa said as she grew increasingly concerned about the stress her husband appeared to be under.

His hand shook as he reached up and buried his fingers in his hair. "No ... no, Louissa. Please, jus' listen."

She caressed his cheek. "I'm listening, Martin. You go ahead, but stop anytime you want."

He inhaled, and the action loosened secretions in his lungs, causing him to cough. He grimaced and a groan escaped his lips.

"Are you all right?"

"Mm." He wiped the pain-induced tears from his eyes. "I could ssmell ... blood on my troussers ... in the car. I could fee'lit

… warm an' wet. I 'membered thad feeling in the sstudy. I wa'zitting on the floor. So mush blood. Blood wass running aroun' me … soaking my troussers thad day, too."

His face was expressionless as he stared up at the ceiling.

"Where was the blood coming from, Martin?"

His head swung lethargically, side to side. "I don' know. My father … he threw me back. He look'dat me … like he 'ated me. My mother … she wass angry. Wass blood on my trousers. An' on the floor. She said …" Martin pulled in a ragged breath. "She said thad I ruin everything. An' then she locked me in the cufferd."

"She locked you in the cupboard … under the stairs?" She brushed her fingers through his hair.

"Mm. I wass on my arm an' …" His breaths were becoming more rapid, but he kept unseeing eyes fixed on the ceiling as his chin began to tremble.

"Martin, I think we should talk about this when you're stronger. You'll remember it later, won't you?" Louisa nodded and smiled encouragingly.

"No, no … no, nooo! Jus' listen!" he protested weakly.

"All right, go ahead." Louisa stroked her fingertips along his forearm.

"I … I could smell id on my troussers, an' my arm hurd, an' it was har'to … har'to breath."

He rubbed at his forehead as he gulped back a sob. "I couldn't breath an' the blood … the ssmell made me veel sick. I vomided. I was scared. I knew Mum …"

Tears escaped and rolled down into his hair, but his gaze remained fixed.

"I peed myself an' … an' things jus' kep' gedding worse. I could hear voices … peeble in the housse. Af'er a long time … I heard the fron'door … an' it got quiet. Mum … she opened the door an' …" He sucked in several ragged breaths.

"She wass angry 'boud the mess. I couldn't ged up. Id hurd too mush to moof. My father pulled me out. Mum said ... go up ... take a bath an' throw ... the clothes in the bin. I did. An' then ... I wen'to bed."

Louisa sat silent for several moments before reaching for a tissue. She wiped the tears from his face and then leaned over, kissing him gently. "I'm so sorry, Martin. I'm so sorry."

"Do you belief me, Louissa?"

"Yes, Martin. I'm afraid I do."

He breathed out an audible sigh. "Good. But Chris iss waiting. He can be im—im— He doesn't like to waid. You should go now."

"Are you sure you'll be okay here by yourself? I mean, after what you just told me ..."

"I'm fine ... the nursses."

She eyed him uncertainly. "I'll stop at the nurses' station ... tell them to call me if you want me, okay?"

"Mm."

"You try to get some rest tonight. Maybe you'll feel better in the morning."

Martin dreaded the nights. He couldn't sleep well, and he was too alone with his thoughts. This night was no different as his father's words replayed in his head. What did he mean when he told him that something had happened because he had a son who lacked even an ounce of sense? Martin could now remember hearing those words said to him as a child, but he couldn't connect them to any incident. Had he been the cause of something terrible?

He tried to forget the words, but even in his sleep, they haunted him.

Physically, Martin was noticeably improved the following day. Ed Christianson stopped in to check on him before starting in with rounds.

"Your vital signs and blood gases all look good this morning, Martin. We've discontinued the midazolam and scaled back a bit on the morphine, but don't hesitate to say if you're needing more. I don't want you in pain."

The surgeon pulled out his pocket torch and looked in his patient's eyes. "How are the headaches? Getting any better?"

"I think so."

"Well, I don't anticipate any more unexpected trips to theatre, so I think we could let you eat something. Think you could keep some food down?"

"I'm not really hungry."

"Maybe not, but we need to be trying to get you off our IV diet. What do you think you might be able to eat?"

"I don't like hospital food."

"Sorry, Martin. That's all I've got."

He shrugged his shoulders. "I don't care then. Bring whatever you like."

Martin's mood was souring quickly when Louisa arrived a bit later.

She walked into the room and spied the bowl of porridge and side of toast on the tray in front of him. "Mmm, that looks good." She leaned over to kiss him. "How are you this morning? Must be doing better if they're letting you eat something."

He gave her an uncivil grunt before pushing the untouched tray away.

"It's a wonder patients get out of hospitals at all," he grumbled.

"You need to try to eat it, Martin," Louisa said.

He looked up at her as she watched him with pleading eyes. He mumbled unintelligibly as he pulled the tray back and reluctantly spooned some of the grey gelatinous material into his mouth, grimacing accordingly.

Chris stopped in a short time later, and Martin was still curmudgeoning.

"I take it you weren't happy with your food?" Chris said, peering at his friend over the patient notes.

"He didn't eat much, I'm afraid," Louisa already looked sapped by her husband's foul mood.

"What exactly is it you're wanting, Mart? Monkfish—no butter?"

"I wouldn't complain!" he snipped as he rubbed at his forehead.

Chris cocked his head at him. "Are you having a headache?"

"I am now! It's probably that mucilaginous grot your culinary geniuses slopped up in the name of breakfast," he said, wagging a finger at his partially eaten porridge.

"Martin!" Louisa hissed.

Chris looked over at Louisa and gave his head a small shake. "It's probably the change in your morphine dose, Mart. I'll talk to Ed about getting you something for that."

"Thank you," he answered crisply.

"You're welcome." Chris looked at his friend askance. "Louisa, could you give Martin and me a few minutes?"

She hesitated. "Sure, I'll run down and get myself a cup of coffee."

Chris pulled a chair up next to the bed. "Okay, what's the problem, Mart?" he asked after the door had closed.

Martin screwed up his face and Chris tipped his head at him. "Mart ... what's going on?"

"It's complicated."

Slouching down in the chair, Chris folded his arms across his chest and crossed his ankles in front of him. "Well, I'm not the brainbox you are, but I suspect if I try really hard I might be able to keep up with you, so let's hear it."

Martin cleared his throat, "I've been having a lot of nightmares lately ... well, for a while now. Really memories from my childhood ... things I'd managed to forget."

"Bad memories then?"

"Mm. After the surgery yesterday, I kept hearing my father's voice, all the belittling things he used to say."

"I know I'm not supposed to speak ill of the dead, but your dad was the worst excuse for a father I've ever met, mate."

Martin pulled in his chin. "Mm, yes."

"Sorry," Chris said. "Go on."

"Most of it I had remembered before, but this I remembered only yesterday ... when I was trying to shake the anaesthesia. Dad said, 'You want to know why this happened? Because I have a son who lacks even an ounce of sense, that's why.' But, I can't remember what happened."

Chris uncrossed his arms and sat up in his chair. "So, it's bothering you that you can't remember?"

"*No.* It's bothering me that I don't know what happened ... if I did something terrible!"

"Why would you think you'd done something terrible? The way your dad was, it could have been something completely benign that he was upset about."

"Mm, could be, but ..."

"But ... what?"

"I had another memory the other day, and I'm worried that the two might be related."

"Go on, Mart."

"I ... I ... well, my father was especially angry with me once. I don't have a complete memory of it, but something happened in his study. I remembered the other day that I was sitting on the floor and blood was running towards me. My father came in and grabbed me by the arm. He yelled, 'Martin, what have you done?' Then he threw me back behind him. When he yanked on my arm it broke. There's more to that memory, but

I don't think the rest is relevant to what I remembered yesterday."

Chris rubbed his hand down his face. "Jeez, Martin, I'm sorry."

Martin screwed up his face. "Ohh, don't look at me like that. I don't want your pity, Chris," Martin said angrily, turning his head away from his friend.

"Don't worry, mate. You're not the pitiful type. So, you're worried that ... what?"

"What if I did something, Chris. What if I'm responsible for ... God, I don't know what!"

"So, you're afraid you might have hurt someone? Is that what you're saying? Mart ... it's just *not* in you."

"I don't know what's in me any more," Martin mumbled. "I've tried so hard to remember, and it's not coming to me. I'm frustrated ... and worried."

Chris leaned forward to put his hand on his friend's arm. "I don't know what else to say, Mart. It just is—not—in you to do anything like what I think you're worried about."

"Mm ... hope not."

Chapter 15

Louisa glanced over at Chris as they drove home that evening. She was not only curious about what he and Martin had discussed earlier, but also a bit insecure. Was there something that her husband could talk to his friend about that he couldn't share with her?

"How do you think Martin's doing, Chris?" Louisa asked.

"His crankiness is probably a good sign that his physical health is improving. That and the headache that started up today is probably related to the reduced morphine dose as well. Will and Robert get back to Truro tonight, and they're planning to check in on him around six tomorrow morning. If they think he seems ready, they'll take him into theatre around half seven. It'll be a big day ... having those wounds finally closed."

"Mm, yes it will."

"Something bothering you, Louisa?" Chris asked as she bit at a fingernail.

"Martin was so irritable today, and I'm just worried. I'm worried about how he's doing with everything, mentally."

Chris squirmed in his seat. He didn't know how much of the information that Martin had shared today was confidential. "He's beginning to feel well enough to be more aware of things going on around him. The long days for one thing, the poking and prodding of the doctors and nursing staff, and the effect that all of this is having on you and James ... as well as Ruth. I'm sure he's probably been thinking about what lies ahead for the two of you, and he's no doubt feeling a bit discouraged."

Louisa pinched her lips together as she drummed her fingernails on the side window ledge. "Chris, I'm sorry, but I have to ask. What were you and Martin talking about?"

He pulled the car into the driveway and shifted it into park. "Louisa, maybe you should ask Martin about it. I suspect he'll tell you anyway. I don't want to betray a confidence."

"It's just that I'm imagining the worst right now. And I might not have a chance to talk with him until Saturday ... he'll be in surgery tomorrow."

Chris breathed out a heavy sigh. "All right, Louisa. Did Martin tell you about what he remembered the other day ... from his childhood?"

"Yes. Did he share that with you?"

"He did. He's worried that he may have hurt someone when he was young, hurt someone seriously; it's eating at him.

"I think that he's linking his memory of what his father yelled at him in the study that day ... the Martin-what-have-you-done bit ... with the old arse's comment that something happened because Martin lacked an ounce of sense.

"Given the fact that he remembers a lot of blood on the floor, he's made the leap to thinking he may have been responsible for someone being seriously injured ... or worse."

Louisa gave a slight shake of her head as her brow lowered. "He told you his father said these things?"

Chris stared back at her for a moment before dropping his chin to his chest. "Oh, bugger," he muttered. "I assumed he'd told you."

"No."

"Well, for Martin's sake, Louisa ... please don't let on you know. I've never given him a reason to distrust me. I've tried to be very careful about that, because I know that trust doesn't come easily to him."

"Yeah, I know. I won't say anything, Chris. I wouldn't do anything to jeopardise your friendship. But ... *Martin* hurting someone? He never would. Not physically, anywa—"

"What is it, Louisa?"

"Mm, it's just ... a few weeks ago, Martin got into a confrontation with a man. Well, the man's a patient of Martin's ... an alcoholic. Martin had stopped at the man's farm for a medical reason, and he found the man had physically abused his son ... broken the boy's arm. When Martin tried to get the man to sign a parental release form so that he could take him to Truro for x-rays, the man went off. He called his son a bastard and said the boy deserved what he got.

"Martin was terribly upset when he got home that night, because he had lost his temper with the man ... knocked him to the ground. He was going to hit him, but our village constable was there; he got him under control. Do you suppose that incident's added to Martin's worries?"

Chris shrugged his shoulders. "I'm not sure what to think, but I do know that what you just told me doesn't sound like Martin at all. I'm rather shocked to hear about it."

"Oh dear, I shouldn't have said anything, should I? You'll have to report this now. Chris, this all occurred about the time that these memories were coming back to him. I think seeing that little boy hurt the same way he had been hurt by his own father made Martin react defensively. *Please* ... don't report this."

"No, no. It's old news now. So, are you feeling better about the conversation I had with Martin?"

"I think so."

"Good. We better get inside or Carole's going to be interrogating me about our conversation on the driveway."

Friday was a big day. If all went according to plan, Martin's wounds would finally be closed and allowed to heal. Robert and Will had arrived in Truro the night before and were in his room shortly after six a.m.

"Are you ready to get this over and done with, Martin?" Robert asked.

"Mm, I'm feeling somewhat nervous about it."

"Don't worry, we're going to take very good care of you, my friend. But let's get some midazolam in you. That should make all your worries go away. Any questions before we muddle that brain of yours?"

Martin shook his head. "Just get it done. And ... thank you for all you've done to put me back together ... both of you."

"We didn't hesitate when Chris called us last week Martin. We were honoured that he asked us to be the knuckleheads in charge of reassembling the pieces, actually," Will said, patting his arm.

A nurse came in a few minutes later and added the midazolam to Martin's drip. By the time Chris and Louisa came through the door, he was feeling much more relaxed.

"Good morning," Louisa said as she kissed his forehead.

"Good morning. I missed you." He reached for her hand.

"Well, you'll finally get those wounds closed up today, and maybe they'll let you out of Critical Care soon." Louisa pulled a chair up next to him and sat down.

"Yes. Maybe James could come visit, too," Martin said, looking at Chris. "You could do that couldn't you, Chris? Get James in to see me?"

"Hmm, let's just wait and see on that, okay? I can't make you any promises."

Martin shifted his gaze back to his wife, and his expressive eyes softened. "Louisa, you are lovely ... absolutely beautiful. Isn't she beautiful, Chris?" he said turning to look at his friend.

"Yes, Martin, she is. You're very lucky, mate."

Louisa glanced over at Chris, puzzled by her husband's atypical behaviour.

"I see you've had the midazolam, eh, Mart?"

"Mmm." He stared fixedly at his wife before reaching his hand out for hers. "Louisa, you never gave me that proper kiss. Do you remember what you said at the school?"

"Yes, Martin. I remember."

"I was thinking about it on the way home that night … what we might do after the kiss. But then I had an accident."

"I tell you what," Chris interjected. "Why don't I step out and give you two a little time to yourselves before they come to take Martin to theatre."

"Thank you, Chris," Louisa said as a flush crept up her neck. "I'll see you in the waiting area."

She turned her attention back to her husband. "Now, what were you saying about a proper kiss?"

"Mmm, just that I never got one. I had an accident and—"

Louisa stood up and leaned over, pressing her lips to his in a very proper and passionate kiss.

"Oh, Louisa," he said hoarsely. "I love you very much. You do know that, don't you?"

"Yes, Martin. I do know."

"Do you know that I love you very much, too?" she said as she brushed her fingers through his hair.

"Do you?" he slurred.

"Yes, Martin, I do."

"Louisa, I've been wanting to tell you … thank you for my letter—the letter with the reasons."

"Well, you most certainly *do* deserve me."

"I'll always treasure it."

"Good. That makes me very happy."

"I want you to be happy," Martin said as he gave her a penetrating stare. "More than anything, I want you to be happy."

She brushed tears from her cheeks and nodded her head. "Well, I see they're coming to take you to theatre now, so I better say goodbye."

"Mmm. Could I have one more proper kiss first?"

She gave him a soft smile and bent down to share a final moment with him before the door slid open and two nurses came into the room.

This surgical procedure went much more quickly, and Louisa was surprised when she saw Chris walking towards the waiting area.

She got up and met him in the corridor. "How did it go?"

Chris took her arm. "He'll be back in his room soon, so let's talk on the way."

They zigzagged through a group of registrars and headed towards the CCU.

"Everything looks good for the most part," Chris said. "Robert's not entirely happy with the end result of the arm and left leg, so I suspect he'll be discussing doing some reconstruction down the road."

"Oh," Louisa said, a shadow of apprehension crossing her face.

"Don't worry about it at this point; just take things one step at a time.

"They put drains in both legs and the arm to try to prevent Martin from developing something called compartment syndrome. It occurs when oedema, or fluid accumulation in the cells, as well as bleeding into the soft tissue causes pressure to build up in a muscle compartment. It can lead to very serious and painful complications."

"How long will the drains stay in?"

"About forty-eight hours. Martin's progress will be assessed at that time anyway, and if all looks good, the drains will come out. By the way, the thoracotomy drains may come out tomorrow. Mr. Christianson will make that call."

Chris and Louisa arrived at the room just ahead of Martin. He was already beginning to wake a bit when they wheeled him through the door.

"Hi Martin, I'm here," Louisa said, taking his hand.

Martin turned his head towards her voice, looking at her through the haze of the drugs in his system. He tried to focus on her, but the image danced around, making him nauseous, and his eyes drifted shut again.

The surgeons stopped in momentarily, checking their patient's vital signs and verifying that all the specifications passed on to the nursing staff had been done completely and correctly.

Robert walked over and adjusted Martin's drip. "Well Louisa, I guess we'll turn him back over to you. Will and I have to be in theatre later this afternoon, so we're going to be leaving. Mr. Christianson and Dr. Parsons," he said, giving a nod towards the two men, "will be in charge of follow-up care. They'll contact us immediately if they foresee any problems."

"Thank you very much, Robert. You too, Will. I can't begin to tell you how much Martin and I appreciate all that you've done to provide him with the best outcome possible," Louisa said.

Will leaned back against the wall, crossing his ankles. "Martin still has a lot of work to do to get full use of those limbs back, but things are looking much better than we ever would have thought possible a week ago."

"Do you think he can get back to where he was before the accident?" Louisa asked, her eyes hopeful.

"We'll have to see about *that*, but I feel pretty sure that with work, he'll end up with fully functioning limbs. Just remember, encourage, but don't push him. He's come a long way. I don't think any of us felt very confident Martin would survive his injuries a week ago."

Louisa looked at Will taken aback. "I didn't realise Martin's injuries were that severe ... I mean, I knew that he'd been seriously injured but no one told me after the accident that he could ..." She hugged her arms around herself.

Robert walked over and leaned forward on the bed rail. "Louisa, do you remember when I was talking to you about the effects of shear forces? That organs of differing densities travel at different rates of speed, causing the less dense organs to pull away from the denser tissues surroun—"

"No, no, no, no, no." Robert's mini-physics dissertation was interrupted by his patient. "Dessity has no effec' ... on the spee' an objec' travels. Gal-aylo had thad figurd ... figurd ou' five hun'red years ago, Roberd. The sof' tissues pull away ... from the more rishid cardi'lash'enous an' bony tissues. *Thass* shear ... forsh."

"Somebody give this clever clogs some more midazolam," Robert said, chuckling.

Chapter 16

Martin was awake off and on throughout the afternoon. He was uncomfortable but not in severe pain as he had been after the previous procedures.

Louisa sat by his bed reading a book, peering up occasionally to watch him sleep. His words to her that morning had been so sweet and, she was sure, heartfelt. But his openness had been medically induced. How difficult it ordinarily was for him to express himself in that way. It seemed to be only in times of desperation, distress, or rage that he could lower the walls that he had built over the course of his life. His emotions were only revealed in moments of impulsivity. Genuine just the same, but not a calculated expression of his thoughts or feelings.

There was a short period of time before and after their wedding when he seemed more relaxed, more open. But as the weeks progressed he had begun to withdraw, to pull away from her.

The day of their wedding had gone better than she could have ever hoped. He had even extended his hand to her before shyly leading her to the dance floor.

Then came the great catastrophe that was their honeymoon. If only he had remembered to open the damper on that fireplace. Ah, and the cold, wet, miserable walk through the forest ... or wood, as Martin would remind her it *technically* was.

She laughed silently as she recalled his false bravado, threatening what turned out to be a horse. She could picture his face, how startled he had been when the animal bolted out of the shadows, barrelling towards them. But in all fairness, she had been as well.

A guilty conscience needled her as she tried to mentally dismiss her mocking behaviour. She had been annoyed with him, and rightly so. If he had listened to her they wouldn't have found themselves turned around in the wood.

But, she had hurt him—wounded his male pride. And he *had* been trying to protect her. No matter that it had been ineffectual.

She got up from her chair and stretched her arms over her head and yawned as she looked down at his heavily bandaged legs. It was hard to believe that this was the same man who had carried her across that icy stream in the wood so that she didn't have to get her feet wet.

Things would have been so different if they had not misunderstood one another about a honeymoon. Why didn't Martin tell her that he would have been open to the idea if it was what she wanted? Why couldn't the man just tell her what he was thinking!

He did try at times, though. Martin ... yes *Martin*, had attempted to initiate a conversation as they wound their way through those trees. A real conversation. She replayed the verbal exchange in her head.

"Can I say something?"

"NO!" She tried to cut him off.

"I think you're being unfair."

"Oh. Right! Thank you."

"Because you say one thing when you mean another. You agree to something when actually you want something else. It doesn't make sense."

She flicked her thumb absentmindedly over the pages of her book as she remembered Dr. Newell's advice—that she needed to spell things out for him, that he wasn't going to be able to intuit what she was thinking or wanted from him. Maybe her expectations hadn't been realistic.

But he didn't need to intuit what I was thinking. He should have wanted a honeymoon—to have that time alone with me. If he had really wanted to go away with me, he could have arranged for a locum.

She laid her book down on the little table beside her and rubbed at her bleary eyes.

Well, I guess I may as well get used to playing second fiddle. I should already have the role down pat—Mum with her boyfriend … Javier, Dad with his flights of fancy, and now having a husband whose job and patients come first.

Martin began to cough, and it woke him from his sleep. "Are you okay?" Louisa asked as he tried to stifle a groan.

"Mm, I'm fine," he said, trying to get his eyes to open completely. "What time is it?"

"Almost half five. Chris will be coming by soon, I suppose. I called Ruth to let her know how your surgery had gone today, and she said to tell you that she'd be coming over tomorrow."

Martin's gaze met hers, and he sighed heavily. "Louisa, we need to talk about what to do from this point on. You have your job, and James needs his mother close at hand. And …"

Louisa cocked her head at him. "And … what, Martin?"

"Well, they'll probably start physical therapy tomorrow, and it would be best if you weren't here for that." He fidgeted nervously with the blanket.

"I think it'd be good if I could see what they do. Maybe I could help you when you get home."

Martin swallowed hard. "Louisa, I'm a doctor; I know what this entails. It won't be enjoyable to watch, and I can't see you upset any more. I'm sorry."

Louisa furrowed her brow. "I don't need to be *entertained* or have it be enjoyable, Martin. And I've survived all of … *this* up to now," she said, her hand waving along the length of him.

Martin rubbed at his eyes, and then his forehead, trying to soothe the pounding headache he'd woken up with. "Physical therapy is inherently painful after injuries like mine, at least at first. I don't want you to ... I mean, you've watched me moan and groan all week. I think it would be best for both of us if you weren't here."

"I'm not sure I understand, Martin. Are you saying that you don't want me here any more?"

The heel of his hand pressed forcefully against his brow before he slapped it down on the bed. "I just don't want you to see me like that! Please!"

Louisa shook her head at him. She'd been by his side for the last week. She'd seen his broken body and wiped the tears from his face when the pain had been so intense that he cried. She'd held his hand when he needed reassurance—when he was afraid. Why this sudden discomfort with her presence?

"Could we talk about this later, Martin? Tomorrow, when you feel a bit better?"

"*No!* I want to have this understood between us right now. I *don't* want you here during my therapy."

Louisa's eyes snapped at him. "Fine, Martin! That's just fine!" she said, grabbing her purse and storming towards the door.

Martin closed his eyes and blew out a long breath, trying to calm himself. "Louisa, come back!" he called out ineffectually. He squeezed his eyes shut as he mentally berated himself.

A few minutes later the door to his room slid open and two nurses came in to roll him over. He clenched his teeth together to prevent the groans from escaping. The only remotely comfortable position for him was on his back, but he had to spend at least part of the day on his left side. The fixators made this miserable. Even with pillows to support and cushion the sensitive areas, it was still painful.

And now that they had cut back on the morphine, he was much more aware of the milder aches and pains, and he had more time awake in which to be tormented by them. He couldn't sleep the day away in a drug induced oblivion any more.

There was someone in his room constantly, it seemed, adding something to his IVs, taking out an IV which had passed its "sell by date" before starting a new one in a different vein, changing bandages, prodding him to eat. It was all wearing on his nerves and contributing greatly to his increasingly foul mood.

He'd been trying to be on his best behaviour for Louisa's sake, but he knew that he would disappoint her once the physical therapy started. He was afraid that he couldn't keep up the facade much longer, and soon the anger and frustration inside him would boil over with a vengeance.

After racing out of her husband's room, Louisa had ducked into the lavatory down the hall from the CCU. She splashed cold water on her eyes and got herself under control, and then headed towards Chris's office. He was taken by surprise when he looked up to see his friend's wife standing in the doorway.

"Louisa! Come in ... please," he said, pulling out a chair for her. He took note of her red eyes. "What's the matter? Did something happen with Martin?"

"Yes," she said, trying to remain composed. "Well, no. Not in the way that you think. He said he doesn't want me here, Chris. I don't understand why. He doesn't want me here for the physiotherapy tomorrow. He doesn't want me to see him like that." Louisa couldn't hold the tears back any longer.

Chris walked over and closed the door before pulling a chair over next to her. "We've cut back on Martin's morphine, Louisa. He's just now becoming fully aware of what's happened to him, the severity of his injuries. He's going to need a bit of time to adjust to it all."

Louisa sat shaking her head. "No, it's more than that. He said that the physiotherapy will be painful, and he doesn't want me to see him in pain any more. He doesn't want to see me upset."

"Yes, I can see why he might feel that way. I know that he's been worried about the stress that all of this has put on you."

"I'm dealing with it just fine, Chris," she said, her lips pursed as she crossed her arms in front of her.

Chris dropped his head to the side. "Look, I'm not saying that I don't think you can deal with it. But if Martin's going to be worrying about you if you're watching him go through this, then maybe it *would* be better for him if you weren't here. I'm not sure that you can be of much help to him during these therapy sessions anyway, and your presence could be a distraction to him. He'll have to focus all of his energy on dealing with the pain from the range of motion and strengthening exercises."

Chris handed Louisa a box of tissues. "Keep in mind that Martin is extremely uncomfortable right now. Up to this point, the morphine's made the pain from the obvious injuries easier to deal with, but it's also masked less serious injuries that he no doubt sustained in the accident—contusions, cuts, abrasions, the general aches and pains that are a result of the unnatural and forceful movements of his body in the crash. And it's common for less serious injuries to be missed initially because our attention is focused on the life-threatening problems. We say, in cases like Martin's, that we have to play catch up for a while. We do what has to be done today and take care of the other problems when they show themselves. So, I'm saying that Martin's pain may be less severe now, but it's also constant, and that's very tiring, very stressful."

"But there must be some way that I can be of help to him. I can't just leave him here on his own," she said wiping at her eyes with a tissue.

"Louisa, much of Martin's time will be spent working with the physiotherapist. When he's not with the therapist, he'll probably be exhausted and needing to rest.

"And ... well, there's something else that you may not have considered. Most men want to be able to protect their wives and children. And, given Martin's history of abuse, I would imagine he feels an especially strong need for that." Chris gave her a knowing smile. "I bet he drives you crazy with his vigilance over your health."

Louisa peered up at him, her taut posture relaxing. "Just a bit."

"I figured as much. But he probably also wants to be able to physically defend you and James, should the need arise, and he's probably feeling rather diminished in that area right now. To have you watching him struggle to even be able stand on his own two feet—"

"I don't care about that, Chris! That doesn't matter to me! We don't *need* that from him."

Chris winced at her words. "Well, it might be best if you didn't let on to Martin about that. He already thinks he's pretty rubbish when it comes to romance. You need to leave the guy with reason to think he serves *some* advantageous purpose in your relationship."

Louisa bit at her lip and sighed. "I just want to be there for him, and it feels like he's pushing me away."

"I understand that," Chris said nodding his head. "But this is about what *Martin* needs right now. It has to be. And Martin realises that he needs to focus one hundred percent on physical therapy at this time.

"You can help him most by holding down the fort at home. Martin's moving into a different phase in his recovery and his needs will be different. What he needs from you is going to change. Make sure that he feels certain that you're there for him in whatever way he needs you to be."

Louisa sat turning her wedding band back and forth on her finger. "Hmm, I hadn't considered all of this. He's not saying that he doesn't want me around any more; he's saying that he can't have me here for the time being. That he needs me to take care of James and things at home so that he doesn't have to worry about anything other than getting well."

"Exactly. Also, Louisa, remember that there are many unknowns for Martin right now. The most immediate concern he probably has is how painful it's going to be to have his limbs being moved around. He knows it'll hurt, but he doesn't know to what extent. And I'm sure the thought of having to put weight on those legs of his is pretty scary as well. Add to that the uncertainty about what the final outcome will be—how it'll affect his job as a GP, not to mention the odds of ever returning to surgery—it's a frightening time for him."

Louisa worried the tissue in her hands. "I don't think I was looking at this from Martin's perspective. I was worrying about what would make me feel better, not what would be helpful to him."

"Don't be too hard on yourself, Louisa. Your intentions were good. And I would imagine that after having spent a week in that chair by his bed, it would be hard not to feel hurt when he told you to stay away."

Chris rubbed at the back of his neck. "Martin finds it difficult to word things in a tactful manner in the best of times. It's hard for him to think straight right now, so try not to take his bluntness today personally."

He got up from his chair and offered Louisa a hand. "Shall we go then? I'm sure Carole has dinner ready by now, and I bet James Henry is wanting his mum."

Chapter 17

Martin closed his eyes that night feeling the lowest he had since the whole nightmare began. He had buggered things up with Louisa again, and after all she'd endured in the last week, he worried that she might not be back.

He fell into a fitful sleep, his slumber repeatedly interrupted by voices taunting him. His father's voice— "You'd have to drug 'em to keep 'em". Louisa's excruciating declaration after their sole date— "I'm sorry, Martin. I'm really, really sorry. But I don't want to see you any more". And his mother's vindictive, but excruciatingly truthful remark after Louisa left him the last time— "I'm not surprised your wife walked out on you. You better get used to being on your own".

Images haunted him—watching the farm buildings grow smaller and smaller as his father drove him away in the car, ever farther from the love and security of Auntie Joan; sitting at the train station waiting to be taken away to live with strangers in an unfamiliar boarding school; watching as Louisa walked down Roscarrock Hill and away from him.

He tried to roll over to get comfortable in bed, but he couldn't move his legs. He drifted off to sleep again. Louisa was holding his hand, comforting him. "I don't want you here!" he yelled, pulling back away from her. He watched her face, the hurt in her eyes before she turned to run away. He ran after her, calling for her to stop. His legs began to crumble beneath him, and he fell to the ground, watching as she ran into the path of an oncoming car. Then he heard the sickening thud. He tried to drag himself to her, but his arm began to give way, turning into a useless piece of rubber.

He woke suddenly, his heart racing and perspiration dampening his brow. The door to his room opened, and a nurse hurried in to check on him. "I'm sorry if I woke you, Dr. Ellingham. The alarm on your heart monitor went off. She took hold of his wrist, noting his damp skin. "Your heart is racing, how are you feeling?"

"I'm ... fine," he said, trying to catch his breath and feeling chagrined.

"Ah, a bad dream?" she asked.

"Mm."

"Well, you've been through a lot in the last week. All that stress and the emotions are going to come out one way or another," she said, gently caressing his arm. "Do you think you can sleep now? I can leave the light on if you like."

"No, I'm fine," Martin said as his pounding heart begin to slow.

"All right. I'll be right outside if you need me. Goodnight, Dr. Ellingham," she said as she slid the door closed.

Martin lay in bed, unable to get back to sleep. He needed Louisa.

As her husband pined for her, Louisa tossed and turned in bed that night. Would he think that she had gotten fed up and left him again? Morning couldn't come fast enough. She needed Martin.

She was up bright and early Saturday morning. It would be a busy day. Ruth would be arriving, and after visiting her nephew, she would take Louisa and James back to Portwenn with her to try to resume some semblance of normal life. But first Louisa wanted to get to the hospital so that she could clear the air with Martin.

Chris walked with her as far as the corridor leading to the business offices. He headed off to make phone calls, and Louisa hurried towards the CCU.

Martin was reclining in bed when she arrived at his room. His eyes were closed when she walked in, but he pulled his head up when he heard the rumble of the door. His brows pulled down as he blinked his eyes. Walking over, she wrapped her arms around his neck and pressed her lips to his head.

"I thought you might not come back," he said softly.

"Martin, I'm sorry."

He pulled his good arm up around her back. "Mm, I'm sorry too."

"You have nothing to apologise for. This one was all me. I s'pose I got my feelings hurt last night, but it was wrong for me to run out on you like that."

"I shouldn't have yelled."

Louisa held on to him as relief that the storm had passed washed over her. "I love you."

"Love you, too," he said, taking in a slow, gentle breath as he nuzzled into her neck.

She pulled back before kissing him on the lips. "Martin, I'll be here for you all the way through this. Whatever you need me to do to help you ... I'll do. Even if that means staying away."

"But Louisa, I don't *want* you to stay away. I just need to work very hard now to get everything I can out of physiotherapy, and I ... and I can't—"

"Martin, I understand. Chris talked with me about this, and I do understand now."

"But, Louisa, please give me some time to get this out ... to get the words right."

"Sorry. Go ahead."

He took in a breath. "I am so thankful for you. The night of the accident, I was bleeding to death. I could feel it. When they started to pull me out of the car, the pain was ..."

He stopped as his breath caught in his throat. "The pain was so intense that I wanted to die. And I could feel the life draining out of me. But then you and James were there with me, and you didn't want me to leave. You ... the two of you are my reason for living. And you've been here for me whenever I've needed you. You've gotten me through this. So *please* ... don't think that I don't need you now."

Louisa brushed the moisture from her cheeks. "That means so much to me, Martin ... to know you need me."

He turned his head away from her.

"What?"

"I ... I had a dream last night. *You* needed *me.* I was useless to you. You'd been hit by that car, and as I ran towards you to help, my legs fell apart. I tried to drag myself to you, but my arm gave way ... like it had turned to rubber. I was useless; I couldn't take care of you."

Louisa took hold of his chin and turned his face towards her. "Martin, you *will* have two arms and two legs that will be fully usable. I have no doubts about that, because I know how determined you are. I also know that the man I married would find a way to care for his family—legs or no legs. You've figured out how to care for your patients despite your blood sensitivity. Hmm?"

"Mm, yes."

She smiled at him. "*Yes ... mm.* Now, I'm going to go back to the Parsons' to pack. James and I'll ride back to Portwenn with Ruth this afternoon. I'll stop back to see you before we leave."

"Louisa, I do want you to come and visit, so you'll need a car. The insurance information is in my wallet ... can you get it and call the man? They should cover a rental, but if they don't, rent a car anyway. We'll get things sorted after I'm home."

The thought brought a smile to Louisa's face. "It's wonderful to hear you use those words ... *after I'm home.*"

Chapter 18

Ed Christianson stopped by Martin's room shortly after Louisa left. He stood at the foot of the bed, silently flipping through the most recent patient notes.

"Well, all went pretty well yesterday. Some reconstruction that'll need to be done down the road, but that should be a walk in the park compared to what you've been through in the last week. How are you feeling?"

"Like I was hit by a lorry. How do you thi—" Martin screwed up his face. "I'm sorry."

"It's okay," Ed said as he slipped the patient file back over its hanger. "I'm sure things look a bit dark right now."

"Mm."

"Just physically?"

Martin huffed. "It hurts everywhere ... places I didn't know could hurt. But ... Well, I'm in a much better place now than I was a week ago, and I ... I have you to thank for that."

"I did have a bit of help, you know."

"Yes."

Mr. Christianson came to the side of the bed and grasped on to the bed rail before lowering it. "So ... physically, not tip top. How are you doing mentally?"

Martin fidgeted. "My wife's going home today. A physiotherapist might be in this morning to start working on range of motion, and I thought it might be best if Louisa wasn't here to see that."

"So, you're losing your moral support?"

Martin shook his head. "I'll be fine."

Ed eyed him for a moment and took in a breath. "How would you feel about moving into a regular room later today?"

Martin pivoted his head quickly and shot the man a wary look. "A room or a ward?"

"Martin, you secured the funding for our air ambulance. I think we can swing a private room for you. And with the physiotherapy, I thought you might appreciate the privacy."

"I would ... very much. Thank you for arranging that."

"No problem. We'll take out the thoracic drains in just a few minutes. Then we'll see how you get on the rest of the day without them. I'm going to send you down to radiology for a chest x-ray before we cut you loose from Critical Care. If there's any sign of mediastinal fluid build up, then we'll keep you here a while longer. If needs be, we'll put the drains back in."

One by one, Ed removed the bandages covering Martin's wounds, checking for any redness or seepage. "Any of the wounds been bothering more than the others, Martin?"

"Mm, my left leg's been throbbing."

"Yep, there's a bit of inflammation and drainage. I think we have some infection starting in there. We'll hit you harder with the antibiotics, and I'd like to get a CT of that leg ... make sure there's no osteomyelitis. You're not febrile, so I'm pretty confident it's confined to the soft tissue. Don't want to take any chances, though. How's the belly feeling?"

"Sore, but bearable."

"And the thoracotomy wound?"

"What one would expect at this point."

"Okay, I'm going to give the go ahead for the physiotherapy. They'll probably want to get you up into a wheelchair for a while ... get you off your back for a bit. They'll work on your range of motion to start with, maybe some strengthening exercises for the thigh muscles."

Ed studied Martin's face before pulling a chair up next to the bed. "How are you feeling about all of this? About all that's happened ... all that lies ahead?"

"I'm trying not to dwell on it."

"I see. Well, humour me and dwell on it for a moment."

Martin picked at a loose thread on the edge of the blanket. "Well, *obviously,* I wish that it hadn't happened. And, of course, I don't like being apart from my wife. I miss my son. I miss him ... very much."

"I have to tell you Martin, all of us on your care team, including those two characters from Imperial ... we're concerned about you.

"Not just how you are physically, but how you are emotionally. This sort of an accident can easily send a patient spiralling into a depression, and we know that you're going to have a tendency to internalise all of this. So, I'd like to send someone by to see you ... someone you can talk to ... see if we can help you deal with all of this in a healthy way and prevent any depressive episodes."

The patient sat unresponsive.

"It would be good if you could give me a little feedback here," Ed finally said.

Martin shook his head. "You don't need to ... send someone by. I have someone I've been seeing. I'll call *him* if you want me to talk to someone."

"I tell you what, give me his name, and *I'll* call him and set something up ... make sure it doesn't conflict with your therapy schedule."

"Barrett Newell. It's Barrett Newell."

"Okay, excellent doctor. I'll give him a call. I, erm ... I'm glad you're agreeable to this."

Martin glanced up at Mr. Christianson. "I just want to get home to my family."

"We'll get you there, Martin. We'll get you there," he said, patting his shoulder.

There was a knock at the door, and Ed got to his feet as Ruth entered the room.

"Am I interrupting?" she asked.

Ed waved her in. "No, no. Come on in ... please."

Ruth extended her hand to the surgeon. "I'm Ruth Ellingham, Martin's aunt. Are you one of the brilliant surgeons who pulled my nephew back from the brink of death?"

"I'm Mr. Christianson," Ed said, taking her hand. "I don't know about brilliant, but, yes, I'm one of Martin's surgeons. It's nice to meet you, ma'am."

"Oh, please don't call me that. It makes me feel like an old biddy." Ruth shot her nephew a warning look, precluding any comment regarding her senescence.

"I was just going to remove the drains we put in after Martin's thoracotomy. We'll see how he does today. If all looks good later this afternoon, we'll move him to a regular room."

"Well, that's cause for celebration," Ruth said, giving her nephew a crooked smile.

"Okay, let's get you rolled on to that left side, Martin," Ed said as he adjusted the sling over his head. The surgeon pulled out the drains, and a nurse came in and dressed the wounds that were left behind before replacing the bandages that Mr. Christianson had removed earlier.

"I'll leave you to visit with your aunt, Martin. With any luck, the next time I see you will be upstairs in more comfortable accommodations. Ruth, it was nice to meet you."

Ruth settled into a chair and gave her nephew an inquisitive once over. "Well, you're still out of commission but on the mend. Have they given you any idea yet as to when you might be able to come home?"

"No. I've been afraid to ask. I would imagine it'll have a lot to do with when I can get myself ambulatory."

"And that will be about how long?"

He sighed heavily. "At least three more weeks I would imagine, probably more like four. Erm, Ruth, do you think we could borrow Al long enough for him to get some things moved around at the surgery?"

"I think that could be arranged. How do you plan to handle moving back home?"

"I'm not sure. The stairs are out of the question, so I imagine we'll use the consulting room as a bedroom for a while. Chris hasn't said how he wants to deal with the practice whilst I'm laid up. Everyone went to Wadebridge before I took the GP position, so I would think they could find their way back there ... if they try hard enough."

Ruth got up and walked to the end of the bed. "Mind if I take a look?"

Martin scowled at her. "Go ahead."

She pulled the blankets away from his legs. "Well, it's not pretty, but it's definitely an improvement over a few days ago. And all that hardware is serving a purpose." Leaning over, she peered closely at his left leg. "Hmm, there may be a bit of purulent discharge seeping through the bandage here."

"Yes, I'm aware of it, and so is Ed," Martin said testily as he tried to flip the blankets back over his legs.

The elderly woman came around to the head of the bed and opened the sling. "There's a significant amount of soft tissue damage isn't there?"

Martin swallowed hard and turned his head away.

The elderly woman eyed him suspiciously. "You *have* looked at your injuries, haven't you, Martin?"

He hesitated. "My gawping at those wounds won't make them heal any faster, Ruth."

"Noo, I don't believe I suggested anything of the sort. I do think that at some point you'll need to face up to this though, and I think you should do it sooner rather than later."

Martin furrowed his brow before turning his gaze away from her. "*Yes*, I will."

"Good."

"Do you have any more pearls of wisdom you'd like to share? You obviously didn't come to cheer me up."

"I'm sorry, Martin. I'm just concerned." Ruth came around the bed and put her hand on his. "You're going to be fine, Martin. But you *will* need help."

He kept his eyes averted, but the old woman could see the sinew working in his jaw.

"Well, I told Louisa that I'd pick her up, so I should get going. She plans to stop in to see you before we head back to Portwenn, but I'll say goodbye now."

Ruth looked sympathetically at him before adding, "You've done very well, Martin. I'm proud of you. And if my brother hadn't been such an idiot, he'd have been proud of you, too. This last week couldn't have been easy, and the weeks ahead won't be much easier, I'm afraid. But I have great faith in you. You've overcome a lot in your life, and I know that you'll overcome this as well."

She leaned over and kissed him goodbye before leaving him on his own.

Chapter 19

Martin had eaten what he could of his lunch. But the vegetables, bland and overcooked to the point of disintegration, and the unidentifiable meat product, which had been shredded by the kitchen staff to facilitate the digestive process, only intensified the persistent roiling in his stomach, a side effect of the potent cocktail of drugs that dripped steadily into him from the bottles hanging overhead. He pushed the tray as far away as he could before laying his head back and closing his eyes, trying to ignore the smell that remained in the air.

He forced his lids open when he heard the soft rumble of the door. A nurse came into the room carrying a tray of the supplies needed to tend to the regular maintenance of the external fixators on his limbs. Fluid continued to seep out around the pins penetrating his skin, hardening into a crust which had to be cleaned off several times a day. This was only a mildly painful process, but given the number of pins in Martin's body, it was also a lengthy process.

He tried to relax, inhaling and exhaling slow, deep breaths. But he soon found himself fighting nausea and light-headedness as the nurse went on with her work.

"Are you almost done? I'm not feeling well," he said. He swallowed back the saliva that had begun to flood his mouth.

The nurse looked up, noticing her patient's growing pallor and the sheen on his face. "Let's take a little break, Dr. Ellingham. Would you like something to drink ... some juice or a soda maybe?"

"God, no," he said, shaking his head vigorously.

She patted his hand lightly. "I'll step out and give you a few minutes to catch your breath."

Gawd, I'm getting tired of looking at this ceiling, he thought as he tried to get his mind off all the poking and prodding that he'd had to endure. He heard the door to his room slide open again, and he groaned internally, expecting the return of the nurse with her instruments of torture.

"Hey, Mart, you awake?"

Martin pulled his head up when he heard his friend's voice.

"Jeez, you don't look so great, mate."

Chris came over and placed his fingers on his wrist, and Martin pulled his hand away sharply. "I'm fine. Those bloody nurses keep coming in and cleaning these damn pins. It's amazing that the other patients get any attention at all with the amount of time your nursing staff seems to spend in here," he groused.

"Ah." Chris nodded, pulling up a chair. "Has Louisa been back yet?"

"No." Martin scowled. "James is usually napping at this time."

"Oh, sure. So ... did Ed take the drains out this morning?"

"Yes." The furrows in Martin's brow deepened. "Can we talk about something other than my health?"

Chris cocked his head at his friend. "What can I do to help you here, Mart? I can bring in a chessboard ... a video ... some of my *BMJs* ..."

Martin sighed heavily. "Sorry ... I'm feeling a bit irritable."

"Does this have anything to do with Louisa leaving?"

"Probably," Martin said, rubbing at his eyes.

"For what it's worth, I feel the same way when Carole's gone." Chris leaned back and put his feet up on the bedrail.

"Erm, Chris ... what are the plans for handling patient care in Portwenn whilst I'm gone?"

Chris laced his fingers behind his head. "I'm actually thinking of turning your surgery into a cafe. It'd be charming, don't you think? Tea and biscuits served up daily. Maybe cream tea served at four o'clock every afternoon. I'm sure the locals would love it; it'd be like old times, you know."

Martin turned his head and gave his friend a dark look. "Very funny, Chris."

"Sorry, mate. I was just trying to lighten the mood. Actually, I thought it would be easiest to have them go to Wadebridge for care. But it's your practice, so feel free to say if you have other ideas."

"No, no. That makes sense to me. I hope it won't be for more than four or five months."

Chris watched Martin's dour face. "I suspect your spirits may improve when you can take a more active role in your recovery, Mart. But don't hesitate to tell me if there's something I can do to make this all easier for you ... please."

Martin rubbed his hand over his head. "There is something."

"Just name it, mate."

"I haven't looked at ... erm, I haven't seen what everything looks like. I really don't see the need, but I promised Ruth. She seems to thinks it's important, and ... well, I can't reach my bloody arm and legs."

Chris put his feet back down on the floor and walked to the door, stepping outside briefly to alert the nurses station that he and Martin were not to be disturbed. He returned, locking the door behind him and pulling the curtain.

"Okay, Mart. Let's do this. You ready?"

Martin hesitated, and then gave him a nod of his head. His heart pounded as Chris pulled the blankets back. As a surgeon, he had repaired severed arteries in patients with injuries nearly identical to his own. He had looked at their repaired limbs with clinical eyes, assuring himself that he could feel an adequate pulse in the foot or hand and that there was no redness or drainage which could be a warning sign of a developing infection. There was always a brief sense of relief in knowing that his hard work was not in jeopardy.

But as he looked at his own legs, he didn't think about adequate blood flow or bacteria that could be proliferating in his wounds. He found himself struggling with the visceral reaction he was having to the metal framework that now merged with his flesh, the impulse to pull the foreign objects from his body. He closed his eyes and slowed his breathing. When he opened them again, he tried to look at his wounds as a doctor evaluating a patient.

"Should I take the bandages off, Mart?"

Martin swallowed hard and nodded his head. Chris peeled back the gauze coverings, revealing an eight-inch vertical line of sutures on the inside edge of each shin and a slightly longer incision under the fixator on the outside edge of his right thigh. He then removed the bandage over the ten-inch diagonal wound extending from the middle of his inner thigh up and across to the outside of his leg. There was a return of the sensation of warmth and wetness that he had felt spreading across his lap as he sat, unable to move, trapped in the twisted metal of the wreckage. He squeezed his eyes shut and took in a deep breath, trying to loosen the growing tightness in his chest.

"You okay, Mart?" Chris asked, holding out a glass of water. "Take a break and catch your breath."

"I'm all right, it's just ... it just ..." He took a few sips of water before giving the glass back to his friend and shaking his head. "It's nothing." He glanced up. "Okay, I'm ready."

"We'll have to move this a bit, or you won't be able to see anything, I'm afraid. Just relax and let me do all the work."

Chris put a small pillow on the tray table next to the bed before moving the table so that it was extending over Martin's lap. He then slid the sling forward slightly and peeled back the

Velcro closures. Holding on to the metal fixator, he slowly lowered his friend's arm down, resting it on the pillow.

Martin stared down at the obvious deformity in his arm, a depression left as a result of the soft tissue loss in the accident itself as well as the repeated debridement of nonviable tissue. He reached over and tentatively removed the bandage covering the worst of the wound. An uneven four-inch line of sutures ran along the top of his forearm. Chris took hold of the fixator, raising the arm up and peeling off the bandage so that his friend could see the damage to the underside, a slightly shorter but equally disfiguring wound.

"Remember, Mart, this will look a lot better after reconstruction down the road."

Martin nodded his head as Chris's voice grew more muffled in his ears, the lights grew dim and the air seemed to be sucked from his lungs. He drew in ragged breaths as various emotions washed over him—the disgust he felt at the appearance of his disfiguring wounds; fear of how his injuries would impact his life, his career; and an overwhelming grief over the the effect his wounds would have on Louisa, the repulsion that he was sure he would see in her eyes.

He turned his face away from his friend, trying to hide the tears spilling on to his cheeks, but his shudders gave him away.

Chris put one hand around the back of Martin's neck as the other rubbed his shoulder in a gentler version of a man hug. "It'll be all right, Mart. Will and Robert still have more work to do. And they're confident that you'll have good use of the arm."

As Chris pulled back, Martin ran a broad palm down his face, wiping away the tears. He inhaled deeply, trying to calm himself.

Chris covered the wounds with clean bandages and then lifted his friend's arm back into the sling. He heard a sharp intake of air, and glancing over, he saw Martin grimacing.

"Sorry, Mart. I was trying to be careful."

Martin shook his head. "No, it's my shoulder. Something snapped."

Chris pressed the Velcro closures back into place, watching his friend intently. "Is it still hurting, or is it better now?"

"Better, I think."

"Good. Make sure you tell Ed if you have any more problems." He finished getting Martin settled before notifying the nurses station that they could come back in.

The nurse who had been cleaning Martin's fixator pins re-entered the room to finish the job. He closed his eyes and tried to tune out what she was doing, but the persistent rubbing away at the crusted secretions was again making him feel ill.

He grabbed for the basin next to his bed and vomited into it.

"I'm sorry, Dr. Ellingham. I'm almost finished here. Should we take another break before continuing on?"

"No! Just finish it up ... *please*."

The nurse completed her job, wrapping each pin with a compression dressing before leaving her patient alone. It was still early afternoon, but he was exhausted, and he drifted quickly off to sleep.

Chapter 20

Martin had been asleep for the better part of an hour when he was awakened by warm lips pressed against his. As he pried his eyes open, the lips moved from one cheek to the other before finally landing with a kiss on his forehead.

"Hello, Martin," Louisa whispered.

He rubbed his eyes and yawned. "What time is it?"

"Just past half three. How's your day been?"

"Mm, I'm not sure you really want to know."

She gave him a look of mock astonishment. "I want to know everything there is to know about you, *Martin*."

He sighed, blinking slowly, trying to wipe the haze from his eyes. "Ed came in and took out the thoracotomy drains, Ruth stopped by, I had my pins cleaned, then Chris came in and we … talked, I had my pins cleaned some more, I threw up, and had some more pin cleaning. Then I fell asleep. You are the nicest and most interesting thing that's happened today, by far."

Louisa smiled at him as she ran her fingers through his hair. "I do realise that I'm being compared to wound cleaning and vomiting, but still … I like being the nicest and most interesting thing."

Martin pulled her back down and kissed her. "How's James?"

"He's just fine. Entertaining Ruth in the waiting area right now. Has a therapist been in yet?"

"No. It's possible they'll wait now until they get me moved to a regular room later this afternoon."

"Martin! They're moving you out of the CCU?" Louisa said, putting her hands on his cheeks. "That's wonderful news!"

"Mm, Ed wants another x-ray first to make sure no fluid build-up has occurred since the drain removal this morning. But if that looks good, then they'll move me."

"It sounds like they think you're making progress," she said, nodding her head vigorously.

"Mm. At least I'm not going backwards any more."

"Well, now I wish I could stay ... help you get settled. But I guess I better get going so we can make it home before dark."

Their eyes met and Louisa leaned over, touching her forehead to his. "You'll call me if you feel lonely ... or just want to talk?"

"Ah. I don't ... I don't have my mobile. I'm not sure where it ended up."

"I'll check with the nurses. I need to get your wallet from them too ... for the insurance information. Be right back," she said placing another kiss on his nose.

She returned a short time later, carrying a brown paper bag, stapled shut across the top. "Got it." Paper rattled as she tore the bag open.

Martin reached his hand out. "Louisa, let me!" he said before she upended the bag and dumped the contents on to the recliner in the corner of the room. Her face crumpled as she looked down at the dissected pieces of her husband's bloodied clothing.

"Oh, Martin!" She picked up his ruined white dress shirt and held it to her face.

He waved his hand, beckoning to her. "Louisa, come here ... come here."

She moved to his bedside and wrapped her arms around his chest. Burying her face in his neck, she released all the emotions that she had kept hidden from him over the course of the previous week.

"Shh, shh, shh, shh, shh." He grimaced and clenched his jaw as her grip tightened over his thoracotomy wound. "It's all right now," he said hoarsely, stroking his hand over her head. "It's all right, Louisa."

Her sobs dissolved into ragged breaths and sniffles as she raised up to look at him. Martin took the corner of the blanket and wiped at the tears on her cheeks. "Better now?" he asked gently.

She sighed. "Oh, Martin, I wanted to be strong for you, and here I am, getting tears and—and—"

"Snot?"

"Yes, Martin ... snot, all over you. I'm sorry."

"No need to apologise. Do you feel better now?"

"Yes, I do." She gave him a scrutinising look. "Are you okay? You're very pale. And you're sweating."

"Mm." He shook his head dismissively.

She hesitated and then headed for the door. "I'm getting a nurse."

"Louisa! No, that's not necessary. Come back."

"Your colour isn't good, Martin. I think someone should check on you."

"Louisa ... it's just that ... well, you were squeezing my chest."

"Oh, gawd, I'm so sorry."

"I'll be all right."

"I'm sorry," she said again, brushing her fingers across his cheek.

"I'm fine now, really. What about my wallet and mobile?"

She went back to her husband's belongings and fished out the requested items. "Hmm, it needs a charge. I'll ask Chris to bring you a charger."

"Thank you," Martin said as he looked at her apologetically. "I'm sorry about all of this, Louisa."

"Martin, I don't want to hear you apologise one more time! I mean it! This is in no way your fault."

She softened her tone. "I guess … I'm sorry about all of this, too. I'm sorry this happened to you … to us. But it did, and we'll make the best of it, won't we?"

"Yes."

"I s'pose I better go. Call me anytime you want, even when I'm at the school. You will *not* be bothering me, so don't even start about that."

"Will you come and visit me?"

She leaned forward again, resting her cheek atop his head, saying softly, "Just try and stop me."

"I'll look forward to that."

She kissed him goodbye and reluctantly left the room.

An aide came in a half hour later to take Martin down to radiology for a chest x-ray and a CT scan of his left leg. Ed Christianson stopped by afterwards to discuss the results. He pulled a chair over next to the bed and took a seat.

"Your films look good, Martin, so I think we can go ahead and move you upstairs to a decent room. I want to keep an eye on that leg, though. We've increased the IV antibiotics, and I'm hopeful that will nip the infection in the bud. But if needs be, we'll open the leg up and pack it off with antibiotic beads again until we have things under control."

Ed slapped his palms down on his knees before getting to his feet. "But for now, let's get you out of here." He patted his patient's shoulder. "One step closer to home, my friend."

Two aides came a few minutes later to move Martin to his new room. After more than a week of looking at the same four windowless walls, the trip through the hospital corridors bordered on exciting, and it bolstered his spirits a bit. He was familiar enough with the hospital to know that the room they gave him was one of a handful of large, suite-like rooms normally reserved for the occasional visiting celebrity or aristocrat. Or for the well-heeled.

He had a west facing window, and he watched as the sun dropped to the horizon. He wondered if Louisa had arrived back in Portwenn, and, if so, whether she also was watching as the muted pink and purple hues of the evening sky faded into grey, the light of the stars becoming just barely perceptible.

There was a knock on his door, and a young man entered the room, introducing himself as Tim Spalding, a physiotherapist on staff at the hospital.

"I won't be the only one working with you, Dr. Ellingham, but I'll be in charge of your therapy. So, if you have any questions or concerns, please feel free to call me ... anytime."

Martin had seen his own patients undergoing therapy, but he had remained fairly detached from the process. However, on the receiving end of treatment this time, he began to feel a sense of panic as the therapist lowered the side rails down on the bed.

"I'll work with you this evening on some gentle range of motion exercises so your muscles don't tighten up on you any more than they probably already have," he said as he went to the sink to wash his hands. "How are you feeling about the physiotherapy ... a bit apprehensive I would guess?"

"I don't really know what to expect. I know it'll be painful, but I don't know how painful. So yes, I'm ... apprehensive."

"I'll start slow and build up to what you can no longer tolerate. That threshold will get higher with time, but the more you can push yourself to do, the better the end result will be and the quicker we'll reach that end result. Ultimately, you call the shots, though. You determine how much is too much."

Tim dried his hands and wadded the paper towel up, rolling it into a ball. It flew across his patient's tray table in a graceful arc before landing in the waste bin on the other side. "Are you ready to do some work then?"

"Mm, yes."

The therapist grasped the fixator on the top and side of Martin's lower right leg, lifting it up and, bending his knee slightly.

Martin groaned as the contracted muscles stretched, pulling on the tendons attaching the muscle tissue to the fractured bones. The therapist released the pressure on his leg before pushing it forward again. He repeated this process, gradually loosening the muscles and decreasing the flexural rigidity in his patient's knee.

"How are you doing, Dr. Ellingham? Hangin' in there, or should we stop for now?"

Martin squeezed his eyes shut and took in a deep breath. "You can go a little more," he said giving his head a nod.

Tim kept at it, working Martin's leg back and forth. "Okay, I think we better stop for now. Are you ready for the other leg?"

Martin swallowed back the nausea that he was beginning to feel. "Could I have a drink first?"

"Sure. Sorry 'bout that. Stop me anytime if you need a breather," he said as he handed him a glass of water.

The patient took a few swallows before passing the glass back to his therapist.

"Okay, Martin, I want to work on increasing the range of motion in this ankle. Then we'll stretch the muscles in your calf," Tim explained as he moved his foot in a circular motion, first one direction, then the other. Martin groaned loudly as the stretching muscles sent searing pain through the bones in his leg. The physiotherapist relaxed the pressure he had been putting on his foot.

"Let's take another break, okay?"

Martin nodded his head while trying to slow his breathing.

The young man took a seat with a clipboard in hand and proceeded to fill in notes as his patient laid his head back and closed his eyes. He got up a few minutes later and returned to the bed.

"So ... are you married, Dr. Ellingham? Any children?"

"Yes ... and yes," Martin answered testily. "Can we get on with this now?"

"Yep. I'll work on that arm and the pectorals next."

Tim removed Martin's arm from the sling and rested it on a pillow atop the tray table. He nudged his hand downward at the wrist, then upwards, loosening the muscles and stretching the tendons in his forearm.

Beads of perspiration began to form on Martin's face, and he clenched his teeth together to try to keep the groans from escaping. When the therapist felt he had pushed him to his limit, he backed off and worked on his stiffened fingers.

The young man moved up Martin's arm, holding on to the fixators on either side, bending and straightening the elbow several times. Martin pushed his head back into his pillow and cried out, trying to pull his arm back away from the source of the pain.

The therapist laid his arm back down on the table. "Another glass of water?" he asked.

Pressing trembling fingers to his eyes, Martin nodded his head.

"You're doing great, Dr. Ellingham," Tim said as he lifted his patient's good hand and pressed the glass into it. "Got it?" he asked before letting go.

"Yes, thank you."

The therapist sat for a while, allowing his patient's pain to subside before again taking hold of the fixators and moving the entire arm side to side and up and down, working the pectoral muscles that had been dissected during the thoracotomy. Martin didn't find this to be as excruciating and began to relax.

The therapist brought his arm diagonally up and over his head. There was a snap, and Martin cried out. Tim brought his patient's arm down, laying it across his stomach.

Martin's face contorted as he reached for his shoulder. "Argh!"

"Dr. Ellingham, I probably don't have to tell you that your humeral head has slipped out of it's socket. Lie still. I'll go and get someone in here to reduce it," the young man said before leaving the room, returning quickly with Ed Christianson.

"Sounds like a bit of a problem, eh, Martin?" the surgeon said, pulling open the snaps on his patient's hospital gown.

"Just ... get it sorted!" he spat back.

"I will. But I want to give you some extra morphine first," Ed said as he adjusted the flow of medication into the IV.

"I suspect you sustained a labral tear in the accident. That's loosened the joint and allowed the humeral head to slip out. Had you been having pain in that shoulder?"

The morphine had begun to take effect quickly, muddling his thoughts and thickening his tongue. "I think juss once. Maybe this afternoon. I'm nod sure about before ... thad."

"Okay, Martin. You know how this works. I'm going to have Tim help me, though, so I don't knock any of your pins loose."

The two men pulled and rotated Martin's shoulder until it popped back into place, and then replaced his arm in the sling.

"Tim, you'll need to be pretty careful with the physio," the surgeon cautioned. "Shouldn't be a big thing to repair though, Martin ... arthroscopic surgery. Simpson can do it when he does the reconstruction."

"Mm." Martin gave in to the combination of pain, stress and opioids and allowed his eyes to drift shut.

Chapter 21

"So, Ruth, did you have a nice visit with Martin today?" Louisa asked as the elderly woman steered her Mercedes down the M-39.

"Yes. You know my nephew, though; I'm not sure that one would call it visiting. We did exchange a few sentences, nonetheless."

"How did you find him?" she asked as she handed a bottle back to James Henry, who was buckled into his seat and chewing on a teething biscuit.

"Definitely improved since I saw him last. It helps to have those ghastly wounds closed up. I suspect he's feeling a bit discouraged and extremely overwhelmed at the moment, though. Wouldn't you be?"

Louisa furrowed her brow. "Hmm, yes I'm quite sure that I would. But overall ... you think he's doing all right?"

"I was concerned when I discovered that he hadn't yet laid eyes on the damage done to him in the accident ... and I told him as much. He needs to face up to what's happened to him. I've seen many a patient develop PTSD symptoms after these horrific car crashes." Ruth paused. "I told him today that he needed to look at his wounds, and sooner rather than later."

The two women rode silently, watching as the terrain began to change from rolling moorland to the more rugged coastal geology.

"He's going to worry about how you'll see him, you know," Ruth said as she stared out the windscreen.

Louisa bit her bottom lip. "I know. He told me about a nightmare he had. About the day of my accident. I'd been hit by that car, and he couldn't get to me to help me because of his injuries. He's afraid he won't be able to protect James and me any more."

"Yes, I'm sure he does worry about that. He'll heal though, and I think that concern will pass when he gets his strength and mobility back. But the scars won't go away. I think Martin's going to worry that you'll find them off-putting."

"Well, that would be very small-minded of me."

"Yes, *I* know that his scars won't bother you, but I can just about guarantee my *nephew* is thinking otherwise. I think he's been afraid to look at his wounds because of it."

"But Ruth, I've seen his wounds. I don't care about how they look."

"Does Martin know that you've seen them?"

"I'm sure he must. I've been there with him every day for more than a week."

"So, that's a yes, then? He's aware that you know how that leg and arm look?"

"Hmm, I guess maybe I'm making an assumption. He's either been asleep or pretty fuzzy on those occasions. Oh, Ruth, do you really think that he's worried about this?"

"Well, I'm not a mind reader, but I suspect he is. It would be quite natural for him to have insecurities, so I suggest that you discuss it with him before he worries himself silly about it."

"I will, Ruth. I really hate having to be away from him. I'm as concerned for his mental health as I am for his physical health at this point."

Ruth steered the car down the hill leading into their little village. How odd it seemed to Louisa to be back in Portwenn without Martin. He had been here for the past five years, and the village didn't feel the same without him.

They pulled into the surgery car park, and Ruth helped Louisa gather the bags and carry them into the house.

"Ruth, would you please stay and have dinner with me? I really don't want to be alone," Louisa said, plunking the bags down at the bottom of the stairs.

"Yes, I suppose I have nothing to get done that can't wait until tomorrow."

"An omelette okay? We probably don't have a lot in the refrigerator."

"That sounds good actually. But why don't you let me do the cooking. You go and unpack ... or do whatever one does with a baby after being away from home."

"Thank you, Ruth. James and I'll be back down in a tick. Let me know if you need anything," Louisa said over her shoulder as she hurried up the stairs with her son in her arms.

"Just what did you mean when you said you were worried about Martin's mental health?" Ruth asked as the two women were finishing up with dinner.

Louisa flicked the toast crumbs from her fingers before taking a sip of tea. "It seems he's remembered a few more details about the incident when he fractured his arm."

Ruth's index finger ran around the rim of her teacup as she peered up at her. "I assume you're referring to the day *my brother* fractured his arm. Let's give credit where credit is due."

"Hmm, yes." Louisa stood and began gathering the dirty dishes together to take to the sink. "He said that when he was trapped in the car the night of the accident it felt much the same in some ways as that day. He said that he could feel a warm wetness spreading across his lap. I would assume from the haemorrhaging ... the laceration to his thigh."

She pulled a clean facecloth from the drawer and ran it under the tap before wringing it dry. "Anyway, he could smell the blood. It put him back, mentally, to that day in his father's study. He remembered feeling a warm wetness soaking into his trousers ... seeing blood running on the floor and pooling up next to him."

Louisa paused to wipe the applesauce from her son's face before glancing up.

The older woman stared absently in front of her as her finger sat poised, seemingly frozen in place on the rim of her cup.

"Ruth? Is something wrong?" she asked.

The old woman cocked her head. "You're sure you didn't misunderstand him—that he thinks it was blood on the floor, not paint?" she asked, her brow furrowed.

"That's what he thinks."

She pulled a hand up over her mouth as she sighed.

"What is it, Ruth? Is there something you know?" Louisa asked as she worried the facecloth in her hands.

The woman shook her head before giving her nephew's wife a forced smile. "No, no. I'm just ... pondering. Do continue."

Louisa lay the applesauce coated facecloth by the sink, and then lifted James from the highchair. "I don't know Ruth. He'd been having some upsetting dreams while he was fighting that infection. Maybe it was all a result of the high fever; I just don't know. I know that Martin seemed very certain of the story he was telling me."

"Does he remember any more than that?"

"He said that his father yelled at him, 'Martin, what have you done?' Then he grabbed him by the arm. Margaret came in and accused him of ruining the floor ... and his clothes."

"Well, that certainly sounds like Martin's monstrous parents." Ruth set her teacup down on the table and reached for a digestive.

Louisa sat back down with James on her lap. "Martin said that Margaret locked him in the cupboard under the stairs as punishment. I think—"

"Locked him in the cupboard under the stairs?" Ruth interjected.

"You *did* know that was a routine punishment for Martin ... didn't you?"

Ruth shook her head as she stared out the window. "Although I suppose it shouldn't come as a surprise. Christopher believed that a crying child was best left alone in a room."

Louisa shook her head and blinked her eyes before returning to the main thread of the conversation. "Anyway, Martin was in the cupboard, lying on his broken arm. He was in pain, and he could smell the blood on his trousers. It was hard for him to breathe, and it all made him nauseous. He threw up. He was afraid of what Margaret would do when she found the mess in the cupboard. Oh, Ruth, the poor child wet himself. There's more to the story, but that's the gist of it."

Tears began to well in the old woman's eyes. "Joan and I failed him miserably, didn't we?"

Louisa hurried around the table and crouched down by her chair with James on one knee. "Ruth, you did *not* fail Martin. I suspect that by this time he had already become a master at hiding his emotions, and you and Joan would have had no way of knowing what was going on behind closed doors."

She got to her feet and put her free arm around Ruth's shoulders before leaning over to kiss her on the cheek. "You have been a source of comfort for your nephew, Ruth. I don't think there was anything that you could have done forty years ago. But he *does* need you now."

Louisa took a seat in the chair next to her husband's aunt.

Ruth sighed. "Well, I can certainly see why you're concerned for his mental health. It's difficult to know if these recent recollections are true memories or a figment of his febrile or medicated imagination."

Louisa rose with James, preparing to take the boy upstairs. "Well, I made the mistake of second guessing Martin when I questioned his thinking about his parent's love for him. I won't make that mistake again. If Martin says it happened, then it happened," she said adamantly. "Please don't feel you need to leave, Ruth. But I do need to get James off to bed."

Ruth got up and walked over to collect her jumper which she had hung on the coat rack by the door. "I should be getting home. It's been a long day for babies *and* old ladies," she said as she put her hand on James Henry's head. "Do keep me posted on my nephew's progress, and let me know if I can be of help," she said as she pulled the door shut behind her.

Chapter 22

The daylight coming in his window woke Martin early the next morning. Chris had stopped by the night before and dropped off a charger, so now that he had a functioning mobile, Martin was anxious to call Louisa. He lay in his bed, not wanting to risk waking either his wife or son, and he watched the minutes tick by.

His door opened and a nurse entered the room. "Good morning, Dr. Ellingham! Lovely day isn't it."

"Mm," he grunted.

"I'm here to get you cleaned up a bit, and then we'll take care of your pins."

Martin found the bed bath to be one of the most humiliating experiences that could be foisted on someone. He tried unsuccessfully to convince the nurse to help him out of his hospital gown and leave him to bathe himself.

"No, I'm afraid I can't do that, Dr. Ellingham. You're in no condition to be doing this on your own. Besides, how would you ever be able to wash between your toes?" she asked, trying to illicit a smile from him.

He erupted. "Why in the world would I need to wash between my toes? Good God, woman! I've not been out of this bed in over a week, and my feet have been thoroughly disinfected before every one of my surgical procedures! I've practically been marinating in betadine!"

Martin immediately regretted the harshness of his response when he saw the disconcerted look on the woman's face. "Just ... go ahead and do what you need to do," he mumbled.

By the time he'd been bathed and his hair had been washed, he had calmed down. And he had to admit that he felt considerably better.

The nurse then started in on the tedious task of cleaning all of her patient's pin sites before wrapping each with a small compression bandage, held tight against the skin with a clip that was fastened to the pin.

"There you are, Dr. Ellingham, fresh as a daisy now," she said as she gathered her equipment together and turned to leave.

"Erm, thank you ... and, I'm ... I'm sorry about my earlier remarks."

"It's quite understandable that you'd be a bit short tempered, Dr. Ellingham. Don't give it a second thought," she said before hurrying out the door.

But Martin did give it a second thought. This was an item on his crap list that he needed to work on. He sighed heavily, wondering if he could ever learn to hold his tongue in situations like this, or if the slightest irritation would always result in a vitriolic outburst. He resolved to try to do better with the nurse if she ever came into his room again.

The clock now read half eight, and even though Louisa was known to sleep later than this on a weekend, James Henry was not. Martin picked up his mobile and dialled Louisa's number.

"Good morning, Martin," she answered.

"Good morning. Did I wake you?"

"No, no, not at all. James has been up for at least an hour. He inherited your early riser genes, I think. Thank you for that."

"Mm, sorry." The tension he had felt since his unfortunate physiotherapy session the day before began to subside. "It's nice to hear your voice. It ... helps."

"I'm glad, Martin. I hate not being there, but I'm glad I can still be helpful," Louisa said as she tried to put James's nappy on with one hand while holding her mobile with the other.

As the baby released a string of chortles and babbles, Louisa held the mobile out so that Martin could hear his son. He felt the stress ease a bit more.

"Did you get into a new room?" she asked.

"Mm, I did. It's actually a suite. I think Chris and Ed are responsible for that. They seem to think that I somehow swung the NHS decision on the air ambulance in their favour."

"Well, you sort of did, Martin."

"Louisa, it's not like I *tried* to have an accident. Let alone time it so that the NHS's committee of idiots would stand around and listen to all the sanguineous details come in over the dispatch radio."

Louisa gathered the baby in one arm and headed for the stairs. "Well, yes, but let them do this for you, Martin. I think they feel a bit guilty that you've had to suffer so horribly, and the rest of us will benefit from it."

Martin furrowed his brow, annoyed at the whole idea that he had somehow saved the day by colliding with a lorry. "They shouldn't feel guilty. It's not as if I intentionally—"

"Martin," Louisa said softly. "Let it go."

"Yes."

"What about physio? Did a therapist stop in to see you?" she asked as she set James into his high chair.

"Yes, a young fellow. I can't remember his name."

"And ..." Louisa waited for a response. "Martin, this is where you tell me what happened, what he did with you ... how it went."

"It went ... erm, fine."

"Martin!" Her husband's sigh into the phone brought a smile to her face. "Was it as painful as you had expected?"

Martin knew this question would be asked, and he also knew that he'd rather not discuss it.

"It wasn't ... it ..." Another sigh. "All right, yes it *was* painful, but I survived. And it doesn't help to talk about it!" he answered testily.

"Martin, calm down. It's just that when I'm not there to see for myself how things are for you, then I want to know all the details. It helps me to feel closer ... not so detached from it all."

"I would think you might appreciate being detached from it all. *I* would."

He sighed again, and Louisa sensed that there was something he hadn't told her. "What is it, Martin? Is there something I should know?"

"It's nothing to be concerned about. It seems there's been some damage to my shoulder that we weren't aware of before."

"What do you mean by *damage*?"

He grimaced. "There was a bit of a problem during the physiotherapy. The therapist was moving my arm, and the humeral head slipped out of it's socket," he explained. "But Ed was able to reduce it immediately, so you don't need to worry about it," he added quickly.

"Oh, *Martin!* That's what happened to the old man with the chickens ... the one who held us hostage on our honeymoon night. You told him he'd be in agony!"

"Yes, but if I remember correctly, you told the man that I didn't mean it like that."

"*Martin* ... Are you all right? Does it still hurt?"

"Like I said, Louisa, Ed reduced it right away so there's no need to worry. They'll get some pictures to pinpoint the problem, and Will should be able to fix it when he and Robert do any later procedures."

Louisa closed her eyes and exhaled slowly, trying to quell her growing frustration at her husband's reluctance to answer her questions.

"Martin, I'm in Portwenn, and if you want me to stay here in Portwenn, rather than running back over there to check up on you, then you need to tell me what I want to know. I'm asking you if it hurt when your ... whatsit came out of the—the socket, and I want to know if you're in pain at the moment. If you can't answer my question, then I'll have to come over there to see for myself!"

There was a period of silence before Louisa heard her husband's voice again.

"Yes, it hurt. And it aches now," he answered flatly.

"Thank you," she replied. "I'm sorry for getting angry with you, but I'm very anxious about being apart from you right now, and I need to trust that you're not hiding anything from me. Don't think for one minute that you're sparing me worry and stress by having this distance between us. I'm going to worry and stress about you until you're completely well again. It helps me to have as much information as possible. I don't like surprises. You *do* understand what I'm trying to say ... don't you?"

"Yes."

She huffed out a breath. "What's your room like?"

Martin glanced around him. "Erm, it's big ... there's a window, and there's a bathroom ... which I can't make any use of ... obviously. There's a sofa and a table in one corner." He waited for a response, and, not getting one, he added hesitantly, "The walls are white."

She tapped a fingernail on her mobile as a smile came to her face. "What's the bed like?"

Martin looked quickly up and down his mattress. "It's ... it's ..."

"Is it big enough for two?"

"It wouldn't be a comfortable fit. It's just a standard, twin-sized mattress. Patients aren't typically admitted in pairs, Louisa. But I suppose if ... Ah, you were joking?"

"Yes, Martin. I was joking."

"I see."

There was an awkward silence before Louisa spoke again. "Martin, I really miss you."

"Mm. I miss you, too." The door opened, and a woman entered his room. "Erm, Louisa, I should call you back; someone just came in."

"Oh, sure. Well ... I love you."

He glanced over at the stranger who had taken a seat in the corner and cleared his throat. "Me, too," he said as he rang off.

"Hello, Dr. Ellingham. I'm Meredith Conrad, your physiotherapist today. Sorry to interrupt your phone call."

He waved off the woman's apology.

The therapist grasped the bed rail, lowering it to the side. "I've been told things didn't go very well yesterday, so we'll be cautious with that arm. I want to get you sitting up on the edge of the bed today."

Martin's heart began to pound as he watched her move the tray table out of her way and turn back the blankets.

"I'm afraid it's going to be a couple of weeks before Mr. Christianson will allow you to be doing *any* weight bearing on those legs, so we'll start getting you accustomed to using a lift to get you in and out of a wheelchair," she said.

She repeated the exercises that Tim Spalding had done the day before and showed him several exercises he was to do on his own to strengthen the muscles in his lower extremities. She then had him sit up before slipping his broken arm into a sling and helping him to manoeuvre his hardware clad legs over the side of the bed.

Blood rushed to the now lowered body parts, triggering a painful throbbing. Martin squeezed his eyes shut as he tried to stifle the long groan that escaped.

"I know ... it hurts. Give your body a few minutes to release endorphins," she said, rubbing a hand on his back.

Gradually the pain became less intense, and Martin began to relax. He had been lying on his back for most of the entire nine days that had elapsed since his accident. The simple act of sitting normally made him feel less a medical specimen and more human.

"Okay, Dr. Ellingham, let's see what we can do about getting you into a wheelchair," she said before stepping out into the hall and manoeuvring a Hoyer lift in the door. "I've been told you don't care to have your time wasted, so *you* tell *me* ... should I explain anything before we get started, or are you familiar with this process?"

"I know how the bloody thing works. Just get on with it," Martin grumbled.

The therapist helped him to lie back on the sling which had been positioned across the mattress. He clenched his jaw as his traumatised abdominal muscles tightened.

The young woman wrapped the canvas around his sides, hammock-style, before fastening it to the piece of hydraulic machinery. The whole process took less than five minutes, but Martin was emotionally and mentally spent by the time he was lowered into the wheelchair. The ordeal put a large exclamation point on his feelings of helplessness.

The therapist elevated his legs and wheeled him over near the window.

"Would you like to sit for a bit before we get you back to bed, Dr. Ellingham?"

Martin nodded his head, but said nothing. He felt utterly dispirited.

Chapter 23

Martin sat watching out the window as people hurried up and down the sidewalks, going to and from their cars in the adjoining car park. It was the same car park where, just a little over a week ago, he himself had walked on two good legs from Dr. Newell's office over to Chris's office downstairs. He was now unable to even get himself from his bed to a wheelchair without assistance.

Hearing a rumbling and feeling a familiar vibration in his stomach, he looked up at the clock. It was past noon; the food service staff should have been around with the lunch menu by now. *I can't believe I'm actually looking forward to a hospital meal,* he thought. *Gawd, what a pathetic sod!*

His therapist had left the room momentarily, so he would have to wait until she returned to inquire as to the whereabouts of his dinner. He heard the rattle of the knob on his door and looked up as the Parsons walk into the room.

"Mart! Look at you, you're upright! Very well done, mate," Chris said as he walked over and immediately began an inspection of his friend's wounds.

"How's the infection in that left leg doing?"

"I don't know. I haven't checked."

Martin turned his attention back to the car park below as Chris peeled the bandage away from his leg. He crouched down to get a closer look at the incision. "Has Ed been in today to check up on you?"

"No, why? Is there a problem?"

"Not necessarily. You take a look; tell me what you think," Chris said, still fixated on the wound.

Not getting a response, he glanced up. Martin's face had blanched as he sat with his eyes closed.

"Hey, Mart, it's okay. Let Ed and me do the doctoring on this, all right?" he said as he recovered the wound.

Martin nodded his head and wiped his face dry with his palm.

"Are you okay?"

"Yeah, just ... you know."

Carole stepped out from behind her husband. "Hi, Martin, I hope you're hungry. We brought your dinner."

"Yeah, we thought you might appreciate something other than hospital food," Chris said as he pulled the tray table over to his friend's wheelchair.

Carole set a large flat container in front of him and pried the plastic lid off. A wonderful aroma worked its way upward to Martin's olfactory receptors, heightening his already hearty appetite.

He looked back and forth between his friends, wide-eyed and with a hint of a smile. "It's monkfish ... and steamed vegetables."

"Yep, and we brought you something else." Chris presented him with an insulated cup, removing the lid so that the deep roasted fragrance of espresso could reach his nose.

"This is very ... it's ... very nice."

Carole took the plate from the box and set it on the tray table, laying a knife, fork, and spoon next to it. "We're just doing our part to get you well, Martin ... and fattened up a bit. There *is* butter on the fish, I'm afraid. You have no say in the matter."

Chris reached into the plastic box and withdrew a brightly coloured, paisley napkin, laying it on the table. "In your case, Mart, the fat's good for you. We'll make sure you get at least one home cooked meal every day, but you have to promise to follow it up with a dish of ice cream. You need the calories and the calcium."

"Thank you," Martin said before clearing his throat uncomfortably.

Chris headed towards the hallway. "I need to get some papers from my office, so we'll leave you to enjoy your meal."

"There's more where that came from, Martin," Carole said over her shoulder as she and her husband disappeared behind the closing door.

Martin sat in the sunshine, enjoying the wonderful meal in front of him. Auntie Joan had cared for him in this way when he was a small boy, but that was a very long time ago, and the response he was having to the Parsons kindness now felt foreign and unsettling.

The therapist returned shortly to get Martin back into bed. Once he was settled, she worked his limbs to keep the muscles from contracting and potentially displacing the bones that Mr. Simpson had so carefully pieced together in theatre.

"You know, Dr. Ellingham, you'd probably find therapy more comfortable if you had your own pyjamas rather than our conventional hospital attire. Maybe a vest and a pair of boxer shorts. Just make sure they're roomy enough to fit over the hardware."

"I'll mention it to my wife, but it might be next weekend before she visits again."

"Where are you from?"

"Portwenn. My wife is the head teacher at the primary school, so she needs to be back to work tomorrow."

"I'm sure you miss her ... especially when things get particularly rough for you here."

"Yes," Martin said, thinking about how the mere sound of Louisa's voice comforted him.

Ed Christianson entered the room, and the therapist wrapped up the stretching exercises, leaving the two men on their own.

"Chris called me," the surgeon said. "He's a little concerned about this incision, Martin. I wouldn't be able to sleep tonight if I didn't lay eyes on you myself, so let's take a look." The man's features tightened as he pulled the blankets back and removed the dressing.

"There a problem?" Martin asked.

"I don't think our antibiotic cocktail here is doing the job," Ed said, gesturing to the bag of fluid hanging next to the bed. "I want to get a swab culture ... see what grows. If need be, we'll open up the wound and debride ... get another culture that way, then pack it off with beads again. You know the drill."

The surgeon tapped his fingers on the bedrail. "Any questions?"

Martin shook his head, avoiding eye contact with him.

"All right then. I'll go get a culture tray."

The door closed behind the man. Martin blew out a breath of air and pressed his palm to his face, steeling himself for not only the discomfort of another procedure, but the disappointment and worry that would come with another setback. Infections like these were common with his type of injuries, but Martin had hoped that he would be one of the lucky ones and would stay infection free.

Ed came back a few minutes later with the necessary equipment in his hand. He set the tray down and pulled open the drawer next to the bed, removing a thermometer. "One hundred point eight," Ed said, glancing up at Martin.

He went to the sink and scrubbed his hands before donning gloves and opening the sterile pack. Then he put a towel under his patient's calf before proceeding to rinse the wound thoroughly with saline solution. "Be right back." Ed peeled off his gloves and binned them, and then returned to the sink to scrub up again.

"Okay, Martin ... with or without a local? I'd highly recommend the local."

"Whatever you think." Martin tried to focus his thoughts on James and Louisa ... what they might be doing at the moment.

Ed picked up a syringe and injected the local anaesthetic around the incision. He then took a swab and inserted it into the wound between the sutures. He repeated the process with two more swabs before wiping a final swab down the incision line, using a zigzag motion.

"All done, my friend," Ed said looking up from his work. "How are you doing ... okay?"

"Yeah," Martin said, swallowing the lump in his throat. "You'll keep me apprised of any results?"

"You'll be the first to know. Try not to worry. We'll get things under control. I'll stop in tomorrow morning to check up on you and to take those drains out. Get some rest if you can."

Martin waited for the door to close and then rang Louisa's mobile.

"Hello, Martin."

"Hello. Is this a good time?"

"I just put James down for a nap, so yeah, it's perfect. How's your day going ... better than yesterday?"

"In some ways, yes. I sat up on the edge of the bed for a while. It may not sound significant, but it felt like a big step forward."

"That's wonderful, Martin! You'll be up and walking in no time at all."

"Louisa, that's still a long way off."

"I didn't really mean it, Martin."

He tipped his head and blinked his eyes. "Then why did you say it?"

"Because I didn't expect you to take me literally. I wasn't thinking."

"I see."

"Oh, Ruth drove me over to Wadebridge today, and I picked up a rental. The insurance *will* cover it, by the way."

"Good. I was worried about you not having transportation in the event that James should need a doctor ... you know."

"Yes, I do. I also feel better knowing that I have a way to get to you if you need me ... or want me." She dropped down on to the sofa. "Did a therapist come in again today?"

"Yes, twice. The first time she got me into a wheelchair, and I sat by the window for a while. I had my dinner there, actually. The Parsons brought in a home cooked meal ... monkfish and steamed vegetables. And a good cup of espresso."

"Oh, how sweet of them. I feel much better knowing that someone's looking after you while I'm back home."

"Mm. Carole intends to make it a daily event. She thinks I need fattening up."

"You *do* need fattening up."

"Louisa, the therapist suggested that I wear a vest and boxers now ... to make the therapy more comfortable. Could you bring some with you the next time you come to Truro?"

"Certainly. You know, maybe you'd find that attire more comfortable at home as well."

"Very likely. They would be easier than pyjamas to get on over the fixators."

"That's true. Not exactly what I meant, but true."

"Erm, Louisa ... Ed came in a while ago. The antibiotics I've been receiving don't seem to be effective against the pathogens in the lower left leg wound. He took some cultures. We'll have to wait to see what they grow, but hopefully they'll show us what we're dealing with."

"What do you mean, what we're dealing with? Are you saying you have an infection in your leg?"

"Yes, but once they've determined what's causing it, it can be treated more effectively."

"So, are you saying that the test will tell you what antibiotic will get rid of it?"

Martin rubbed at his eyes as he began to feel fatigue and an uneasiness. "It's more complicated than that. Some bacteria grow rapidly—within twenty-four hours. Others can take days ... or even weeks to grow. If it's a pathogen that grows rapidly, then yes, it should help us to know what would be effective."

"And if not?"

"Then they'll open the wound back up and pack it off with the antibiotic bead pouches again."

"And that'll clear it up?"

Martin swallowed, trying to loosen the constriction that was growing in his throat. "It should but ..." His unease intensified. "God, I wish you were here," he said, his voice cracking.

Louisa could hear her husband's heavy breathing, and she knew that he was fighting to stay in control of his emotions. She struggled to keep her own sense of panic in check. "Maybe you should tell me what's worrying you, Martin," she said softly.

His breathing became more ragged.

"Martin, what is it?"

"I don't want to lose my leg, Louisa. I'm afraid I could lose my ..."

His distress tore at her, and both of them were regretting their decision to part ways.

"Martin, you're a doctor. I know that this is a very real and legitimate concern, but maybe you should try doing what Dr. Newell had you do ... take yourself out of the equation and imagine a nameless patient in your place. Are the chances of a good outcome better than your worst fears?"

It got quiet on Martin's end of the call before she heard him take a deep breath. "You're right. I was letting myself focus on the worst-case scenario."

"I know you're going to be fine, Martin. I just know in my heart that you're going to be fine."

When Martin closed his eyes that night, he allowed himself to trust in Louisa's heart as he fell asleep.

Chapter 24

Louisa quickly realised how many household chores Martin ordinarily took charge of when she found her usual routine in chaos Monday morning. He had a way of doing things so quietly and efficiently that she often overlooked his efforts.

She was accustomed to a bath in the morning while Martin, having been up much earlier, would already be dressed and getting James ready for the day. He usually fed their son his breakfast, and he would quite often have a hot breakfast ready for her when she entered the kitchen.

She was running well behind schedule when Poppy arrived.

"I'm really sorry about your husband's accident," the childminder said as she slipped her coat over a peg behind the door.

"Thank you, Poppy. It's been a very difficult week. I really appreciate you being so accommodating."

"It's no trouble, Mrs. Ellingham. Just let me know if you want me to watch James so you can go back to the hospital."

Louisa dumped a few more bits of dry cereal on to the high chair tray before reaching for her cup of coffee sitting, now tepid, on the counter. "Mm, I actually intended to stay with Martin at least through this week, but we decided it would be easier for him to focus on physiotherapy if he was on his own."

"Is he doing any better?"

"Much better, Poppy. I'll tell you more about it later, but I really need to get to school. I have a favour to ask though. Could you stay late tonight?"

"Erm ... yeah. That should be okay."

"Great. I'd like to run some things over to Martin this afternoon, and I don't know what time I'll be back."

Louisa tapped her fingers against her cup. "Would you be comfortable spending the night with James if I need to stay over there?"

The young woman hesitated. "I get kind'a nervous on my own at night. But yeah, that'd be okay."

"Oh, thank you Poppy. That would be a huge help. I'll stop by and make sure you have everything you need before I head out." Louisa looked at her watch. "Gosh, I've got to run." She grabbed a pile of books and her satchel from the table before planting a kiss on the top of her son's head.

"Be a good boy, James. I'll call you when I have a better idea about my plans, Poppy," she said as she dashed out the door.

Thirty miles away, Martin's morning was off to a much rougher start. He woke in the night, sick to his stomach, feverish, and his left leg was pounding. He didn't need to look to know that the infection had worsened.

Chris and Ed had been informed by the nursing staff of the situation, and they had arrived at the hospital as the sun was breaking over the horizon.

"Let's take a look, Martin," Ed said as he pulled the bandage away from his patient's incision, revealing an angry red wound oozing a purulent discharge. He picked up the silicone bulb attached to the end of the drainage tube, his brows knitting together at the sight of the yellow-green colour of the fluid in the bulb.

"Chris, would you get a temperature on him, please." The surgeon went to the sink and began to scrub and disinfect his hands before inspecting his patient's other wounds.

"One hundred and two," Chris said.

"Feeling pretty lousy I bet, aren't you?" Ed said, as he came back over and opened the sling before removing the bandage on Martin's arm.

Martin lay with his eyes closed as he fought to quell his nausea with a swallow.

Leaning on to the bed rail, Ed breathed out a heavy sigh. "All right, we can't hang about waiting for bacteria to grow on agar plates. We're going to head into theatre ... get that leg cleaned up and packed off again.

"I also want to add cefazolin to the mix in your IV. I really don't think this is MRSA, so hopefully the cefazolin will do the trick. But I don't want to wait around any longer. I'll leave Chris to see that you're prepped. I'll go scrub up. You okay with all of this, Martin?" he asked, backing away from the bed.

"Mm," Martin grunted back softly, not daring to open his eyes lest the room begin to spin again.

"Chris, tell them to bring him down as soon as he's ready," Ed said as he headed out the door.

Chris put his hand on his friend's shoulder. "I'll be back, Mart. I need to chase somebody up to get you prepped."

A red-haired nurse toting a metal tray came through the door a few minutes later. "All right, Dr. Ellingham, they want you down in theatre again, I hear." She set the tray down on the table next to the bed and picked up a syringe, pulling the cap from it before injecting additional midazolam into the IV line.

By the time Chris returned with a male nurse to help move Martin to theatre, he was barely lucid.

"How are you doing?" Chris asked as he waited for the nurse to finish disinfecting his leg.

"Mmm, I don' ... don' feel well. Zumthing'ssrong."

"Martin, you have an infection in your leg. We're going to take you to theatre again."

"I fee'like ... crrab."

"Yeah, I bet you do. You ready to go get this thing done, mate?"

He watched his friend for any response, but Martin had given up his battle with the medication.

Chris walked with him as far as the theatre doors before calling Louisa to inform her of the turn of events.

She was just arriving at the school when her mobile rang. Chris's name displayed on the screen, eliciting an immediate sense of unease.

"Chris, is something wrong?"

"Well, Martin's had a bit of a setback. Some infection has developed in his left leg."

Louisa stopped inside the doors and sat down on a bench in the hallway. "He mentioned it when he called last night. "

"It worsened overnight, Louisa," Chris said, leaning back against the wall. "He's just gone into theatre. Ed Christianson's going to open up the wound, remove the nonviable tissue, and wash out the nasty stuff that's accumulated in there. Then he'll pack it off with the beads that were used before and wrap it up again."

Louisa felt a heaviness settle in her, the uncertainty of Martin's future again weighing her down. "Is this something that I should be ... I mean, how serious is this, Chris?"

Chris pushed himself away from the wall and began to pace slowly up and down the hall as he explained the situation more completely to his friend's wife.

"It's serious, Louisa. But remember, this is actually something we were all anticipating ... prepared for ... Martin included."

A small group of children tumbled through the school doors, giggling and chattering. They quieted when they saw Louisa and moved on down the hall.

"Chris, Martin was afraid last night that he could lose his leg. He was blowing things out of proportion ... wasn't he?"

"It's scary, but this is usually a manageable problem. It's the relatively small but very real possibility of the infection not responding to treatment that makes us all uneasy."

"What do you mean by a *relatively small* possibility that it won't respond?"

"It's difficult to say. The incidence of trauma wound infections rises exponentially with the number and severity of the injuries. Those same variables influence how easily the patient can fight off any infection that does develop. I've seen patients with more devastating injuries than Martin's, but ... well, his injuries were severe. So, I guess the best I can do to answer your question is to say that chances are good that we'll be able to get a handle on the situation."

"Can we talk more about this when I get there, Chris? I want to get going as soon as I can."

"Sure, sure. Just drive safely. Give me a call when you arrive, and I'll come down and meet you."

"I will. How was Martin this morning? Was he upset?"

"I think he was too miserable to be upset— headache, fever, dizziness. He'd been vomiting in the night and having nausea this morning. I'm sure it'll help a lot to have you here."

Louisa rang off and hurried down the hall to get things in order at the school before leaving for Truro.

Martin had been returned from theatre, but he was still sleeping when Chris showed Louisa to his room.

"He has a high fever. We would hope to see noticeable improvement by tomorrow morning, though, maybe even later today," Chris said as he pulled a chair over by the bed for her.

"What will he feel like when he wakes up ... any pain, I mean?"

"He'll no doubt have some pain. It's been another invasive procedure. But I think he'll feel more fatigue and general body aches. He won't be real perky for a while, but hopefully we won't see any nightmarish moments like we had last week."

Martin began to mumble softly, and his eyelids fluttered before opening slowly.

"Hi, Martin," Louisa whispered to him as she held her hand to his hot cheek.

He tried to bring her face into focus. His gaze met hers, and he breathed out a soft sigh before squeezing his eyes shut tightly. "I missed you," he whispered hoarsely, wrapping his arm around her back and pulling her to him before pressing his lips to her head.

"I missed you, too. Now try to go back to sleep ... work on getting well."

"Promise me you won't leave."

Louisa pulled back. "I promise you, Martin, I will *not* leave your side."

Martin slept fitfully for the next three hours, waking up several times, retching from the nausea he was experiencing. A nurse came in around noon with lunch for Louisa. "As requested by Dr. Parsons," she explained as she set a tray down in front of her.

"Thank you, but I'm not really hungry."

The nurse gave a nod towards Martin's bed. "You need to take care of yourself, if not for you, for him. He'll heal more quickly if he's not worrying about you."

Louisa gave the woman a smile and picked up the dinner tray. "I'll eat what I can."

Early in the afternoon, Martin began to mumble in his sleep. His hand, which had been lying loosely in his wife's, tightened, and he became agitated.

"Martin, you're dreaming," Louisa said as she gently shook his shoulder. He pulled in a breath and woke, looking at her wildly with glazed and unfocused eyes.

She reached up to caress his face, and he flinched, bringing his hand up quickly. "Martin, you're dreaming," she said again.

A nurse hurried through the door and reached for his wrist to check his pulse, and he pulled his arm away. He thrashed around, trying to roll himself off the bed.

"Your husband's delirious, Mrs. Ellingham. Help me to lay him back down, please," the nurse said as she pressed the call button.

He pulled frantically at his arm in the sling, pleading with whatever antagonist his fevered mind had conjured up to release him.

"Led go! It hurds! Led go!"

The more Louisa and the nurse struggled with him, the harder he fought to get away. A second nurse hurried through the door and adjusted the infusion pump before Martin slowly began to relax. Louisa held on to him as his body slumped back on to the bed.

Rapid footsteps could be heard coming down the hall before Ed entered the room.

"He just had more midazolam, Mr. Christianson. He was pulling on his arm ... trying to get out of the bed," the nurse said.

Ed removed his patient's arm from the sling and unsnapped the top of his hospital gown before palpating his shoulder.

"What's happened?" Chris asked as he approached from behind.

"His temp's higher. He woke up delirious ... tried to get out of the bed and was pulling at his arm. The pins all look secure but he's dislocated that shoulder again. Can you help me with it ... make sure I don't knock anything loose?"

Chris gave Ed a nod before turning to Louisa. "It would be best if you waited outside. This won't take long, and then you can come back in."

She shook her head. "No, I'm staying here. I promised Martin that I wouldn't leave his side."

"We'll just be a minute, Mrs. Ellingham," Ed said.

"I was in the bloody trauma centre with him; I think I can handle this." She directed a steely gaze at the two men, and then took hold of her husband's hand.

She caressed his good arm as the two men pulled and twisted, easing the bones back into place.

Ed rubbed a hand roughly over his head. "I want someone to get him fitted with an abduction orthosis. But have them consult with me first," he instructed over his shoulder as he strode quickly towards the door.

Louisa cocked her head at Chris.

"An abduction orthosis is a brace that'll support Martin's unstable shoulder," Chris explained after the surgeon had left the room.

"I see," she said. "What about the fever ... is it a bad sign that his fever is higher?"

"No, no. It's typical. It's the body's way of killing off bacteria. So, in a sense, it's beneficial ... to a degree. If it goes much higher we'll need to take measures to bring it back down, but he's okay for the time being." Chris glanced at his watch. "I need to get back to my office. I have to meet with someone in ten minutes. I'll check back in an hour or so."

"Thanks, Chris."

Louisa dropped on to the sofa and blew out a long breath before leaning her head back and closing her eyes. She woke later to the sound of her husband's voice.

"Louisa? Louisa!" he called out to her.

"I'm right here, Martin," she said as she hurried to his bed. His fever had broken and he was sweating profusely. He pushed weakly at the blankets, trying to uncover himself.

"Louisa, I'm hot. Help me get these off. I'm hot!"

As she began to peel the blankets back, Martin suddenly grabbed at them, attempting to pull them back up.

"I thought you were hot." she said. He glanced at her, wide-eyed, keeping a firm hold on the coverings over his legs.

"You sit tight, and I'll be right back." Louisa went to the nurses station and returned with a dry gown. Then she took a facecloth from the cupboard by the sink and ran it under the tap before wringing it out. Returning to her husband's bed, she unsnapped the sweat soaked gown that he was wearing before wiping him down with the cool cloth, being careful to avoid the large bandages over his thoracotomy and laparotomy wounds.

"I'm going to rinse this," she said, before returning to the sink. When she returned, she reached to pull the blankets back and Martin grasped her wrist.

"Louisa, please don't."

"Martin, I don't care about what's under there," she said. "It doesn't matter to me. Do you remember the list of reasons that I gave you?"

He cocked his head at her as his brows pulled together. "Yes."

"Well, *those* are the reasons you deserve me, but they're also the reasons I love you. The scars that you'll always have won't offend me in any way. They'll be a reminder to both of us of a very difficult time that we got through together ... a reminder that if we could get through this together, we can get through anything ... *together.*"

She leaned over and kissed him. "I've seen everything already you know."

Pulling the covers back, she caressed his legs with the cloth. He watched her, askance, but saw no indication of antipathy as she cleaned around his bandaged wounds and hardware.

She reached for the clean gown and snapped it in place before giving him a gentle smile. "You want the blankets back on, or are you still hot?"

His gazed avoided hers. "Mm, maybe just the sheet."

Sighing softly, Louisa closed her eyes for a moment. Then she returned the shroud to its proper place.

Chapter 25

Louisa was uneasy about leaving Martin alone in Truro that night, and Martin wasn't ready to let her go for fear there could be a turnaround in his condition. But the fatigue that he saw on her face caused him concern, and he insisted that she sleep at the Parsons', away from the constant disruptions that came with the hospital environment.

When she arrived the following morning, she found a much-improved Martin sitting on the edge of the bed. "Look at you!" she said as she walked into the room, smiling broadly. "Are you feeling better?"

"I am. The new antibiotic seems to be effective." His cheeks nudged up slightly, and his eyes sparkled as he looked back at her.

"*That* ... is wonderful news. I brought you something." She held up the hot breakfast which had been prepared by Carole. "You have orders to clean your plate."

"That won't be a problem."

Louisa set the container down and removed the plastic sectioned tray inside, placing it on the wheeled table next to the bed.

"I can't remember when I've seen you eat like this," Louisa said as she watched him tuck into the generous helping of poached eggs, oatmeal with nuts and raisins, and heavily buttered toast.

Martin stopped eating, his fork poised in the air, and he looked at her sheepishly. "Mm, sorry ... I was hungry."

"Oh, Martin, don't apologise—just eat."

Ed Christianson stopped in a short time later. "The cultures we took grew Staphylococcus, so I feel pretty confident that we're on the right track with the cefazolin, Martin. Now the challenge will be to get you ambulatory."

"When can I start putting some weight on my legs?" he asked.

"Patience, my friend. I'll have the physiotherapists come tomorrow, but I do *not* want them doing anything with that left leg until I give the go ahead. We'll give the wound a few days before we close it up again."

"Mm, yes. Did you talk with Barrett Newell yet?"

Louisa glanced over at her husband as her head tipped to the side.

"Yes, I did. He was actually planning to stop in yesterday, but I didn't think you'd feel much like talking, so I called him ... told him to hold off. Would it be all right by you if he stopped in this morning?"

"Mm, that'd be fine ... good."

"Well unless you have something else crop up, I'll plan to check in on you again tomorrow."

Louisa watched as Ed disappeared down the corridor before turning to her husband. "You didn't mention that Dr. Newell was stopping in to see you. Is ... everything okay?"

Martin grimaced and sucked in a breath. "Would you help me change into my boxers and vest before we discuss it? My legs ... hurt. I need to get them elevated."

"Martin ... maybe ..." Louisa eyed him, biting at her lip as he leaned towards his left side, trying to shift weight from his fractured femur.

He raised an eyebrow at her. "Did you bring them?"

"Yeah ... yeah, I did. But maybe I should get a nurse to help. I don't want to hurt you."

"You won't hurt me. And I'll be needing your help at home so ... please ... I'd rather have you."

For the second time in as many days, Louisa felt her husband pulling her to him instead of pushing her away. "Let me get your things," she said as she hurried over to the bag she had brought from home.

She unsnapped the gown he was wearing and let it fall across his lap. Then she took a step back to evaluate the situation.

Martin squirmed under her intense gaze. "Perhaps it *would* be better to have a nurse help with this."

"No, no, no! I'm just planning my strategy," she said, holding his vest up in front of her.

"Ah, I see."

"Okay, let's see if we can get the sleeve over those contraptions," she said as she pulled at the fabric first, attempting to stretch it out a bit.

She worked the right sleeve over his fractured arm first before slipping the neck over his head.

"What about the IV?" she asked, wagging a finger at the plastic tubing attached to his left arm and the central line snaking out from just under his collarbone.

"Slide the little blue tab over first," he said, extending his arm out to her. His eyes settled on the neckline of her top as she leaned over in front of him. He blinked and refocused his attention on the task at hand. "Yep, yep ... that's good. Now, unscrew the red piece."

Louisa's slender fingers handled the small bits with ease. "How 'bout that ... I did it," she said, giving her husband a smile.

"Yes," he breathed out. His eyes locked on hers, and he leaned forward to place a lingering kiss on her lips.

"Mm, that was very nice. But I s'pose we better finish this up so you're not half dressed the next time someone comes in," she said, caressing his cheek.

Martin instructed her on how to disassemble the tubing running to two of the three ports on his chest, and then he slipped his good arm through the sleeve of the vest before telling to his wife how to reconnect the IVs.

"Okay, now the boxers," Louisa said, scrutinising the situation at hand. "What about the catheter?"

Martin shook his head. "They took it out this morning." He scratched at an eyebrow and breathed out a heavy sigh. "I think you better help me lie back before we attempt this."

"What do you need me to do?"

"Just lift my legs up on to the bed."

Louisa looked at him uncertainly before reaching down to put her hands behind his calves.

"No, no, no, no, no. Grab hold of the fixator bars ... on the anterior— Sorry, the front side of my legs."

Louisa's eye widened, and she gave a theatrical shudder. "Oh no, Martin. I can't do *that*."

"It's actually less painful than if you put pressure on the soft tissue. You want to avoid pulling on the skin around the pins." He gave a sharp downward nod. "Just grab the bars and swing my legs up on to the bed. Go slow ... turn with me." He grimaced again before adding, "But we need to get a move on."

She reluctantly did as he asked, finding her stomach churning as she grasped on to the cold metal penetrating his flesh. She followed his body around as he painstakingly pivoted on the bed. Pulling his chin to his chest, he tried unsuccessfully to stifle a groan.

Louisa focused intently on what her husband needed her to do, unaware of the tears filling her eyes.

Martin leaned back on his good arm and pulled in a breath as a sharp jolt shot through his left leg. He swallowed hard and gave her an approving nod of his head. "Well done. The boxers now?"

"Yeah." Louisa picked them up from the tray table and then wiped at her eyes before turning towards him. She looked from her husband's legs back up to his face. "This will be interesting," she said, giving him a strained smile.

"Just pull them up over the hardware. You'll have to work one side at a time. Be careful to not let the fabric catch and pull on the pins."

She slipped the boxers over his bruised and swollen feet and leaned over, instinctively applying gentle kisses to each one.

Martin stared back at her, and his eyes grew moist before he quickly looked away.

"Okay, here we go," she said, giving him an encouraging nod. Martin rocked himself back and forth while Louisa worked his shorts carefully up and over all the metalwork protruding from his legs. She took a step back, inspecting him carefully. "I think you're presentable now."

The foam blocks used to elevate his legs were repositioned. Then she pulled the blankets back up over him.

"Now ... your arm?" She nodded her head towards the sling.

"Better wait on that. My shoulder makes it tricky."

Louisa went to the sink and came back with a wet flannel.

"Here, I can do it," Martin said as he reached for the cloth and wiped his face before handing it back to her. "Thank you for doing that, Louisa. I'm much more comfortable now."

"Good. You look more comfortable." She smoothed out his hair, tousled during the wrestling match with his vest.

"Now, you were going to tell me about Dr. Newell," she said, handing him a glass of water.

"Mm, it's nothing really. Ed ... as well as Chris, Robert and Will evidently ... seem to think I need to talk to someone about the accident. Ed was going to line someone up, but I told him about Dr. Newell. That's really all there is to it."

Louisa sat down on the edge of the bed. "I think it's a good idea. It's been a very traumatic experience. I'd like it if *we* could talk about it sometime, too ... you and me."

Martin cocked his head. "Why?"

"Because ... there's a lot I don't know about."

Martin furrowed his brow. "What do you mean? I would imagine you know more than I do. You were conscious through the whole thing."

"Hmm, that's true. But I wasn't there when it happened, was I?" She stroked her fingers across the back of his hand. "Do you think you might tell me about it sometime?"

He hesitated. "You could stay while Dr. Newell's here. But perhaps ... if I need to talk to him alone—"

"I can give you some privacy ... whenever you want it. You just tell me, and I'll step out for a while." Louisa leaned over and pressed her lips to his forehead before whispering, "Thank you for including me in this."

She got up from the bed and moved towards the door. "I'm going to run down to the canteen. Is there anything I can get you?" she asked.

"No, I'm fine."

"All right, I'll be back in a tick then."

She made a stop at the lavatory before spotting Ed Christianson in the corridor. He was involved in a conversation with someone.

The man turned as she approached. "Hello, Mrs. Ellingham. I was just on my way down to see your husband," Dr. Newell said.

"Yes, he's expecting you."

She turned to the surgeon. "Thank you, Ed, for insisting that Martin talk with someone."

"You're welcome. Your husband's taciturn nature is legendary in the British medical community. We were afraid he'd keep this bottled up."

"I suspect you're right." She gestured towards the canteen. I was just going for a cuppa ... maybe a biscuit. But I'll be back in just a bit."

"Could you give me a little time alone with Martin ... a half hour or so?" the psychiatrist asked.

"Certainly, I'll see you then." Louisa glanced at her watch before continuing down the hallway.

Martin was sleeping when Dr. Newell reached his room, but he woke when he heard the door open.

"Hello, Martin. I just spoke with your wife. I think she'll join us a little later."

"Yes, she went to the canteen."

"Sounds like a pretty brutal week and a half for both of you."

"Mm, things are getting better now though."

"How have things been going otherwise ... the depression and nightmares?"

Martin shifted his weight to get more comfortable. "The symptoms of depression have been better. I was actually hungry this morning and ate a big breakfast."

"Mm-hmm. And the other?"

"I've had a few since the accident."

"About the accident, or something else?" asked Dr. Newell as he leaned against the bed rail.

"About the accident ... yes. But also about ... things that have happened."

"Care to elaborate?"

"I, er ... I remembered something the night of the accident ... when I was trapped in the car. It wasn't paint on the floor in my father's study; it was blood. I remember more about that day now."

The therapist pulled a chair over and took a seat. "Go ahead."

"You're aware of what happened after my father came in. But my mother came in shortly after that. She was angry. She said I'd ruined the floor, my clothes ... that I ruin everything. She grabbed me by the arm ... the broken arm."

Martin winced, and unconsciously pulled his left arm against himself. "She led me to the hallway ... to the cupboard door. I looked at her face and ..."

He laid his head back on his pillow and closed his eyes, taking in a ragged breath.

"Sorry," he said as he wiped a palm across his face. "Where was I?"

"You were telling me about your mother's face. What was it about her face that's upsetting you now?"

Martin's gaze shifted to the window. "The hatred and disgust that I could see in her eyes. She, erm ... she shoved me into the cupboard and the lock clicked. I'd fallen forward and was lying on my arm. The pain was intense. I could smell the blood on my trousers ... like the night of the accident."

His head tipped to the side. "The pain and the smell made me sick to my stomach, and I vomited."

Dr. Newell waited for a few moments. "Do you remember any more?"

"Mm, yes. I could hear people outside. I didn't know what was going on. My mother liked parties, but I hadn't heard her talk of having one."

Martin turned his head towards the therapist and furrowed his brow. "I don't know why the people were there, but after a while, I heard them going out the front door and ..."

He hesitated as a fleeting sensation passed through him before quickly evaporating.

"What is it, Martin?"

He sighed and shook his head. "I don't know ... it was a sound ... a familiar sound but ..."

He squeezed his eyes shut, grasping for the memory he knew was there. He brought his fist up, hitting his forehead in frustration before letting his arm drop back to his side. "It's gone. I can't remember," he said, throwing up a hand.

"Why don't you go back to the cupboard, Martin. What happened after the people left?"

"I could hear my mother's shoes. They made a certain sound ... a harsh click when her high heels hit the hardwood floor. Her footsteps sounded angry. I was afraid of how she was going to react when she saw the mess I'd made in the cupboard ... afraid of what she might do. I ... I wet myself, which made things even worse."

He shook his head and sucked in a ragged breath. "My heart was pounding. I heard her stop. Then the key was turning in the lock."

Dr. Newell could see a growing panic in his patient's eyes. "All right, let's stop for now. You can finish the story later." He handed him a glass of water and waited quietly until his posture relaxed. "Better now?" he asked.

"Mm, yes ... I'm fine," Martin said, clearing his throat. "I need to finish ... to tell you before I forget again."

"I don't think you'll forget these things again, but if you feel you're ready, go ahead."

He pulled in a breath. "She opened the door, saw the mess, and yelled at me to get out. I couldn't move. I was stiff, and I'd been lying on my arm. It hurt to move. My father came, grabbed me by the collar and dragged me out into the hallway. I was confused. I didn't understand. I *still* don't understand what I did wrong."

Dr. Newell nodded slowly. "Martin, do you remember anything about what might have happened in your father's study ... where the blood came from?"

"No. But I had some dreams ... or memories. Once when I was febrile and again as I was coming out of anaesthesia. It was my father's voice ... the things he said to me in the past. Belittling things about my job in Portwenn, my not joining the navy. But ..."

"Yes?" Dr Newell leaned his forearms on his knees.

"It's something else that he said that ..." Martin licked his lips. "In his study that day ... when he came in, he yelled, 'Martin, what have you done?' And when I was coming out of the anaesthesia, I kept hearing the belittling remarks. But there was something I hadn't remembered before. He said, 'You want to know why this happened? Because I have a son who lacks even an ounce of sense, that's why'.

"I don't know when he said it ... why he said it or if he even said it at all. But I'm afraid the two comments could be connected."

"Why is that? In what way do you think they're connected?"

Martin blinked at the man. "Well, if both remarks were in reference to the incident in his study ... Well, it stands to reason, doesn't it? *I* was responsible for the blood on the floor."

Dr. Newell pulled his ankle up over his knee. "Martin, there are many unknowns regarding this incident. We don't even know if all these bits of memories are even related."

"Yes, but if I hurt someone in some way, or if I caused someone's death, it would explain everything."

"What would it explain?"

Martin stared absently across the room. "I suppose I could then understand why I wasn't loved ... wanted."

"It's natural, Martin, that you would want to be able to make sense of what happened that day ... to make sense of your childhood and your parents' behaviour and attitude towards you. But keep in mind that it's human nature to want to make the pieces fit neatly together ... to have explanations for things. You and I are both scientists ... living proof of this, but you may very well never be able to fit those pieces together.

"It's important to remember that you were a child. You were a little boy whose brain was immature. Regardless of where the blood came from or what your father's words meant, you need to remember—you were a little boy."

The therapist looked at his watch, noting that Louisa would be back soon. "I think we should shift gears, Martin, and come back to the incident in the study the next time we talk. Let's take a short break. Louisa's planning to join us, so I'm going to get a cup of coffee, and we'll continue once she's arrived. Can I get a cup for you?"

Martin shook his head. "I don't like hospital coffee."

After Dr. Newell and Louisa had both returned to the room, the psychiatrist pulled up another chair. "There you are, Louisa," he said, taking a seat next to her.

"So, Martin, tell me about your accident. This happened after your appointment with me. Did it have anything to do with our session?"

"No, nothing like that," Martin said. "I had a meeting at the hospital after I left your office, so it was well after my session with you when I headed home."

"So, how did it happen?"

"A lot of it's fuzzy for me, but I can remember coming up to the River Camel bridge. Headlights from a car on the other side blinded me momentarily. The next thing I knew, there was a lorry coming at me, drifting into my lane. There was no place to go. A collision was inevitable." Martin sighed. "Everything gets sketchy after that."

Dr. Newell sat quietly for a few moments before looking up at him. "I'm sorry," he said shaking his head. "I was just trying to imagine what that would be like ... seeing something coming at you like that ... waiting for the impact."

Martin shrugged his shoulders. "It really wasn't like that. It happened so fast that ..."

Seconds passed before he began to speak again. "The guardrails ... I didn't know what to do. I didn't know if it would be better to move left or right or ... I didn't know what to do. I was afraid ... for James and Louisa."

Louisa got up, standing by the bed as she took hold of her husband's hand.

"Can you explain to Louisa what you mean by that?" the therapist said.

"I was afraid of leaving ... of leaving them alone ... no husband ... no father."

He pressed his fingers to his eyes and continued. "Then there was a jolt. I can't describe it. I could feel the energy behind that lorry go through me. I could feel it in my bones. And then nothing at all until I heard someone talking to me. And the pain started to ..."

He stopped, attempting to slow his breathing. "I tried to cover my eyes to block out a bright light, but I couldn't move my arm ... it was caught. I tried to pull it away and pain shot through it.

"There was someone in the car with me. They told me to stay still. I sat there ... waiting for them to get me out of there. I could feel blood running down my arm ... across the palm of my hand. My fingers felt odd ... numb. But the blood running off of them tingled. I could feel my lap getting warm. I thought at first that I'd ... that I'd peed myself, but then I noticed the pulsing in my leg, and I knew ..." He swallowed hard. "I knew I was bleeding out. I was sure that I was going to exsanguinate before they got me out of there."

"But you didn't, did you?" Dr. Newell said.

"No. I wanted to die at one point, but I thought about Louisa and James ... how I finally have a family ... a family who loves me and ... and I didn't want to die. Louisa and James saved me."

Louisa leaned forward and kissed her husband's cheek.

Martin's face warmed and he pulled in his chin. "I don't remember much after that."

The therapist shook his head. "I was shocked when Louisa called to tell me what had happened ... to cancel your upcoming appointments. I'm very glad that you're here to relate the story to us today."

Martin felt his wife's fingers wiggle in his hand, and he squeezed back.

Dr. Newell got up from his chair. "You look very tired, and I promised Mr. Christianson that I wouldn't allow you to overdo it. I'll give you a couple of days to recuperate and stop back again. Will you be here on Friday, Louisa?"

"I can make a point to be. Whatever you think is best for Martin."

"Well, I asked because I suspect there may be some issues you'd like to discuss as well. But for now, we'll call it a day," he said, stepping towards the hall.

Louisa waited until the door had swung shut behind him before leaning over to rest her head on her husband's shoulder. "I am so very, very glad to have you still with me."

"Mm. I'm glad to still be here," Martin said as he pulled her closer.

Chapter 26

The soft rattle of the doorknob and the crescendo of hallway noise caused Louisa to stir as she lay napping beside her husband later that morning. Martin had shifted over on the bed after Dr. Newell left so that she could lay with him, and they had both drifted off to sleep. She propped herself up on an elbow and brushed the hair back away from her face.

The young woman in the doorway pulled up her shoulders. "Sorry to disturb you," she said softly. "I'm Megan White. I'm here to fit Dr. Ellingham with his shoulder brace."

Louisa slid from the bed and jostled her still sleeping husband. "Martin," she said softly. "There's someone here to see you."

He released a long groan as he slowly opened his eyes.

"Does something hurt?" she asked, placing her palm against his cheek.

"No. I just ... it was ... it was nice with you here," he mumbled sleepily. "Climb back in here with me."

"How 'bout we pick up where we left off a little later. There's someone here to see you right now." Louisa glanced in the visitor's direction.

Martin turned his head quickly towards the door. A wave of heat spread up his neck when he saw the orthotist observing their interactions. He grumbled unintelligibly and raised the head of the bed.

"Sorry to wake you, Doctor. I'm Megan White. I'm here to fit you with your shoulder brace."

He wiped his palm across his face and cleared his throat. "Mm, yes."

"Mr. Christianson's on his way down, so I'll wait for him to arrive. He evidently has specific instructions for me."

"Will this brace keep Martin's shoulder from slipping out again?" Louisa asked as she wrapped her arms around herself.

"There's no guarantee of that, but it certainly will make it less likely. It'll also keep his arm elevated, even when he's up and about. That'll be important as he gets more mobile and is spending more time out of bed."

The door opened again, and Ed hurried into the room. "Hi, Megan. Thanks for waiting. Let me show you what we're dealing with. Hopefully, we can come up with something that will protect the shoulder without compromising all the work that we've done here," he said as he lowered Martin's arm down and opened the closures on the sling.

The surgeon and the orthotist discussed the concerns and options and came up with a brace design that Ed could live with.

The surgeon scratched at an eyebrow. "Sorry, Martin. This will be an improvement but still rather uncomfortable, I'm afraid."

He moved to the foot of the bed and pulled the blankets back. "I may as well check on this wound while I'm here," he said before removing the bandage on the problem leg. "Looks pretty good," Ed said, patting his patient's foot."

He pulled a clean bandage from a supply cabinet and redressed the wound. "I'll stop by in the morning ... make sure we're still on track," he said as he binned the empty bandage wrappers and headed towards the corridor. "But I think we can plan on closing things up on Thursday, okay?"

"Mm, that would be good," Martin said, giving a nod of his head.

"Thank you, Ed." Louisa waited for the door to close behind the surgeon and orthotist before turning to her husband.

"Now, what was it you were saying before we were so rudely interrupted?"

"*Ohh,* I embarrassed myself," he moaned.

She sat down on the edge of the bed, stroking her fingertips back and forth across his chest. "You mean because you were cuddled up in your bed with your wife?"

Martin batted her hand away. "Yes, Louisa! That orthotist will probably exaggerate the entire incident and rumours will spread around this hospital faster than the bubonic plague in the Middle Ages!"

"Mm, rumours," she purred. "If rumours are going to spread anyway..."

"Louisa, I'm *serious*. I have to interact with these people on a professional basis. I can't ..."

She walked her fingers up her husband's torso, stopping when she reached his face to trace a finger along his jawline. Then crawling up on the bed she took his chin in her hand and began to place amorous kisses on his mouth.

Making a half-hearted attempt to pull away from her, he shook his head. "Louisa ... we shouldn't. Someone's going to—to walk in," he said, his voice faltering.

"Martin, I nearly lost you in a car crash. If someone wants to spread rumours because they see me loving you, then they can *just—sod—off*."

"Mm, yes," he said as she nestled in against him.

When Carole Parsons came to the room a short time later she found Martin sound asleep and Louisa curled up, her head resting on his shoulder.

Louisa raised her head up and put a finger to her lips. Carole set the container holding the lunch she had prepared down on the tray table. Louisa mouthed the words 'thank you' before she slipped from the room.

More than an hour later, Martin began to stir. When he opened his eyes, his wife was watching him.

"Hello."

Martin yawned, "Hello."

"Are you hungry? Carole brought us lunch."

"I *am* hungry."

Louisa slid from the bed and went around to pull the table over. She watched her husband inquisitively as he ate his salad and sandwiches.

He glanced up at her. "What is it?"

She hesitated. "I'm just curious ... it didn't bother you that Carole saw us in bed together?"

He gulped down a mouthful of salad as his brows drew together. "No." Taking a bite of sandwich, he washed it down with milk. "Louisa, strictly speaking, we weren't *in bed together*. We were in *a* bed together. Regardless, I consider it payback for the innumerable times I walked in on Chris and Carole pawing at each other on my sofa," he said flatly.

"Martin Ellingham, I never thought you'd be the vindictive type!" she said, shaking her head as the corners of her mouth pulled up.

She leaned over the bedrail and rested her forehead against his. "You're quite cute when you're vindictive."

"Mm, I don't know about that," he mumbled as his cheeks reddened.

She straightened back up. "Erm, when do you think you'll want me to head back home? I'm happy to stay as long as you want me here, but I should make some plans if I won't be back at work this week. And I need to make sure things are settled with James."

Martin stared down at his plate as he picked at his bread.

"I don't want to leave here until you feel ready for me to leave." Louisa brushed her fingers across his cheek.

"No, you should be with James. I'll be fine here now." He bit at his lip, and then reached for his glass.

"Hmm, why don't you think it over this afternoon. Let me know at the end of the day," she said.

"No. I'm sure it'll be fine. You should get back ... take care of things at home. I ... I'm just going to miss you. Could you come back this weekend?"

"I will most certainly be here this weekend," she said, placing a kiss on his head.

She stayed for several more hours before heading back to the Parsons' to pick up her belongings.

"How does he seem to be doing? Better physically, I know. But emotionally ...?" Carole asked as she and Louisa sat, having a cup of tea.

"Okay, I think. It can be hard to tell with Martin. He says he's ready for me to be going back home, but I think he's going to be lonely."

"Well, you said that physiotherapy starts back in tomorrow. Maybe that will keep him busy ... and tired out."

"That's possible. But ... would you mind checking in on him now and then? Let me know how he seems to you?" Louisa asked hesitantly. "You've done so much already, I hate to ask more of you."

"Oh, Louisa. We've been happy that we could be of help through all of this. And a real blessing that's come from it all is our new friendship. I don't know *how* long it would have taken for us to meet if it had been left up to our husbands."

"I doubt we ever would have met," Louisa said with a giggle. Her smile faded and she reached across the table to take her friend's hand. "I'll always feel a special bond with you and Chris. I know Martin's accident took a toll on your husband. I can't imagine what it was like for him to listen to the play by play over the ..." Her voice caught in her throat. "I'm sorry." She reached into her pocket for a tissue.

"There's no need to apologise. It was much worse for you. But you're right, it just tore Chris up to see the condition Martin was in when he arrived in the Trauma Centre."

Carole sipped at her tea as she gazed absently over Louisa's shoulder. "Those two were quite close friends when they were in medical school. Well, once Chris finally broke through that tough shell your husband has, that is. They drifted apart after they finished school, but I'm hoping they'll make an effort to see more of each other now."

"Well, no matter what our husbands do, I intend to nurture the friendship that *we've* developed," Louisa said.

"You're always welcome here, Louisa. This whole ordeal for Martin's far from over. Our door is open whenever you want to stay."

"Thank you, Carole. One day at a time."

Martin spent much of the remainder of *his* day either staring out the window or aimlessly flipping through channels on the television, pausing occasionally to watch a few minutes of a programme before muttering and tossing the remote on to the bed.

Whoever coined the phrase 'it's a dog's life' has never spent two weeks tethered to the end of a leash, he thought as he gave the sling entrapping his arm a sneer. He let out a long groan before the soft creak of the door caught his attention.

Chris walked in carrying a cardboard box. "Hey, Mart. Carole told me Louisa left you to your own devices here, so I thought you might appreciate a few diversions," he said, setting the box down by his friend.

"The latest *BMJ* ..." Chris waved the journal in the air before tossing it on to the tray table. "Laptop and earbuds ... chess set ..." He stacked the items on the table next to the bed.

"And this is something I happened upon in a used bookstore in Plymouth a few years ago. I would have given it to you before now, but I never really found an opportunity when I didn't think you'd find it a bit overly demonstrative. This seemed like the right time." He handed Martin a very worn copy of a book titled *A Horologist's Reference*. "Thanks mate," he said, patting his friend on the shoulder, "for all you did to get me through medical school."

Martin looked down at the book for several moments and then back up at Chris as a crushing pressure built in his chest. The air raced from his lungs, and he struggled to catch his breath.

Tears welled in his eyes and Chris grimaced. "Oh, God, Mart. You're not going to get *emotional* over this, are you? You'll embarrass us both, mate."

Martin stared through him.

"Hey, Mart, are you okay?" Chris asked.

Chris's voice became a hum in Martin's ears, and his surroundings began to blur. The light in the room grew dim before fading into darkness as the book slipped from his fingers and on to the floor.

Chapter 27

Chris leaned over, putting his ear to his friend's chest. The colour had drained from Martin's face, and his breathing had grown rapid and shallow.

Reaching across the bed, Chris pressed the call button repeatedly before hastily removing his arm from the sling and tipping the bed back.

"Martin!" Chris said as he shook his shoulder. "*Martin*, can you hear me?" A nurse came through the door, and he reached his hand out, snapping his fingers. "Give me a stethoscope!" he barked. The woman pulled the instrument from the pocket on her tunic and slapped it into his hand.

"Call Mr. Christianson. Tell him that his patient's tachycardic." The nurse took several steps towards the door before Chris called after her, "And get a crash cart in here!"

He pressed the stethoscope to Martin's chest and listened. His heart was racing. "Martin, can you hear me?" Chris asked again, pinching the back of his hand in an attempt to elicit a response.

There was a commotion as two nurses pushed a metal cart through the doorway, banging it into the jamb. Chris grabbed a plastic pouch from the cart and tore it open before pulling up Martin's vest and slapping ECG patches on to his chest. "Give him six milligrams of adenosine," he ordered the nurse next to him. "We need to get his heart rate down."

Ed Christianson's shoes slid on the floor as he skidded to a stop and rounded the corner into the room. "What the hell happened?" he asked as he came to Chris's side.

"I'm not sure. He's tachycardic ... just seemed to crash as we were talking. He was looking at me for a while, but he was unresponsive to my questions. Then he lost consciousness."

The two doctors watched the monitor as they listened to the steady beeps of the machine gradually begin to slow.

"Do you see anything out of the ordinary?" Chris asked.

Ed studied the ECG screen. "There are some inverted T waves and a slight ST depression. Nothing's screaming out at me, though. I'll go chase up someone from cardiology to take a look. Make sure there's been no ischemic damage."

"From the hypovolaemia?" Chris asked.

"I think we need to rule it out." He tipped Martin's head to the side and inserted a thermometer in his ear. "Normal."

He tossed the instrument on to the cart next to the bed and pulled his stethoscope from around his neck. "Well, he seems to have stabilised now. What were you two talking about? Anything that might have triggered this?"

"No. I brought in a box of stuff to keep him entertained now that his wife's gone back home ... that's it."

Ed noticed Martin's fingers twitch slightly. "He's coming around." He took his patient's hand and squeezed his fingers. "Martin ... Martin, can you hear me?"

Martin's eyelids fluttered before slowly opening. He looked up at Chris and Ed hovering over him, blinking several times before his eyes darted around the room.

"I'll go find someone from cardiology," Ed said as he hurried out the door.

"Hey, Mart. Can you tell me where you are?" Chris prodded, leaning forward on the bed rail.

Time and place were intangible, and Martin began to feel a growing sense of panic. His eyes shifted between his friend's face and his surroundings as his breaths grew rapid again.

"Hey, mate, it's all right. You're in hospital. You were in a car accident, and we've been taking care of you," Chris said as he raised the bed.

Martin's memories of that horrific night and the nightmarish days that followed began to seep back into his consciousness. "What's going on?"

"You tell me. We were talking and suddenly you were unresponsive to my questions. Then you lost consciousness." Chris pulled a pocket torch from the medical cart and checked his friend's pupillary reflexes. Turning, his foot collided with the book that had been dropped on the floor. "Maybe it was the shock of receiving a gift from me," he said, handing the book to Martin with a teasing grin.

Martin glanced down at it, quickly handing it back. "Lay it on the table for me."

"Martin, did my gift upset you for some reason?" Chris asked, noting the tremor in his friend's fingers as well as the shift in his affect.

Martin pressed the heel of his hand to his forehead and he squeezed his eyes shut. "Just ... leave it, Chris."

Ed re-entered the room and walked over to the bed, putting his hand on his patient's shoulder. "Catherine Arneson, one of our staff cardiologists, is on her way down, Martin. She's a crack doctor ... knows her stuff. We need to make sure that the hypovolaemia didn't do any damage to your heart."

Ed turned as he heard footsteps approaching. "Ah, here she is now," he said as a tall slender woman with long blonde hair stepped into the room. "Catherine, this is Martin Ellingham. Martin's the GP who single-handedly saved our air ambulance."

Dr. Arneson held out her hand. "Well, Superman in the flesh! How can I be of assistance?"

The woman's gesture went unnoticed as Martin stared at his lap, his brow furrowed.

Chris eyed his friend suspiciously as he and Ed took turns explaining the details of what had transpired with their patient.

"Maybe Chris slipped some kryptonite into that box he brought you, Martin," Ed joked.

He raised his head and stared blindly past him. "No. It was something else."

The cardiologist looked at the ECG strip and then pulled the stethoscope from around her neck and pressed it to Martin's chest. "Well, I'm not seeing any red flags, but just to be on the safe side, let's keep you on the monitor tonight. I'll get an echocardiogram set up for in the morning."

"Thanks, Catherine," Ed said. "Erm, you'll want to check in with the PT people before scheduling that echo. They're planning to work with Martin in the morning as well. Just don't want anyone getting their toes stepped on."

"Will do."

The cardiologist headed out of the room, and Ed pocketed his stethoscope, turning to follow after her. "I'll check in with you tomorrow, Martin. Are you going to stay a bit, Chris?"

"Yeah, you go on ahead," Chris said as he pulled a chair up next to the bed.

The door closed behind the surgeon, and Chris breathed out a heavy sigh. "Okay ... you want to talk about it?"

Martin laid his head back on the pillow and closed his eyes.

"What do you think happened tonight, Martin?"

He shrugged his shoulders.

"Was it a panic attack, Mart?"

Martin whipped his head around and glared angrily at his friend. "How the hell should I know!"

"Martin ... I'm only trying to help," Chris said softly.

"I didn't ask for your help!" He shook his head and waved a hand towards the door. "Just ... leave me alone."

Chris held his hands up in front of him. "Okay, you win. I'm going home. You have my number. Call me anytime, day or night, if you want me for anything."

Chris paused at the door and turned. "Goodnight, Mart. I'll stop by in the morning."

Martin watched the door swing shut before grabbing the basin by his bed and vomiting into it. He reached for his mobile, turned it off, and closed his eyes as guilt and grief overwhelmed him.

Chapter 28

Louisa had tried numerous times to reach her husband's mobile Tuesday night, frustrated that he had it turned off. She went to bed disappointed, but her thoughts quickly shifted to her responsibilities at home.

When she couldn't reach Martin Wednesday morning, her frustration grew into worry. But certainly, if he had experienced another setback, Chris would have called to let her know about it.

She pushed her concerns aside as she rushed to get herself and James ready for the day before Poppy arrived. James was out of sorts, but Louisa dismissed his contrariness to their disorganized schedule rather than a brewing illness.

She carried out the morning ritual of placing a kiss on the top of his head before dashing out the door and down the hill towards the school.

It was wonderful to be back at work. If she kept busy, she could almost imagine life as normal again. But during the slower times her thoughts turned to Martin.

She didn't have another opportunity to call him again until noon. Hurrying down Fore Street, she dialled her mobile as she made her way home to share lunch with James and Poppy. She pressed the phone tightly to her ear and pulled her free hand up, cupping it over the other ear to block out the noise of the gulls circling over the fishing boats coming into the harbour.

"Bugger!" she muttered before shoving the device back into her handbag. "What's going on over there, Martin?"

As she trudged up Roscarrock Hill she invented several plausible explanations as to why her husband had not turned his mobile on, or why he had turned it off in the first place. But the niggling doubts ate at her.

She arrived back at the surgery to find lunch waiting for her on the table and James playing contentedly in his high chair with a set of metal measuring cups. He found they produced a glorious noise if banged upside down on his high chair tray.

"Poppy, this is such a treat. Coming home to a comforting hot meal and a happy child. I think my husband is the cleverest man on Earth for having thought to ask you to mind James."

"I'm glad you're happy, Mrs. Ellingham." Poppy pulled up her shoulders self-consciously. "How is Dr. Ellingham?"

"He's definitely doing better, but his injuries were extensive and severe so he'll have a long recovery. It could be another four to five months before he's back to seeing any patients. We haven't met with an occupational therapist yet. I'm not sure how he'll even get around."

"Crutches *would* be tricky on the hills here," Poppy said as she spooned more strained carrots into James Henry's mouth.

"He won't be able to use crutches with his broken arm and the shoulder problem."

Poppy gave her a blank stare.

"I'm sorry, Poppy. I've been so absorbed in what's been going on at the hospital that I'm afraid I've been rather economical with the details of Martin's injuries.

"The fractures to his arm and legs were severe and his surgeons were concerned about infection, so they didn't use screws and plates to fix them.

"He has what are called external fixators ... metal bars on the outside of his legs and arm that are secured into the bones with pins. They kind of make me think of the clamps woodworkers use to hold pieces of wood together ... except they hold the bones together."

"That sounds ... Does it hurt."

"Yes, but he tries not to let on. Martin ... Dr. Ellingham also had several internal injuries that required surgery, but thankfully no spinal cord or brain injuries. In that respect, he's very lucky ... lucky to be alive really."

"I'm sorry for Dr. Ellingham. Tell him that I hope he gets well soon," Poppy said, wiping the remnants of lunch from her young charge's face.

"I will, Poppy." She glared at her mobile. "*If* I can ever get through to him." Louisa slapped the device down on the table.

She hurried back to the school after lunch, hoping to time her arrival so that the students and teachers would be busy in their classrooms. She'd been hiding out in her office all morning, in part because she had a lot of paperwork to get caught up on. But she was also trying to avoid the endless questions about Martin's accident.

As she was walking past Large's restaurant she heard Bert's jovial voice call out to her.

"Hello, Louiser!" he said as he worked his way up the steps, trying to catch her before she went on by.

"Hello, Bert. I was just heading back to school. Sorry, but I don't have time to talk."

Louisa tried to keep up her forward momentum, continuing down the hill. "Good morning, Ruth," she said as her husband's aunt approached from the other direction.

"Louisa! You're going to be late, aren't you?"

"Yeah, I'm a bit off my schedule, not having Martin around and all."

Louisa cringed and groaned softly as Bert's voice grew louder.

Her slight delay to greet Ruth had given the man time to gain ground on her.

"How's the doc, Louiser?" He shuffled up, puffing air. "Everybody's heard about the accident, of course. Is there anything I can do to help?" he asked, his voice laden with dubious concern. "I'd be more than happy to pass on any information you'd like to share with the rest of the village. Spare you havin' to relive that whole catastrophe all over again, you know."

"Oh, that's thoughtful, Bert. I think I can manage any questions that come up, though." She glanced at her watch. "Martin's doing better, but he has a long way to go yet before he'll be able to get around well on his own, let alone get back to seeing patients."

"I had an accident once. No fun ... no fun a'tall, that was. Oh, but that was before your time I s'pose. Me and my Mary hadn't even met yet."

Louisa tried to sidestep the man, but he zigged to the left as she zagged to the right, keeping himself positioned squarely in front of her.

"You know where you turn on to Old Deacons Road? Where there's that little hill just past there, and a little past that hill there's a bridge? Well, there used to be a bridge ... till they—"

"I'm sorry, Bert, but I really need to go," she said, interrupting the man as he prattled on. She circled around him and inched her way down the hill.

"Oh sure, sure. I'm sure you're busy, what with the doc off his feet an' all, trips to Truro, that little lad of—"

"Sorry, Bert. I really need to run. Maybe we can catch up another time."

"Oh, sure, sure. You just say the word if there's anything that me or my boy can do ta help."

"Thank you, Bert." She gave her husband's aunt a jerk of her head as they pulled away from the rotund restaurateur. "Can you walk with me, Ruth?"

"Certainly. How do you think my nephew is faring? Continuing to improve, I assume?"

"Yes, Ruth, he is. Sometimes it seems as though he's not making progress, but if I look back to where he was a few days ago, he's definitely showing signs of improvement. It's just a two-steps-forward, one-step-back process."

"And the leg? Any news there?"

"Well, the infection has cleared. So, barring any further complications, they'll close that wound up again tomorrow."

"Well, fingers crossed then," said Ruth, giving her a crooked smile.

Louisa worried the strap on her handbag. "I take it you haven't heard from him recently, then? He hasn't called you?"

"No, but then it's not really his habit, so I wouldn't *expect* to hear from him. I count on you to provide me with any information I should happen to need. Why do you ask?"

"Hmm, it's just that I've been trying to reach him since last night, and he has his mobile shut off. I'm sure it's nothing though," she said, more to reassure herself than to convince the elderly woman.

"Well, you need to get to school, so I won't keep you," Ruth said as she turned on to Dolphin Street and began to put distance between the two of them. "Say hello to my nephew!" she called out over her shoulder.

"I will!" Louisa shouted back as she rushed past The Slipway Hotel and towards the school.

She had just reached the gate when the students began to pour out of the building, followed closely by their teachers. Her impromptu conversations with Bert and Ruth had slowed her down enough to throw her even further off schedule. Running the gauntlet of questions, she worked her way through to the doors of the school. Retreating to her office, she flipped the lock on the door before sinking into her chair. Perhaps the best course of action would be to call a meeting and get all the questions answered at once.

She stepped back into the outer office. "Pippa, would you please notify the staff that there'll be a brief meeting at the end of the day? I may as well give everyone the information they're wanting about Martin so I'm not constantly fielding questions. I don't have the time, and to be honest, it's just too difficult to keep talking about it."

"I'll make sure everyone knows, Louisa. Meet in the conference room I assume?"

"Yes, thank you Pippa." Louisa returned to her desk and dropped back into her chair, knowing that she now needed to allot time to prepare herself for a question and answer session.

Tim Spalding was with Martin when Chris stopped by his room that morning. He watched, unnoticed, as the therapist worked through the exercises with his friend's limbs. Martin lay quietly during the manipulations, which Chris knew were painful and should be eliciting more of a response from him.

He waited until Tim finished up with the session, catching him in the hall as he came out of the room. "I know you don't know Dr. Ellingham very well, but did anything seem amiss to you, today?" he asked.

"Well, I didn't seem to be getting much of a response from him. It's not uncommon though for patients to go through a delayed emotional reaction to an accident like this. It's definitely something that needs to be monitored though."

"Do you think he was having pain?"

"Oh, I know he was feeling it. The involuntary responses were there; sweating, trembling, tears in his eyes. But he hardly said a word to me the entire time I was in there."

"Well, Martin *never* has much to say. But I saw the same thing you did." Chris turned and looked down the hall towards Martin's door. "I'll go and visit with him a bit, see if I can get anything out of him. Thanks, Tim."

Martin looked over when he heard the door to his room open.

"Morning, Mart. I just saw Tim Spalding in the hall. What time did they have you up this morning? It's not even half eight yet."

"I didn't notice." Martin laid his head back and closed his eyes.

"Martin, something's going on in that brain of yours. It would help if you talked about it ... you know that."

"I'm really tired, Chris."

"Okay. So, you won't talk to me. Will you talk to Barrett Newell?"

"Just leave it, Chris. Just ... leave it."

Chris folded his hands behind his back and leaned against the wall. "No Mart, I won't leave it. You either talk to me, or you talk to Barrett. But, I can't in good conscience ... *leave it.*"

Air hissed from Martin's nose as he felt anger building in him. His stomach had knotted up, and his head was beginning to pound. His mind had prevented him from remembering it for the better part of his life, and he was now being asked to pour it all out to someone, having had less than twenty-four hours to come to terms with it himself.

"Come on, Mart," Chris urged gently. "What do you want to do?"

Martin erupted, grabbing at the water glass on his tray table and throwing it across the room in frustration. It struck the wall on the other side and shattered into pieces.

"Don't ... push me! God! It's taken me forty years to remember this! Give me a chance to get my head around it!"

His good hand clenched and unclenched, his knuckles whitening. "I don't—want—to talk about it!"

"Martin, I'm sorry. I don't understand what's going on, and I'm worried about you," Chris said, pushing himself away from the wall. He sat down on the edge of the bed. "You tell me, Mart. What can I do to help?"

Martin sat silently for many seconds before shaking his head. "I think ... I suppose I could talk to Dr. Newell."

"Okay, I'll give him a call."

"I'm sorry ... for yelling at you," Martin said as his eyes scanned over the broken glass strewn on the floor. "And for ..." he said, gesturing towards the mess.

"It's okay, Mart. We got it sorted; that's what's important." Chris walked over and began to pick up the glass left in the wake of his friend's outburst. "I'll have someone come in and tidy up. Maybe you can get a little rest." The largest fragments clinked together as they landed in the bin. "How 'bout we have lunch together later?" Chris suggested. "We could have someone get you in a wheelchair. I could take you out for lunch in fact ... well, just to the canteen. But it'd be a change of scene."

"Yes, that would be fine ... good."

Chris left the room, and Martin's head dropped back against his pillow before he gave in to his fatigue.

Sleep was fleeting, however. It was less than a half hour later when two nurses came to take him downstairs for his echocardiogram. He was back in his room by ten o'clock. Ed Christianson and Catherine Arneson stopped by a short time later to discuss their findings.

"You have a perfectly healthy looking heart, Dr. Ellingham," the cardiologist said. "I saw absolutely no evidence of ischemic damage. We'll check things out again in a few months, but I really don't think we'll see anything different at that time either." Dr. Arneson put her hand on his shoulder. "You're just fine, Superman," she said before patting his arm and exiting the room.

Martin cringed at what he found to be a ridiculous and distasteful moniker, but he was too tired to take issue with it.

Ed walked to the foot of the bed and moved the blankets aside, pulling the bandage from his patient's leg. "Hmm. I'm pleased with the looks of this, but I'm not sure this wound is where I want it to be quite yet. I think it would be best to hold off with surgery until Saturday. Hopefully, this'll be the last of the setbacks." He glanced over at his patient's dour expression. "I'm sorry, Martin. I know you were hoping to have this over and done with tomorrow. How are you doing otherwise?"

Martin eyed the surgeon suspiciously. "What is it you want to know?"

"Just a general question. You hanging in there with all of this?"

"I'm fine."

Ed came around and leaned on to the bed rail. "You've been through quite an ordeal, Martin, and you have a tough road ahead of you. Don't turn down help if it's available to you. And don't hesitate to ask for it either."

Ed signed off on the patient notes before heading out the door.

Martin laid his head back on his pillow and drifted quickly off to sleep. An occupational therapist woke him an hour later. By the time Chris arrived to take him to lunch, the therapist had him sitting in a wheelchair.

Leaving the confines of his hospital room quickly felt like a risky proposition to Martin. His painful legs were much more exposed to possible bumps with all the people moving through the corridors and in the canteen. He nervously guarded his body, ready to fend off any unintentional assaults to his injured limbs.

The outing proved stressful, and Martin was exhausted by the time Chris returned him to his room. The two friends sat by the window, discussing the different options for easing Martin back into his medical practice.

"It's a long way off yet, but it's good that you're thinking these things through and setting some goals," Chris said. He stretched out his arms. "I er, spoke with Dr. Newell. He's planning to stop in this afternoon."

"Fine." Martin turned to gaze out the window.

"You don't have to talk about anything you're not ready to talk about, Mart. What does Louisa have to say about this? I'm assuming you've discussed it with her."

Martin rubbed his tired eyes and sighed.

"What? Did you two have a row over this or something?"

"I haven't told her," Martin mumbled.

"Why didn't you discuss it with her when you two talked on the phone last night? I thought you called her every night."

Martin looked sheepishly at his lap. "I didn't want to talk to anyone about anything, so I shut my mobile off."

"Oh, Martin! You can't keep things like this from your wife! It's the last thing you wanna do."

"I know." He groaned as he rubbed his palm across his face. "I've mucked things up again."

Chris watched his misguided and very vulnerable friend. "Well, it wasn't the most brilliant decision you've ever made, but it's not the end of the world. Just call Louisa ... explain what happened last night. But mate, she's not going to trust you if you keep secrets. It never comes out well in the end. I speak from experience."

Chris got to his feet and moved towards the door. "Let me know how the phone call goes. Prepare for the worst and hope for the best, my friend," he said as he left the room.

Chapter 29

An occupational therapist arrived shortly after lunch to help Martin back into bed. Being moved with the assistance of a hydraulic lift can be a frightening experience, and Martin, due in great part to his past experiences, found it terrifying. He was completely helpless in the lift, suspended in the air with the very real fear that operator error could send his already injured and painful body plunging to the floor.

He had never completely trusted anyone in his life, looking upon human beings as innately untrustworthy creatures. He now had to trust a total stranger to safeguard both his physical well being and his dignity.

The image of the clock on the wall swayed side to side as he was lifted from the chair, setting in motion a cascade of sensations and memories taking him back to that night in boarding school so many years ago—hanging helplessly out that second story window and over the pavement below.

Her patient's obvious strong visceral reaction to the transfer procedure did not go unnoticed by the therapist. "All right, Dr. Ellingham, you're all safe and sound again," she said as she straightened the blankets and pulled them up around him. "I'll leave you to rest now."

"Yes ... thank you," Martin said, clearing his throat in an attempt to hide the waver in his voice.

He fell asleep quickly. Stress is tiring, and he had been immersed in it for the better part of twenty-four hours. He was still asleep when Dr. Newell's arrival roused him several hours later.

"Sorry to wake you, Martin. I would imagine sleep's a commodity that's been in short supply lately." The therapist went to the sink and pulled a facecloth from the cabinet before running it under the tap. "I certainly wouldn't sleep well hobbled by all that hardware."

"Mm." Martin rubbed at his eyes and shook his head, trying to clear the mental sluggishness.

"Here," Dr. Newell said, handing his patient the wet cloth.

Martin wiped his face and tossed the cloth on to the tray table.

"So, is the infection under control?" the psychiatrist asked as he pulled a chair up to the bed.

"Yes. Ed Christianson will close the wound on Saturday."

"That's great, Martin. Sounds like progress."

"I suppose it is."

"Have Ed or Chris given you any idea as to when they might cut you loose?"

Martin screwed up his face. "Does it matter?"

The therapist tipped his head at him. "That's not the answer I would have expected. Aren't you anxious to get back home ... to your wife and son?"

"I don't know ... I ... I don't know." Martin rubbed the heel of his hand against the side of his head.

"Headache?"

"Mm. I'm tired. People keep waking me up," he grumbled.

Dr. Newell sighed softly and pulled an ankle up over his knee. "Well, you and I both know that I'm not here to check on your physical progress. I'm here to listen and only if you'd like to talk. If you'd prefer to spend the time talking about the price of wool in Scotland, that's fine by me."

Martin groaned. "I know Chris is hoping I'll spill my heart out to you about what happened last night, but I'll tell you the same thing I told him ... leave it be."

"That's fine, Martin. But I'd like you to keep some things in mind when you're trying to work through this on your own. Are you open to that?"

Martin lifted a loose hand, letting it fall back to the mattress. "I don't care, go ahead."

The psychiatrist uncrossed his legs and leaned forward, resting his elbows on his knees. "I'm not sure what happened last night, but given what Chris Parsons shared with me, I'd guess some rather potent memories hit you. If that is indeed what you're trying to deal with, please remember that the human brain is very adept at filling in the blanks. Adept, but often unreliable. So, what you're remembering could very well be historically accurate, or it could be your brain very efficiently filling in the voids in your memory with whatever fits inside the parameters provided.

"Please also keep in mind, Martin, that if this is a memory from childhood, your brain was still developing at that time. Children don't have the benefit of the experiences that help adults to put the square pegs in the square holes and the round pegs in the round holes. So, they tend to either adapt the pegs to fit the holes or stretch the holes to accept the pegs. They do what they need to do to make sense of the world."

Martin had fixed his gaze on the window, but the man's words were not going unheard.

Dr. Newell continued. "Also, bear in mind that your childhood memories may have been shaped, or distorted rather, by how those around you reacted to a particular event ... to the event and to you. And their reactions may not have been appropriate.

"What I'm saying is that you shouldn't judge yourself harshly when thinking through these memories. Give yourself the benefit of the doubt. I can guarantee that your wife and I will afford you that courtesy."

He eyed his patient as he sat silently. "How much of this have you shared with Louisa?"

Martin shifted his focus to his lap. "I need to call her ... to apologise."

"Did you say something you shouldn't have?"

"No. I didn't say anything at all. I shut my phone off last night, and I haven't turned it back on. I ... I just couldn't talk to anyone, not even Louisa. I felt like I was drowning ... like I needed to focus every ounce of energy on keeping my head above water. I was afraid that if I didn't stay focused, the memories ..."

Martin pulled in a sharp breath of air. "It felt like the memories would take me under. I was awake all night ... couldn't sleep at all. This morning I felt guilty for not sharing all of this with her last night, but I put off calling her. I still haven't called her, and I'm afraid to now."

"Why are you afraid to call her? What do you think she's going to say ... or do?"

"I didn't talk to her about this, and she's going to be hurt by that. I know she'll be unhappy about it, and I'm afraid that ... that she'll ... She has left before and ... This has all been a tremendous strain on her. I'm aware of that and now I've added to it."

Dr. Newell nodded his head. "You're afraid she'll be unhappy and leave. That you'll be on your own at a time when you're very vulnerable."

"Mm."

"This is probably quite similar to how you felt as a boy, I would imagine. You were vulnerable. You couldn't count on anyone to be there for you, to be in your corner when you needed them."

Martin swallowed hard, trying to loosen the constriction in his throat.

"You're going to have to take a leap here, Martin. The trust that's grown between you and your wife in the last months is being tested. This won't be the last time that trust will be tested either. But every time you take that leap and Louisa's there to catch you, your confidence in the relationship will be strengthened."

Martin sat quietly for a while before nodding his head. "Okay. Okay, I'll call her."

Dr. Newell slapped his hands down on his knees and smiled. "I think I'll go down to the canteen for a bit, then stop back and see how you're doing. Can I get you anything while I'm there?"

"No ... thank you."

Martin waited for the door to close behind the psychiatrist and then reached for his mobile before ringing his wife.

Louisa was preparing to head to the conference room for her meeting when her phone rang. She grabbed for it hastily, breathing a sigh of relief when her husband's name appeared on the screen.

"Martin?"

"Hello. Can you talk?"

"Martin, I've been trying since last night to get you! Is everything all right?"

"Yes, I'm fine. I'd turned my mobile off because—"

"Martin, don't *ever* do that again. I was about ready to call Chris. I was afraid you'd had another setback or something."

Martin could hear not only the annoyance in his wife's voice, but also the worry. "Louisa, I'm sorry. It's just ... it's just that something happened, and I couldn't talk to anyone."

Louisa paused. "Martin, you need to be more specific. What do you mean, something happened?"

"I remembered something, and I just couldn't talk about it with anyone ... not even you. I wanted to call you this morning, but I was afraid that you ... I was an idiot to cut you off like that."

Louisa swivelled around in her desk chair, watching out the window as the students began to stream out of the building to go home. "Martin, are you all right?"

"I didn't get much sleep last night; my mind was racing."

"I tell you what, I have a meeting in a few minutes, but when I'm done with that I'll come to the hospital and we can talk, hmm?"

"No. I don't *want* to talk about it ... yet. But it helps to hear your voice. I'm sorry, Louisa ... that I turned off my phone."

"That you pushed me away again?"

"Mm, yes. I'm sorry, I keep bollocksing things up."

"I do feel hurt that you couldn't talk to me ... that you chose to keep to yourself rather than confide in me."

"It's not like that, Louisa. I do want to tell you. I just don't know what you're going to think of me, how you'll feel towards me. The things you wrote in your letter ... I'm not that person, and I'm afraid ..."

Louisa could hear the waver in his voice. "Martin, what can I do to help?"

"Will you bring Ruth along when you come over for our appointment with Dr. Newell on Friday?"

She hesitated. It was not the request that she had anticipated. "Yes, if she's available I can. But why do you want Ruth there, Martin?"

"If I do decide to talk about this, I don't want to have to tell the story more than once. So please have her there."

"Okay, Martin. Can I call you later to say goodnight?"

"I'd like that."

"All right, later then."

"Mm."

Martin laid his mobile on the tray table and collapsed on to his pillow. He was relieved that Louisa wasn't angry, but he felt ashamed that he had hurt her feelings.

Dr. Newell returned with a cup of coffee in his hand and stood by his patient's bed.

"I called her. She's not angry, but I hurt her by not sharing this with her ... by shutting her out."

"Well, that's understandable. Martin, it's commendable that you're trying so hard to be a better husband, but don't try to be a *perfect* husband."

"I don't think there's much chance of that," he grumbled.

The therapist gave him a smile. "I'm just saying, we *all* make mistakes. You look pretty knackered, so I'll leave you to get some rest. I'll see you on Friday."

"Yes. Thank you."

Chapter 30

Louisa didn't have time to think about her husband's phone call. She hurried down the corridors of the school and went to the front of the conference room. "Hello, everyone. I know this meeting wasn't on your schedule, but if you could give me just a few minutes, I feel the need to clear up some of the questions many of you have about my husband's accident."

She folded her hands in front of her and gazed across the group of intent faces. "As is typical of our wonderful little village, it seems there's been a lot of misinformation making its way through the grapevine. So here are the facts, and I would appreciate it if you could pass the *correct* information on to others. It would ease the strain on me a bit.

"From what I understand, there have been several different accounts of Martin's accident being passed around the village, *none* of them accurate. So, if Martin's accident is going to be discussed amongst you, and in all likelihood on Radio Portwenn, I would prefer that it be the truth."

Louisa continued on, sharing the facts necessary to put to rest rumours and satisfy curious minds, stopping occasionally to answer questions. It was obvious that her co-workers had come to the meeting eager to get all the juicy details about Martin's condition. But as she told the story, she saw their expressions shift to reflect the empathy that they were feeling for her, and she hoped even for Martin.

She paused to check her emotions and then continued. "When Martin finally gets to come home, he'll have metal bars on the outside of his legs and arm that are fastened into the bones by a number of metal pins ... they call them external fixators.

"I don't know how he's going to manage the hills in this village, but if you see him out and about, the less said about his health the better. Just wish him well and don't ask questions. I know that you'll look out for him and be there to help if he needs it. But you know my husband, you may get an earful about it.

"He has a very long struggle ahead of him before he can get back to seeing patients, probably four to five months. But he'll be pushing to make it in three, I'm sure," Louisa said. Thinking of her husband's determined spirit, a smile crossed her face.

"Please, be encouraging. Martin's doctors didn't expect him to survive his injuries that first night. I know his rather brusque manner rubs many people the wrong way, and he's probably even insulted some of you by things he's said, but he's my husband, and I ..."

Louisa batted at tears that managed to get past her resolve to stay composed. "I love him very much. And despite what many people think, he loves me and is good to me. And he's a wonderful father to our son.

"Everyone in this room has benefited in some way from Martin's brilliant skills as a doctor, either personally, or you have a friend or family member who has. Please remember that and remind others of that."

She bit at her lower lip and rubbed her palms together. "Well, I think that's the gist of what's transpired. Any questions?"

A hush fell over the room before Louisa began to work her way through the well-wishers, keeping a smile frozen on her face as she moved towards the door. She had answered the questions, and her desires had been expressed. Now, she hoped her beloved villagers would take her words to heart.

The beautiful late summer day turned into a lovely evening. Louisa settled James into his pushchair and headed out after dinner for a walk along the Coast Path. They stopped at Ruth's before heading back up Roscarrock Hill towards home.

"Well, this is a pleasant surprise," the elderly woman said as she ushered Louisa and James in the door. "How are you getting on as a single mother?"

"It's a lot harder than I expected," Louisa said as she picked James up and took a seat at the kitchen table. "Martin does more around the house than I realised."

Ruth raised an eyebrow at her. "I suspect he does. Would you like a cup of tea?"

"Yes, I would. Thank you, Ruth," she said, giving James a bounce on her knee. "I'm so glad we found Poppy before all this happened."

The old woman set cups on the table and turned the tea kettle on to heat. "Did you ever reach my nephew?"

"I did. He called me, actually."

"And ...? Were your worries justified?"

"I'm sure they were justified. Anything could have happened you know," Louisa said defensively.

"I didn't mean to suggest otherwise. But I do know that Chris Parsons would have called immediately if there had been any deterioration in Martin's health." Ruth poured water into the cups and peered at her nephew's wife. "So ... it wasn't a medical issue, obviously. What did cause the lapse in communication?"

Louisa adored her husband's aunt, but she found her a bit too forthcoming at times. "Martin rang me this afternoon. You're right, he's fine ... physically. It seems he remembered something that he feels unable to talk about. He said he couldn't talk to *anyone* last night, and he didn't get much sleep. Don't bother to ask for more information than that though, because I don't have it. I'm worried about him, Ruth. He sounded different today."

"Do you mean more tired than usual?" Ruth asked as she passed Louisa a plate of biscuits.

"No, he sounded ... defeated. Like the life had gone out of him. He said that he's not the man I think he is. I wish I knew what he meant by that, but I don't."

Ruth's finger ran up and down her cup handle as she stared absently. "Hmm, perhaps he's discouraged. It *has* been an awful two weeks for him. And what he has ahead of him must seem insurmountable at the moment."

Louisa shook her head. "I don't think so. Martin's a very determined man. He's been wanting to get started with the physiotherapy ... wanting to get everything he can out of it." She sighed. "I guess I'll just have to be patient and hope it's all out in the open soon."

She glanced up at Ruth before brushing the biscuit crumbs from her fingertips. "Ruth, Martin has a request."

The old woman looked at her, eyebrows raised. "Well, go on. I can hardly say yes if I don't know what it is."

"He wants you to come with me on Friday ... to his appointment with Dr. Newell."

Ruth reached for a biscuit. "Well, that's a relief. I was afraid he was going to ask me to find something buried in that old barn at the farm. My patients at Broadmoor could hide their victims in there, and it would be years before anyone would find them," she said dryly.

"No Ruth, nothing as taxing as that." Louisa stood and carried James to the doorway.

"In answer to your question, yes, I can come with you on Friday. It could prove quite interesting."

"Well, for your nephew's sake, I hope it's not *too* interesting."

The elderly woman carried the pushchair down the porch steps and Louisa strapped James into it.

I'll pick you up at half two," she said. "The appointment's at four, but I'd like a little time with Martin first."

"I'll be ready. Say hello to him when you talk."

Though Louisa had a peaceful night's sleep, Martin's sleep was interrupted by disturbing images and voices. He woke several times, shaking and in a sweat. The night dragged on, and it came as a relief when sunlight began to dilute the inky blackness of the sky outside his window, and he could begin to make out the colourless shapes of the trees and buildings.

Tim Spalding came by at seven o'clock that morning and pushed Martin's limbs through the painful range of motion exercises.

"This should begin to get less uncomfortable over the course of the next several weeks, Martin. You're a doctor, so I don't have to tell you that you're at the peak of the inflammatory stage with your bone healing."

Martin grimaced and groaned as the young man rotated his left foot, sending sharp pain through his lower leg.

"Sorry about that," the therapist said, patting his foot before lowering the leg to the bed. "Everything's looking good so far, Martin. No loose pins, and your range of motion is excellent considering the severity of your fractures. We'll go easy on you for the rest of this week, but next week's therapy sessions will get more intense. We'll push you harder so be prepared for that," Tim said as he stretched the muscles on the back of Martin's right calf.

Martin gripped on to the bed rail as the therapist pushed his foot back a little farther before moving his hands to his knee, stretching the hamstring muscle on the same leg.

Tim raised the head of the bed, lowered the rail, and positioned the tray table over his patient's lap in preparation for the manipulation of his arm and hand.

Martin wagged a finger at the injured appendage. "What can I do to improve my dexterity? I don't know if I'll ever go back to surgery, but I'd like that to be my decision, not the decision of some idiotic lorry driver."

"I'll show you a couple of exercises I learned when I was taking piano lessons. They're very effective at stretching the tendons in the fingers and hand. They'll also help to strengthen the muscles and improve muscle control," Tim said, laying Martin's arm on the tray table. "Lay your hand flat, then tuck your middle finger under your palm."

Martin winced as the movement sent pain shooting up his forearm.

The therapist gave a nod of his head. "Good. Now, one at a time, tap the other fingers on the table."

The young man demonstrated the second exercise, and Martin grunted. "I'm familiar with these."

"Well, do them several times a day. I think you'll find them helpful. But if you start having persistent pain you need to take a break."

The therapist finished up shortly before eight-thirty, and Martin quickly nodded off to sleep, not waking until the orthotist stopped by early in the afternoon to fit him with the brace that had been custom made to protect his damaged shoulder. Ed Christianson came down to give it the final stamp of approval.

It was more comfortable than the sling, but it was also bulky. A support, which rested against his side under his arm, put pressure on the ribs left sore by the thoracotomy. It was uncomfortable, but, in the end, Martin decided the new brace was an improvement over being tethered to the sling.

An occupational therapist came in shortly before dinner was to be served and moved Martin to a wheelchair. Once the stressful transfer process had been completed he found that it lifted his spirits to look out the window. Especially, to feel the comforting warmth of the sun's afternoon rays as they met with his bare arms and legs.

No menu delivered to his room before a meal meant that he would be seeing either Carole or Chris coming through the door soon, carrying a tray of food. It was, as Carole had promised, a daily occurrence, but Martin never knew which meal would be the special home cooked version or at what time of the day it would arrive.

Though he grumbled and complained about it each time, he held up his end of the bargain, finishing the daily deliveries with a calorie and fat laden bowl of ice cream, courtesy of the Royal Cornwall Hospital.

Today's visit from the Parsons came in the evening, and both Chris and Carol stopped in to see him. Carole watched, feeling a touch of disappointment as their friend picked away at his food. Chris had told her about the tachycardic episode that Martin had experienced. She had also spoken with Louisa earlier in the day and was aware of her concerns about her husband.

Martin would never be described as outgoing, but Carole had always admired the fire in him that had allowed him to reach the top level attainable in surgical medicine. Tonight, however, that fire seemed to have been extinguished. He seemed withdrawn and distracted.

"I spoke with Louisa earlier. She mentioned she'll be coming over tomorrow," Carole said. "Does she plan to spend the weekend?"

Martin shook his head. "I don't know. I don't know what her plans are."

"Well, please let her know that she and James would be more than welcome to stay with us again."

"Mm."

The strained conversation continued for a few more minutes before Chris suggested they leave and let Martin rest.

He was alone with his thoughts again. Perhaps it was the sun's rays that had soothed his soul to some extent, or perhaps the company and caring of friends, but Martin decided as he stared out the window watching people going about daily life, that he wanted that as well. He would tell his story tomorrow.

But would Louisa want to go on with life with him once she heard what he had to say? He went to sleep that night trying to come to grips with the possibility of life without his wife and son.

Chapter 31

Martin endured another sleepless night. All the possible outcomes of the upcoming session with his psychiatrist played through his head. He had begun to have doubts about the wisdom of telling Louisa what he had done. He couldn't imagine a scenario where she could see him in anything but a negative light.

She was a teacher, a teacher of young children. He knew that she would be forgiving, but that wasn't his concern. He worried about how this would change her view of him.

Morning brought yet another session of physiotherapy, followed by a visit from an occupational therapist in the afternoon to discuss some of the problems that he would have to deal with once he was home. Life would be different, and both he and Louisa would need to adapt to a different lifestyle. Hopefully, it would only be temporary.

Shortly after half three Martin looked up from the laptop, brought in by Chris, to see Louisa standing in the doorway. He felt his lungs fill with air, expanding his chest. He released the air slowly and felt himself relax.

She gave him a smile and walked to his bedside before taking his face in her hands and kissing him gently. "How are you?"

"Mm, better now."

"Kind of a rough couple of days?" she asked, her thumbs stroking the dark circles under his eyes.

"Just a lot to think about ... worry about."

"Oh, Martin. The last thing you should be doing right now is worrying."

"I can't help it, Louisa. I'm just ..." He shook his head and then craned his neck to see around her. "Didn't Ruth come with you?"

"Yes. I asked her to stay in the waiting area for a little while. I wanted to greet my husband properly," she said, leaning over and kissing him again, a little less gently this time.

"Mm, you did that already."

"Yes, Martin, I know. I'm in arrears, so I'm just getting caught back up," she said before laying kisses first on his forehead, then on his cheek and nose. Her lips finally settled on his.

"Did you have a good trip over? How was the traffic?"

"Fine ... and fine. Ruth's good company, so it seemed like no time at all to get here. What did you do today? Or should I say, what did they do to you today?"

"Yes. Erm, the usual ... physiotherapy, occupational therapy, and they threw in a bed bath today," Martin said, scowling.

"You do look especially nice." Louisa brushed a hand across his head, taming a rogue tuft of hair.

He gazed at her for a moment before wrapping his arm around her and pulling her closer for a kiss.

There was a knock and their attention shifted to the doorway.

"Sorry to interrupt. I know I'm running a bit early," said Dr. Newell.

Martin pulled his arm away from his wife and busied himself straightening his blankets.

The therapist strode into the room. "Feeling any better, Martin?"

"Yes, I'm progressing," he replied before quickly turning back to his wife. "Louisa, is Ruth going to come in?"

"I'll go collect her," she said, leaning over to kiss him one last time before heading out the door.

Martin gave his therapist a sideways glance as the colour rose in his cheeks.

"We have a couple of minutes alone here, Martin, so let's make sure that I'm on the same page with you about your session today. Do you want me to bring up the subject of your most recent memory?" the man asked.

Martin leaned his head back and closed his eyes. "It's not that I'm not ready to talk about it. I think I am, but ... I'm afraid to talk about it."

"What do you think is going to happen?"

"I don't know for sure, but I can't see how this won't have a negative impact on how Louisa sees me ... the kind of man she thinks I am. And Ruth ... I know how my father reacted to this, and I would imagine she might have similar feelings."

"Well, you tell me what to do."

Martin pressed a hand to his eyes. When he pulled it away, Louisa was walking towards him with Ruth following behind. He turned to Dr. Newell and nodded. "Yes, go ahead."

The psychiatrist left the room and returned with an extra chair which he placed by the bed for Ruth. Then, after locking the door, he came back and pulled up a chair for himself. Louisa perched next to her husband on the edge of the mattress.

"Well, we all know why we're here, I think. Martin, before you begin, I'd like to remind you that we're just here to listen. This isn't the time for deep exploration or for judgments to be made.

"Things aren't always as they first appear with memories, and everyone here needs to remember that. I'm in no way implying that you're not to be believed, Martin. I promise you that I will not doubt your story. But you remember the incident from your perspective only. A completely different story might be told from another perspective."

Dr. Newell leaned forward, his elbows resting on his knees. "Can you tell us about what happened the other day ... what you remembered?"

Martin rubbed his eyes and drew in a nervous breath. "I guess I need to start with the day I broke my grandfather's pocket watch. You remember that, don't you, Ruth?"

"Yes, I do. Although, as you know, I wasn't actually there when it happened. But I got *all* the details from your lovely mother a few days later. One would have thought you'd stolen the Crown Jewels."

Martin turned to his wife. "I was at my grandfather's house with my parents. I ended up alone in my grandfather's bedroom, and I saw his pocket watch on the table by the bed. He'd shown it to me before. I was intrigued by it, and I couldn't resist picking it up.

"I wasn't supposed to touch the watch. My grandfather had made that clear. I didn't hear my father coming down the hall until he yelled at me to put the watch down. I was startled, and I dropped it. The cover broke off, and the gears stopped."

Louisa put her hand on his arm. "Is this the watch you said you had offered to mend ... when you were seven?"

"Mm. My grandfather was understanding, but my father was angry. He grabbed my collar and dragged me out to the shed. He used his belt. I'd embarrassed him, and that was something he wouldn't tolerate. It only made matters worse that I had embarrassed him in front of his father."

Louisa's hand slid down, resting on top of his, and Martin gave her a wary glance as he licked his lips.

"I told my grandfather later that I could repair the watch for him, but he wouldn't allow it."

"I doubt he thought a seven-year-old was up to the job, Martin," Ruth said.

"Mm, yes." He turned to Dr. Newell. "Could I have a glass of water?"

"Certainly, take a break whenever you like, Martin." Dr. Newell filled a glass and handed it to him.

He swallowed down half the glassful, but when he opened his mouth to speak, the words still caught in his throat.

"Martin?" Louisa squeezed his hand.

Dr. Newell tapped his steepled fingers against his lips. "Think about what I told you the other day. You need to make the leap ... to trust."

Martin tried to swallow the massive lump in his throat before focusing his eyes on the church bell tower he could see through his window. "It was a few days later. My mother and father were building up to a row. There had been tension in the air all day. The maid was cleaning upstairs, so I sat on a chair in the entrance hall, trying to stay out of the way. Their voices were getting louder and angrier, and I ... It was frightening when they fought."

He cleared his throat. "The grandfather clock at the bottom of the stairs chimed five o'clock. It was almost dinnertime, so I hoped they might stop arguing soon.

"Then the doorbell rang, and I went to answer it. My father came storming over and yanked me back before pulling the door open. It was my grandfather. He told Dad that he wanted to have a few words with me. My father told him to take me into his study ... that he and my mother were in the middle of a discussion.

"When we got to the study, my grandfather took a small box out of his coat pocket. It was a present ... wrapped in paper, and it even had a ribbon on it. I wasn't sure what to do with it when he handed it to me. I was confused. I assumed it was for my mother, but he said it was for me. He told me to open it.

"It was a pocket watch. Not an expensive one like his, but nice. He said it was broken ... that he was going to show me how to fix it. He pulled a book out from under his arm ... *A Horologist's Reference*. It was a book about how to repair timepieces—the same one that Chris gave me the other day," Martin said, gesturing towards the table.

Louisa picked up the book and rubbed her palm across the cover. "That's what brought all this back?"

"Mm." Martin stared at the book in his wife's hands for a moment before continuing.

"We sat at my father's desk, my grandfather next to me. He pulled a little set of tools, wrapped in a cloth sleeve, from his coat pocket. It's the set I still use. He showed me how to take the watch apart ... how to organise the pieces so that I didn't lose anything. Then he asked me if I could figure out why the watch wasn't working. It was exciting for me. I'm sure most people would find it terribly dull, but to me it was like diagnosing a medical problem. And I had someone there who wanted to diagnose it with me ... who had confidence in me.

"My parents' voices were getting louder again, and I turned around to look out into the hallway. Grandfather told me to focus on the watch.

"I looked through the pages of the book and found a diagram of the movement I had laid out in front of me. It only took me a few seconds to identify the problem. There was a tooth broken on the escape wheel. My grandfather looked pleased. He said that I was a clever lad and that ... that he was proud of me."

Martin paused, his eyes shifting towards the door as someone in the corridor dropped something, creating a loud metallic clattering.

Quiet returned to the room, and Dr. Newell gave his patient a nod. "Go ahead, Martin."

He cleared his throat again. "The voices outside the room kept getting louder. When my mother called my father a cheating bastard, my grandfather got up and shut the door. He was walking back to the desk when he collapsed on to the floor. I sat looking at him for a few seconds. I didn't understand what was going on. He was holding on to his chest. He looked over at me ... asked me to help him. I ran over and dropped on to the floor beside him.

"He looked afraid. I'd never seen an adult look afraid before. He told me to get my father. I started for the door. I had my hand on the knob, but—" Martin pulled in a sharp breath, grimacing at the pain it triggered in his chest.

Louisa got up from the bed and put her hand on his cheek. "Martin, maybe you should finish telling us when you're feeling be—"

"No!" He pushed her hand away. "Just let me ... let me get this out."

Dr. Newell gave Louisa a jerk of his head, and she sat back down.

Martin batted back tears as he stared at the wall in front of him. "My father's voice erupted, and Mum started screaming at him to get out. I jerked my hand away from the doorknob and ran back to my grandfather. I got down on my knees next to him. He couldn't breathe. He kept saying, 'Martin, go get help'. But I was afraid to leave the room. I just *sat* there!" Martin spat out. "God, I just *sat* there! I just sat watching him, because I was too afraid to leave the bloody room!"

He took in a ragged breath. "It got quiet, and I heard the eight notes strike on the clock—five-thirty. I thought maybe they had stopped fighting because the cook had set dinner on the table. My grandfather kept pleading with me to get help. I *wanted* to. I started to get up, and then there was a loud crash ... glass breaking ... and Dad called Mum a—"

Martin shook his head. "I felt trapped, like no matter what I did, something terrible was going to happen."

He was breathing rapidly, taking in gasps of air. He paused, and, closing his eyes, he tried to regain his composure. "I don't know how long I sat there trying to get up the courage to go through that door. I heard the clock chime again, so I know it was at least fifteen minutes." He shrugged his shoulders. "It seemed like an eternity."

"Grandfather's lips started turning blue, and I could see sweat breaking out on his forehead. He kept pleading with me to help him."

Martin glanced over at Ruth and swallowed back a sob. "He coughed ... and ... and blood came up. It fell on my hand. His face was pale. He looked at me, opened his mouth to say something, and ... and ... blood started to pump from his body ... out of his mouth. He said '*Martin, help me*'."

Louisa's heart ached for her husband as he struggled to not cry in front of his aunt. She took hold of his hand. It was cold, moist, and trembling.

He continued. "His words were hard to understand. They were garbled by the blood as he tried to pull in air. His skin had turned blue, and he kept staring at me. His eyes were pleading with me to do something, and I just *sat* there. His mouth was open, and I could see his teeth. They were outlined in blood. It ran down the side of his face, puddling on the floor next to me and soaking into my trousers."

Martin was fighting now to get the words out between his sobs and gasps for air. "I grabbed the front of his shirt and started shaking him. I didn't want him to leave me alone in that room, but he just stared. He stared straight at me. I was clinging to him. I laid my head on his chest and I could hear his faltering heartbeat. I knew something was wrong. It should have been steady, like the ticking of his pocket watch.

"I watched the blood coming from his mouth, pulsing out with every heartbeat, getting slower and slower, less and less as his heart got weaker ... as he exsanguinated. His eyes, as he stared at me, were ... I'd let him down."

Martin pressed his hand to his face. "And then the blood stopped, and I couldn't hear his heart beating any more.

"Dad came in after a while. He yelled, 'Martin, what have you done?' He grabbed my collar and tried to pull me away but I'd been gripping my grandfather's shirt so tightly and for so long that I couldn't open my fingers. He grabbed my arm and yanked me back. I felt my fingernails ripping away from the fabric.

"You know what happened after that. After Mum unlocked the cupboard, I went upstairs to take my bath and bin my clothes, and then I went to bed. My father came in my room a few hours later and sat down next to me so that he could reduce the fracture in my arm. I asked him why that had happened to Grandfather. He said, 'You want to know why that happened? Because I have a son who lacks even an ounce of sense, that's why'."

Martin turned to look at his wife. "I just sat there and watched him die, Louisa. I just *sat* there and did nothing. I let him die."

Chapter 32

Louisa sat, shocked by the story that her husband had told and fought back the tears that had been threatening to escape. She wanted to take him into her arms and comfort the devastated little boy in him.

"Ruth, let's step out of the room for a bit." Dr. Newell said, getting to his feet and extending a hand to the elderly woman. "I'll buy you a cup of coffee."

Louisa gave the man a weak smile. "Thank you."

The door closed, and she looked back at her husband. He glanced at her before his eyes darted away again. "Oh, Martin," she breathed out. "I'm so sorry."

She swung her legs on to the bed and reclined next to him, burying her face in his shoulder. Then she cupped his cheek in her hand as his body shuddered, and he broke down completely.

When he had quieted, she went to the sink for a flannel. "Martin, I can only begin to imagine what the last two days have been like for you, trying to come to terms with this on your own."

He held the cloth over his face.

Louisa nestled against him, and they lay quietly for some time. She finally reached up and tugged gently at his hand and pulled the cloth away.

"You should have told me you needed me. I could have been here in less than an hour."

He shook his head and turned away. "I couldn't."

"Why not?"

"Because I was ... I was ashamed. And I needed to be alone with this for a while ... to think it through."

Louisa slipped from the bed, and they looked towards the hall when they heard the door open. Ruth and Dr. Newell stepped back into the room and reclaimed their seats.

Martin turned his head back to his wife. "This changes everything—why you say you love me, why you say I deserve you."

She looked at him quizzically. "Martin, this in no way changes why I love you. This takes nothing away from the qualities that I love in you ... that attract me to you. If anything, I think that you deserve me even more. Look at what you've done with your life despite all of this."

He shook his head and looked pleadingly at his therapist.

"What is it, Martin? Why do you say this changes everything?" Dr. Newell asked.

Martin turned to his wife. "You said in your letter that I deserve you ... that you love me, because I'd been cheated out of the things that every child should have ... parents who love them ... encourage them. How *could* my parent's love me? Especially Dad. I let his father die! I could have done something and I didn't. I was a coward. I understand their hatred now ... the disgust in their eyes. Ruth, I'm sorry. He was your father, and I ..." Martin turned to find the elderly woman's chair empty. He released a resigned sigh. "He was her father."

Dr. Newell leaned forward, resting his arms on his legs. "Martin, try not to jump to conclusions. I spoke of different perspectives before you started to tell your story. Wait to hear what your aunt has to say. She may see this from a very different perspective than your father did."

Martin let his head drop back on to his pillow and he closed his eyes. "Louisa, I don't think my motives for becoming a surgeon were as altruistic as you believe them to be. I think I've spent my life trying to put things right ... trying to make up for what I failed to do for my grandfather. I've been attempting to redeem myself; there's nothing noble in that."

Louisa took his face in her hands. "Martin, you— were a little—boy," she said softly. "A frightened little boy. If this had happened to James, I wouldn't have broken his arm and locked him in a cupboard! I would have taken him in my arms and held him ... told him that it wasn't his fault."

Martin shook his head again and slapped his fist down on the bed beside him in frustration. "You don't understand what this is like, Louisa! I see my grandfather's face every time I close my eyes ... every time I blink. His face is as clear to me now as if this happened yesterday. All I had to do was open that door to my father's study and call for help. It *was* my fault." He slumped back against his pillow again.

Dr. Newell stood and leaned on to the bed rail. "Martin, remind me ... how old were you when this happened?"

"Seven. I'd just turned seven. It was my first year at boarding school, and I was home for the holidays," he said, rubbing at his throbbing head.

"You're seeing this through your seven-year-old eyes ... through the eyes of a seven-year-old who had been physically and emotionally abused ... emotionally neglected. A seven-year-old whose parents shifted their own culpability in this incident on to their son.

"Through no fault of your own, Martin, we have a snarled mess to untangle. But you're not on your own with this. We'll keep working on it. It's certainly not something we'll be able to accomplish today, however. And to be honest ..." Dr. Newell tipped his head to get a better look at his patient's drawn face, "I think we need to wrap this up and let you get some sleep."

The therapist waved his hand at Louisa. "Could you walk out with me? We'll go see if we can find your aunt, Martin. I'll speak with Christianson or Parsons about getting something to help you sleep. In the meantime, try not to worry too much about this. We'll get it sorted."

"I'll be right back," Louisa said, giving her husband a gentle kiss.

Ruth came in from the hallway as Louisa started for the door.

"Ruth, is everything okay?" Louisa asked.

"It is now. Sorry for the hasty exit. I'm an old woman with an old bladder," she explained dryly.

Her remark provoked some smiles, but Louisa noticed her swollen eyes.

"Ruth, I think that your nephew thought you may have left because of what he told us today. That you may harbour some resentment towards him," said Dr. Newell.

Ruth made her way around the bed. "Martin, this didn't take me completely by surprise. I had my suspicions when your wife told me that you had remembered the blood on the floor. But I didn't want to put false memories in your head. Not to mention that I wasn't actually there to witness the unfortunate event. I only have memories of the awful aftermath."

"I'm sorry, Aunt Ruth," Martin said, averting his eyes.

"What exactly is it that you're sorry for?"

"I should have done something. Dad was right, his father might have lived if I had just gone for help. He was your father too, Ruth," Martin said, unable to look at her.

"Martin, do you know what killed my father—your grandfather?"

He nodded. "All the signs would point to some sort of pulmonary event, possibly embolic ... more likely an aneurysm."

"Yes. It was a ruptured pulmonary artery aneurysm. Do you really think there was anything a seven-year-old boy could have done?"

"There was a chance that he might have made it to hospital. It almost certainly started as a slow leak. I sat there next to him for a long time before he died. There may have been time if I'd gotten my father. You know that as well as I do, Ruth."

"Yes, there is that possibility. But Martin, vascular surgery, as we know it today, was in it's infancy at the time. Must I insult your intelligence by reminding you that Blalock had introduced his techniques just a few years prior to my father's death. Hardly established surgical methods."

"That's *not* the point! I should have done something, and I didn't. For that I'm at fault!"

"Oh, for goodness' sake, Martin! If there's any blame to be assigned here, it should fall squarely on the shoulders of your abominable parents, not on the shoulders of a seven-year-old boy!"

Martin sat quietly before starting to speak again. "Ruth, I do appreciate your generosity, but I feel guilty for not having done what I should. And I can't get the image of my grandfather's face out of my head. I hear his voice. I'll always feel guilt for this."

Ruth closed her eyes and let out a long slow breath. "I wish that I could take this burden away from you, Martin, but I can't. I can assure you, however, that in no way do I hold *you* accountable for what happened. I do feel heartsick for that little seven-year-old boy who was abandoned to deal with this on his own. For that I am truly sorry.

Chapter 33

"How's our patient doing?" Chris asked as he approached Barrett Newell in the corridor.

"He's exhausted. Is there something you and Christianson can add to that cocktail he's been getting? Something that might slow his thoughts down a bit."

"Let me consult with Ed, but I think we can come up with something. I'm not asking you to breach patient confidentiality, but what can you tell me?"

The psychiatrist hesitated. "Well, let's just say that he's remembered something particularly traumatic. I just let him talk today, but we'll explore the incident together when he's more rested and has had a few days to think things through. My immediate concern is his fatigue and stress level. I don't want this to have an adverse effect on his physical recovery. He needs a solid eight hours tonight. I don't think he's slept much at all in the last couple of days."

"Well, from what I've seen since he was admitted, I'd say that if you want Martin to sleep, put the lady coming down the hall in bed with him." Chris nodded at Louisa as she walked towards them.

"Louisa, were you planning to spend the night with Carole and me?" Chris asked.

"Thanks, Chris, that's kind of you. But I don't want to leave Martin here alone tonight. I was going to ask if I could stay the night ... sleep on the sofa in his room."

"Dr. Parsons was just saying that he thought Martin would benefit from you being here. I understand he sleeps better when he has you with him." The psychiatrist gave her a smile.

Chris shoved his hands into his pockets. "I'll have them move another bed in. You'll be more comfortable, and you can be closer to Mart."

Dr. Newell rubbed his hand over the back of his neck as he turned to Chris. "Would it be possible for James to spend some time here? I don't want to put Martin at a higher risk of developing any sort of an infection, but if you and Ed think it would be safe, I'm sure it would boost Martin's spirits to spend some time with his son. It might also help him to see this most recent memory in a different light."

Chris hesitated. "Let me bounce it off Ed, and I'll get back to you. Would that even be feasible for you, Louisa?"

"Chris, that would make Martin so happy. Ruth's heading back to Portwenn in a little while to relieve Poppy. She's going to stay the night with James and bring him with her when she comes back tomorrow."

"Well, bear in mind that Ed has Martin scheduled for surgery tomorrow, so he may want to hold off on a visit. It would probably be best not to mention anything to Martin just yet."

Chris called Ed Christianson to consult with him about a sedative and to discuss the pros and cons of James spending time with his father. Like Chris, Ed was usually averse to having children, with their petri dish qualities, mingle with patients, especially immunocompromised patients like Martin.

But given his emotional needs as well as the fact that his son was cared for at home rather than in a day-care setting, they made the decision to allow the visit, provided that one of Martin's doctors examine the boy first to limit the chances of his being exposed to an infectious illness.

"I'd suggest we up the midazolam to help Martin sleep. He tolerates it well and we know it's effective for him," Ed said, addressing the other area of concern. "I'll get that ordered up. He's on the theatre schedule for seven o'clock tomorrow morning. Should be in and out pretty quick as long as there are no surprises when we open things up. I would think by afternoon he'd be feeling up to company."

Ruth and Louisa had dinner in the canteen together before Ruth left to return to the village. When Louisa arrived back at Martin's room, she found him asleep.

A nurse came in and helped to get Louisa settled and familiar with where to find all the necessities. "Feel free to make use of the bathroom, Mrs. Ellingham," a nurse said quietly. "We'll have to be in and out every couple of hours to shift your husband, but we'll try not to bother the two of you any more than necessary. Can I get you anything before I leave?"

"I think I'm fine." Louisa looked over at Martin uncertainly. "But ... I didn't expect this," she said, gesturing to the bed abutting her husband's.

"Doctor's orders, Mrs. Ellingham. You must be very therapeutic," the nurse said before moving swiftly from the room.

Once she had been left alone, Louisa changed into her pyjamas and crawled into the bed next to her husband. She lay looking at the ceiling, thinking about the story that he had shared that afternoon. The resiliency of children and their ability to cope with adversity always amazed her. After watching his grandfather die, Martin had done what he had to in order to move on through life ... he forgot the incident ever happened.

Louisa imagined a seven-year-old boy, a vulnerable and sensitive boy according to Ruth, trapped in a room with the kind of horror that Martin had witnessed. What she would give to be able to go back in time and comfort that little boy, give him a different future. She rolled on to her side and watched him in his drug induced slumber. Shifting her body, she nestled up against him, resting an arm carefully across the left side of his chest. Then she closed her eyes and let his soft breath sounds lull her to sleep.

She woke sometime later to the rustling sounds of medical staff tending to her husband. She moved back on to her own bed and watched as they worked, checking Martin's vital signs, injecting something into his IV line, and shifting his body to stave off the development of bedsores. Louisa wondered how much pain he had been hiding from her when he groaned softly as the nurses shifted his legs.

"I'm sorry to disturb your sleep, Mrs. Ellingham. I think we're done here now," whispered a young women before slipping quietly from the room.

Staff returned at regular intervals throughout the night, repeating the earlier ritual but adding the drawing of blood on their final visit to the room.

The soft glow of daylight began to cast shadows on the wall, and Martin's eyes opened slightly. He turned towards the familiar sound of his wife's soft snores, and he watched her through a hazy gaze.

Her eyelids fluttered briefly before opening completely. "Good morning," she said as he blinked his eyes at her.

She propped herself up on one elbow and smiled at the befuddled expression on his face.

He lifted his head and looked around the room, trying to make sense of the confluence of the beautiful woman lying on the bed next to him and his surroundings.

"What are you doing here?"

She brushed her fingertips along his jawline. "I'm keeping you company. According to Ed and Chris, you sleep more soundly when I'm in bed with you. I guess I have a sedating effect."

"Mm, I see." He wrapped his arm around her and pulled her close, burying his face in her hair and inhaling her fragrance.

Pulling back to kiss him, Louisa saw tears in his eyes. "Martin, is something wrong?"

He shook his head and opened his mouth to answer, but the words refused to come. Swallowing hard, he forced out a whispered, "No, I just missed you," before pulling her back to him again.

Chapter 34

"Mmm, this is absolutely lovely Martin," Louisa said, inching herself over on the bed so that she could get closer to him.

"Yes. What are your plans for the rest of the weekend?"

Louise tipped her head back, peering up at him. "I thought I was going to be staying."

"Right."

"Of course, I don't have to. I'll just head on home then, shall I?" she lightly teased.

"Noo, I'd like that." He tightened his hold on her.

There was a soft knock on the door and Ed Christianson stuck his head in. "Good morning."

"Good morning, Ed." Louisa slipped from the bed and pulled on her dressing gown. "Come on in."

"Sorry to disturb you. I wanted to see if either of you had any questions before we take Martin to theatre."

Louisa folded her arms across her chest, shaking her head. "I think we both know the drill by this point." She gave him a smile.

"How are you feeling this morning, Martin? You ready to give this another try?" the surgeon asked.

"A little apprehensive, but yes ... I'd like to get it over with," Martin said as he tried to shift himself to a more upright position.

Ed pushed the extra bed aside and slid a hand under his patient's good arm, pulling him upright before raising the head of the bed. "All right, I'll send someone in to collect you. I'll see you in theatre in," he pulled up his hand and glanced at his watch, "about a half hour. Louisa, we'll have him back here between eight-thirty and nine. Fingers crossed that this is the last time you're in theatre for a few months, Martin."

"Mm, yes."

"I'll go scrub up and see you in a bit."

Louisa waited until the door closed behind him before going into the bathroom to wash and dress. A short while later, two male aides came and wheeled Martin away for what he hoped to be his final procedure for a while.

Mr. Christianson was pleased overall with the appearance of Martin's wound. He cut away the nonviable tissue that had developed since the last time he was in theatre, washed the surgical site out thoroughly, and sutured the clean tissue edges together.

Louisa was lying on the sofa when they wheeled him back from surgery. She stood back and watched as the aides and nurses got his IV lines straightened out, checked his wound for excessive bleeding, and elevated his legs. Then they packed the left leg in ice. By the time the room cleared, Martin was beginning to stir, mumbling in his sleep.

"I'm right here," Louisa said softly in his ear.

He struggled to open his heavy lids. "Louissa"

"I'm right here, Martin. They're all done."

"Louissa, my leg ... hurds." He grimaced and reached for his iced limb.

"I'm sure it does, but you need to leave it be."

She caressed his cheek until he dozed off again. Ed Christianson entered the room a few minutes later.

"How's he doing?" he asked as he removed the ice and bandage from the wound.

"He woke up a few minutes ago and was trying to reach for his leg. He said that it hurt."

"Ah. Let me see if we can make him more comfortable." The surgeon stepped out momentarily and returned with a nurse who injected something into the IV line.

"The procedure went well," Ed said, redirecting his attention to his patient's wife. "I was pretty pleased with how the wound looked overall. We'll hope it heals now with no more trouble from infection, but Will and Robert will need to do some work down the road. The immediate concern is getting those bones to mend though. Do you have any questions?"

"Do you think that he'll be up to a visitor by this afternoon?"

"We'll play it by ear, but I think he'll be a lot more alert by noon or so, and we should be able to get the pain under control as well. I'll plan to stop in around lunchtime and take a look at him. I can give you a definite answer then," Ed said as he moved towards the door.

"Would you change the dressing on his leg please," he directed the nurse. "And let me know if that bleeding continues," he said over his shoulder as he hurried out and down the corridor.

The nurse finished up tending to Martin's leg and left the room, leaving Louisa alone with him. She settled herself on the bed, lying on her side with her back against him, before opening up the book she had been reading.

A little more than an hour had passed when she felt the pressure of his hand on her back. She rolled herself over and looked into his groggy eyes.

"Hello," she said as she brushed her hand through his hair.

"Hello. What time is it?"

Louisa propped herself up on an elbow, stretching to see the clock behind him. "It's almost eleven. How are you feeling?"

He rubbed at his eyes. "Tired ... a bit nauseated."

"How's the pain in your leg now?"

"Bedder. Did Ruth stay at the Parsons' last night?"

"No, she volunteered to go back home and spend the night with James."

Louisa watched as her husband's eyes drifted closed before he grimaced suddenly, his body tensing.

"Martin, if you're having pain you should let the nurses know. They can give you more medication if you need it."

"I don' wan' it, Louissa. It makes me nauseous. An' is's hard to think."

"You don't need to think while you're in hospital, you know. But you do need to be comfortable so that you can sleep. And I've been reading that pain can actually slow the healing proce—"

"I don' wan' it! Jus' ... drob it, Louisa! Drob it!"

She took in a deep breath and tried to set aside the sting that she felt from the harshness of his words. He had done remarkably well controlling the anger and frustration that she knew he must be feeling with his situation.

Taking his hand in hers, she brought it to her lips, and Martin turned to look at her.

"I'm sorry. I'm jus' gedding ..." He sighed and pulled his arm up over his face.

Louisa stroked her fingertips back and forth across his chest, trying to ease the stress that was beginning to overwhelm him, and she felt a shudder go through his body.

"Martin, are you all right?" she asked softly.

He kept his eyes covered as he shook his head slowly.

Pulling her knees under her, she knelt next to him. Then, moving his arm, she wiped the tears from his face.

She leaned over, placing her cheek against his and talked softly into his ear. "It's going to be all right. You're not on your own with this. I'm here, Ruth's here, and you have Chris and Carole who care about you. You are *not* on your own with all of this."

When she felt his body relax, she went to the sink and came back with a wet flannel. He took it from her and wiped his face.

"Better?" she asked as she sat down on the bed, crossing her legs in front of her.

He handed her the cloth. "Mm. Sorry. I'm sorry for ... for yelling ad you."

"It's all right. I understand."

"No ... no, it's nod all right," he said shaking his head vigorously. "I don' wan' you to think that I'm angry with you. I'm ..."

"The pain's worse again, you're tired, and maybe just a little bit discouraged?"

"Mm."

She caressed his cheek. "You've been so remarkably strong through all of this. You haven't complained, you've been so stoic. Which I know you're doing for me by the way, and it's completely unnecessary. And you've been making an effort to be nice to people when I know you want to lash out."

"Mm, don' ged too used to the last one. It jus' hurts to yell," he confessed.

Louisa furrowed her brow at him. "Oh, dear. Maybe you should warn me when it doesn't hurt any more."

"I suspect you'll know," he said with a glint in his eyes.

Louisa kissed his forehead. "I'll take it as a good sign then, hmm?"

"Yes."

A short while later, Ed Christianson stopped back in. "Well, it looks like you've come around nicely. How's the leg feeling?"

"It hurds a bit."

Louisa caught Ed's eye and gave him a sharp nod of her head.

"A bit or a lot? And I want an honest answer," Ed said firmly.

Martin threw him a dark look and tried to push himself back on the bed. The movement sent searing pain through his recently violated leg, and his stifled groan came out as a very audible grunt.

"Okay, you answered my question." Ed unwrapped the bandage on his patient's leg, revealing a blood-soaked dressing underneath.

Louisa averted her eyes as she felt her stomach turn. She could hardly stand to see her husband's wounds any more. Not because of the physical appearance of them, but because she knew that they were causing him pain.

Ed rushed out of the room, and Louisa heard a flurry of heated words before he returned with a nurse.

"And you don't think this is excessive?" he barked. "If I remember correctly, I distinctly said that I was to be notified if the bleeding continued! You haven't even checked this wound have you? If you had, you would have noticed the oedema!"

The nurse opened her mouth to begin to speak but was cut off abruptly. "Don't even try. There's no excuse for this! Go and chase up Mr. Sturm and have him come in with a drain pack."

The nurse hurried off and Ed rubbed his hands over his head. As Louisa watched the tension in the man's face, she realised how stressful the life of a doctor could be. Ed was concerned for Martin, and he knew that the nurse had failed to do her job properly, potentially jeopardising the outcome for his patient.

A very youthful looking doctor came in carrying a tray of bandage materials and instruments.

"Martin, we need to put a drain in this leg. You have more fluid build up in there than I anticipated. I don't have to tell you that it's causing you a good deal of discomfort. Dammit, Martin! You've got to tell us if you're having pain!"

Ed looked at Louisa. "I apologise for my outburst. It'll be fine, Mrs. Ellingham. But we do need to get a drain in that leg to relieve the pressure." He walked over and adjusted the drip on his patient's IV.

Louisa held her husband's hand while Ed and Mr. Sturm, the on-call registrar, inserted the drain into his wound. The men finished the procedure, and Mr. Sturm left the room.

"Okay, Martin, that should make you a lot more comfortable," Ed said. "Now, can you tell me why you didn't let me know that you were in so much pain?" The surgeon crossed his arms across his chest. "Come on, Martin. I know that hurt."

Martin hesitated for what seemed to Louisa to be a very long time. "Id's ... my thoughts seem to be all jumbled. I was idiotic; I wasn't thinking about compardment syndrome. I just don' wan' more drugs in my system. I wan' to feel like myself again."

"We're getting there, Martin. We're getting there. But until then, all you need to do is tell us when it hurts, where it hurts, when you're hungry, when you need to pee, if you're having trouble sleeping ... Let *us* do the thinking for a while. You're going to be a bit muddled for quite a lot longer you know. You'll have to relinquish some of that control you're so loathe to share."

Martin grumbled under his breath. Ed moved towards the door. "I need to finish my rounds, but I'll check back before I leave for the day," he said before giving Louisa a jerk of his head and slipping out the door.

"I'm going to grab a cup of coffee, I'll be right back," Louisa said as she hurried out to catch up with the man. She found him waiting for her down the hall, and she looked up at him expectantly.

Ed rubbed at his jaw. "Martin's feeling pretty discouraged, isn't he?"

"He's trying to not show it, but yes, he is. What do you think about James?" Louisa asked, nodding her head in tacit encouragement of the visit.

"You have my blessing as long as Chris or I check the boy over first. I'll be anxious to hear how it goes," he said, giving her a grin.

Louisa rang up Ruth to check on her whereabouts. She and James were in the canteen having lunch with the Parsons, so Louisa hurried down the corridor to join them.

Chapter 35

In anticipation of a visit, Chris had already given James the prerequisite check up. Louisa hoped that the surprise reunion would be the magic elixir that would help her husband turn the corner, both physically and emotionally.

She ate hastily and listened distractedly to the discussion going on between her friends and Ruth. After forcing herself to stay an appropriately polite amount of time, she made her apologies. "I hate to rush off, but I better get James down to see Martin before he's ready for his nap," she said, putting the final spit and polish on her son. She glanced up quickly, adding, "Before *James* is ready for his nap, not *Martin*. Or ... hmm, I guess it could be the other way around, couldn't it?"

Ruth raised an eyebrow, giving Chris and Carole a wry smile. The younger woman's nervous excitement was unmistakeable.

Louisa gathered the toddler into her arms. "Let's go find your Daddy, shall we James!"

"Good luck," Chris said. "Hope all goes well."

"Oh, it will. I'm sure."

She walked quickly through the corridors, praying that James would be on his best behaviour. Then, slowing as she came to her husband's room, she stopped to peek through the door. Putting a finger to her lips, she gave her son a soft, "Shhh, your daddy's sleeping."

Her plan to wake Martin quietly was foiled when the child let out a loud squeal after catching sight of him.

He woke suddenly, temporarily disoriented, but, once he had made sense of what was going on, a smile spread across his face.

"*James?* Louisa, what's James doing here?" he asked as he reached his hand out for his son.

"He missed you," she said as she tried to control the boy who was struggling desperately to get to his father. She set him down on the extra bed, and he scrambled quickly to Martin's side. James had already latched on to him before she could react. Martin encircled the child's body with his arm as the two touched foreheads.

The toddler finally loosened his grip and plopped back on to his bum.

"How are you, James?" Martin asked as he brushed the backs of his fingers across the baby's cheek. He glanced up at his wife with tired but happy eyes. Baby James had brought about an immediate improvement in his affect.

The toddler's attention quickly shifted to the tempting gadgets on his father's arm as well as the IV lines running into his body. The electrodes and lead wires for the heart monitor, which had yet to be removed from the morning's surgery, seemed to be of particular interest to the boy.

"No, no, James ... don't touch," Louisa said, holding on to the child's hand while Martin pulled the wires free. This injustice set off a firestorm of protest in the form of wails and kicking feet.

Louisa looked over at the clock. It was past the child's usual naptime. She began to dig through the nappy bag for a book, but it appeared to be an item overlooked by the child's great-aunt when she packed the bag before setting out that morning.

Martin pulled the extra pillow over and patted the bed next to him. "Come over here James. We'll have a story," he said as he pulled Chris's copy of the latest *BMJ* off the tray table.

Louisa giggled. "Oh Martin, that may have worked when he was two months old, but I think he expects a bit more now."

Martin looked at her, his brows pulling together. "I think he might find it interesting."

"Well, it's just not the same as one of his children's books. I mean, there aren't any colourful pictures."

"Of course there are colourful pictures." He rifled through the publication to find a suitable example. "Here, this is a very well researched article on traumatic amputations of the upper limb, *with* colourful pictures," Martin turned the magazine towards his wife to prove his point, eliciting a grimace and a curl of her lip.

James reached out a chubby hand and grasped the *BMJ*, pulling it down to his lap.

"See, James likes it," Martin said. Now vindicated by his son's apparent interest in the article, he gave a see-I-told-you-so nod of his head.

Louisa looked sceptically at him, but sat back on the bed next to the toddler and picked up her own much more benign story. She kept one eye on the baby and one ear on the rather gruesome medical tale being read to him.

The child pulled his knees under him and nestled in next to his father, allowing himself to be lulled to sleep by the sonorous voice.

Martin yawned and laid the journal back down on the tray table before settling in for a nap himself.

Having finished the chapter she had been reading, Louisa dropped her book on to the bed, watching her husband and son. *Both* were so helpless and dependent on her now. Slipping quietly from the bed, she grabbed her mobile and snapped a picture.

The door open and she hurried over quickly, quieting Ruth and the Parsons before they entered the room.

"They're both sleeping. Martin read to him from that *BMJ* that you brought in Chris," Louisa whispered.

"Put him right out I bet," Chris replied softly. "I sat in on one of Martin's lectures a few years ago. It had the same effect on me."

"Oh, Christopher! Poor Martin. Couldn't you have made an effort to show some interest?" Carole scolded, giving her husband a scowl.

"It's *was* interesting. Martin just has one of those voices."

"Why don't you let me sit with my nephews for a bit, Louisa. You go have a little break from this room," Ruth said, directing more than suggesting.

Louisa looked hesitantly towards her husband and son. "All right, but watch James. He'd really like to get his hands on Martin's fixators ... and lines ... and the wires," she said, wagging a finger at all the medical equipment. "And he can move fast, so don't let him out of your sight."

"*Yes*, dear. Now run along." Ruth guided the trio towards the hall before returning to her childminding duties.

She pushed the tray table aside and pulled a chair up next to the bed, settling in with the latest issue of *BJPsych*. Her attention shifted from an article on neuropsychological testing to her nephew and his son. James Henry looked so similar to what she remembered of a one-year-old Martin.

Her life had revolved around her medical career at the time that he was born, and his arrival was a non-event for her. She hadn't the time for things so trivial as family matters.

She first met the not-so-new baby when he was slightly younger than James. Her mother had died, and the family had gathered for the ritualistic expressions of sorrow. There had been a visitation at Christopher and Margaret's, and the nanny had been instructed to parade the boy through the crowd of mourners where all the appropriate oohs and ahs were made before he was whisked off, out of sight, out of mind again.

The next time she could remember seeing him was at his father's graduation from medical school. Again, a family gathering where the child was fittingly put on display.

She had no further contact with her nephew until he was a bit older and no longer confined to the nursery. He was a vulnerable and sensitive four-year-old, hiding behind the full skirt of whichever nanny happened to be in employ at the time.

Ruth accepted a job at a mental health facility in Manchester, which meant that she went a period of time without seeing her brother's progeny. She had just moved back to London to take a position on staff at Broadmoor Hospital when her father died.

Baby James began to stir, raising his head up to look around. Ruth hurried to pick him up before he woke his father and then carried him out to the corridor in search of his mother. Louisa waved to them as they approached and quickly wrapped up the conversation she'd been having with Ed Christianson.

"My boys are awake I see," she lilted as she reached for her son.

"Only one, actually. The big one's still sleeping."

"James will need a nappy change. I'll do it in the lavatory down the hall and then take him to get a snack. Would you like to join us, Ruth?

"Yes, I would actually. This dry hospital air has left me in need of a cup of tea."

Martin began to stir shortly before Ruth and Louisa's return to the room. He looked around in a state of confusion. It at first seemed that his son's presence had been but a blissful dream. However, the lingering warmth and the physical sensation of the boy's small head pressed against his chest was palpable. Martin cursed the drugs in his system for the unpleasant side effects that he was feeling. Had James been there and fallen off the bed?

He tried to wake himself completely, but he couldn't shake the drug induced haze. He called out to the boy but heard none of the usual baby chatter that his father's voice normally elicited.

Martin searched for the call button, spotting it on the tray table which had been moved aside and was now just out of reach. The longer he worried about James's whereabouts, the more convinced his muddled mind became that something terrible had happened to him.

He began to fear that perhaps his mother had taken the boy, and panic set in. His memories of his mother's recent visit became incorporated with the sundry of possible dangers to his son. He could picture her hand that morning in their kitchen, grabbing at his wrist as he reached to pick the plate up from the kitchen table. His hand jerking back in an involuntary attempt to protect himself from the same kind of pain that had been inflicted on him as a child.

He pulled at the bed rail, trying in vain to lower it so that he might be able to reach the call button. Failing at that attempt, he turned his efforts to dragging himself across the spare bed to his left. His elevated leg dropped from the foam block that it had been resting on, sending a deep tearing sensation through the limb.

The intensity of it sucked the air from his lungs. He struggled to get his chest to expand enough to pull in the oxygen that his body needed. The pain began to abate as did the spasms in his diaphragm, and he used his left arm to pull himself to the edge of the bed. Looking around below him, he still could not see his son.

He was desperate now and managed to swing his legs over the edge of the mattress. Attempting to stand, his weakened legs gave, and he fell to the floor, the impact sending pain signals screaming through his nerve fibres as he cried out in agony.

Louisa and Ruth were approaching the room when they heard his wail. Louisa handed James to the older woman and pushed through the door, while Ruth hurried to the nurses station to get assistance.

Dropping down next to him, Louisa wrapped her arms around her husband, trying to keep him from thrashing about and causing himself further injury.

Ed Christianson raced down the hall and into his patient's room. Two male aides followed closely behind. Ed gave Martin a fast acting, short duration sedative. He lost consciousness almost immediately, and hospital staff were able to get him back into the bed.

Ed examined him thoroughly, head to toe, checking all of his wounds for torn sutures and the external fixators for the tightness of the pins. The IV stands had been pulled to the floor with him, but neither the catheter in his arm nor the central line had been dislodged.

He finally turned to Louisa who had been standing back out of the way, fearing the worst. "Well, I'm not seeing that he's done himself any harm, but I'm sending him down to CT all the same. We'll see what the pictures tell us. Do you know what happened in here?"

Louisa shook her head. "He was napping with James. When James woke up, Ruth took him out of the room so that he wouldn't wake Martin. No one was in here when this happened."

Martin began to move, wakefulness returning. He looked wildly about, his eyes settling on his wife.

"Louisa, find James. My mother has James! Get James!"

"Martin, *Ruth* has James. He's just outside in the hall," she said, rubbing his arm.

He pulled away from her and tried to sit up. "She'll hurt him, Louisa. You have to get him away from her!"

Ed tried to push Martin back down on to the bed, but he continued to struggle.

"Louisa's going to get James, Martin," Ed said as he gave her a jerk of his head. "Calm down."

Louisa hurried into the corridor, returning quickly with their son in her arms.

Martin crumpled back, his head dropping on to the pillow. "I thought she had him ... I thought she'd taken him," he said, covering his face with his hand.

Ed loosened his grip on his patient. "Martin, I suspect you're having an adverse reaction to the analgesics. I don't want to make any changes to your medication yet, but I want someone here in the room with you at all times until you're thinking more clearly."

The surgeon looked apologetically at Louisa. "I'm very sorry, Mrs. Ellingham. This sort of a reaction can be upsetting to witness."

"He's all right then?" Louisa asked nervously.

"I believe so. Once we have some pictures we'll know for sure."

Louisa brushed her fingers against her husband's cheek. "It's all right, Martin. James is perfectly safe."

Martin reached his arm out and pulled at his son. Louisa set him down beside his father, and the boy gave him a partially toothless smile.

Chapter 36

James played on the bed next to his father, his simple presence doing more to ease her husband's anxieties than her words ever could.

Ruth had explained to her that as Martin's body adjusted to the morphine he'd been receiving, a higher dose was needed to achieve the same level of pain relief. After his surgery earlier in the day, the dose had been increased even further in an effort to keep him reasonably comfortable. This higher dose had brought about the anxiety and confusion that had led to his panic over the whereabouts of his son.

Although her husband's irrational concern for James's safety had been drug induced, Louisa knew that the fear that his mother could cause harm to their son was genuine and justified. He had experienced the woman's cruelty first hand.

She crawled across the bed and put her arms around him. "I hope that you can feel how very much I love you," she said, holding him tightly.

"Louisa, is something wrong?" he asked apprehensively.

She released her grip on him and pulled back. "*No.* I love you very much, and I just wanted to make that clear. And I didn't want you to just hear me say the words. I wanted you to be able to feel it. That's all."

"Mm, I see. I love you, too."

She kissed him before relaxing back on to the bed, returning her attention to her son.

"Louisa?" Martin said, his eyes on his lap as he gently rubbed at the painful laceration on his thigh.

"Hmm?"

He peered up at her shyly. "I'm not entirely sure I felt it. Maybe you should try again?"

Around half three, two aides wheeled Martin off to radiology, returning him to his room nearly an hour later, irritable and taking out his frustrations on the young nurse trying to attend to him.

"Get off! I can do it myself!" he snapped as she tried to help him get settled back in his bed.

She reached for the IV line, attempting to temporarily disconnect it so that it could be untangled.

"Oh, for God's sake, woman!" he barked, slapping her hand away. "You're going to raise a hematoma if you keep yanking it around like that!"

She pulled back and took in a deep breath. "Dr. Ellingham, if you could just stay still for—"

"Oh, I see, it's my fault, is it!"

Louisa glanced over at the nurse. "I'm really sorry. He's normally not like thi—"

"*Yes*, I am! Or so you keep saying!" he said, his eyes fiery.

Louisa put her hand on his shoulder. "Martin, calm down."

He slapped at the nurse again as she tried to adjust his blankets. His elbow knocked the pitcher of water from the tray table and on to the floor.

"Now look what you made me do, you clumsy dolt!"

"Martin!" Louisa glared at him, mortified by his behaviour.

Ed Christianson stood just inside the door, watching the scene before walking over to speak to the young nurse. She slipped quietly from the room.

"It's fine, Mrs. Ellingham," the surgeon said as he blotted up the water from the floor. "It's the medication." He tossed the soaked paper towelling into the bin. "Sorry to have kept your husband away so long. The change in his surroundings seemed to exacerbate his confusion, and he wasn't the most cooperative patient."

He picked up the binder on the end of the bed, adding to the ever-growing compilation of patient notes. "We managed though, and everything looked good on the scans, Martin," he said, clicking his biro and slipping it into his breast pocket. "However, we did discover several additional fractures that we'd missed before. It didn't come as a great surprise to see fractures to your sixth and seventh ribs on the left side. The seat belt got you there."

Louisa's face registered immediate concern, and Ed quickly added, "With the lung contusions, rib fractures would be expected, Mrs. Ellingham.

"We also found you have a fractured clavicle. Again, not a great surprise given the problems that you have with your shoulder as well as the trauma to that arm. All of the fractures that we discovered today are non-displaced, and given the severity of your other injuries are really nothing we're concerned about. Just more boxes to tick in the fracture column. The good news is that there was no additional damage done by your tumble to the floor today."

"You're sure everything's fine then?" Louisa asked.

"Appears to be. Let me know immediately if you develop any new or worsening symptoms though, Martin."

Mr. Christianson took a seat in the chair next to the bed. "Now, the issue of your pain meds ... After giving this some thought, I'm inclined to stick with the morphine a bit longer ... wait and see if the problems you've been having with confusion and anxiety ... irritability ... don't resolve themselves once we cut back on your dosage again. You've been tolerating it well overall, and ... well, if it tain't broke, don't fix it, right?"

Louisa shook her head. "I don't know. What if he tries to get out of bed again? I don't want him hurting himself."

"I understand your concern. We'll have someone with him at all times to make sure that doesn't happen," Ed said as he rose from his chair. "Any other questions?"

"No, I don't think so," Louisa said, giving him a nervous smile.

The surgeon glanced over at his patient. "Martin?"

"When can I get out of here?"

Ed blew out a long breath. "I appreciate that you must be getting tired of all this, but you need more work with the physio people, and we need to get an occupational therapist in here."

Martin threw his head to the side. "I'll hire people to work with me at home. I want to ged out of here."

"Let's see how you're doing tomorrow ... talk about this again."

As soon as Mr. Christianson had left the room, Louisa slid to Martin's side and took his hand in hers, tracing over the indentation where his wedding band usually resided. "You'll get home, Martin. You don't want to rush things."

"*Rush* things?" he scoffed.

She stroked her fingers along his arm. "It'll be more difficult at home. There are a lot of people to help you out here. And to be honest, I'm a bit nervous about whether I'll be able to take care of you properly at home."

Martin swallowed as his gaze shifted to his lap. "I'm sorry, I wasn't thinking about what this will be like for you. You have James to take care of, and your ... and your job at the school. Mm. I wasn't thinking."

Louisa turned his face towards her. "I want you home as soon as possible, but we need to trust Ed and Chris to tell us when the time is right. I just want the best possible care for you. You can understand that, can't you?"

He scowled at her before turning his gaze back to his lap. "Yes."

Ruth took James Henry back to the Parsons' with her for the night, and Louisa stayed at the hospital.

A nurse came into the room around nine o'clock and increased Martin's morphine dose. "It's just to ease his discomfort a bit so that he can get a better night's rest," the nurse explained. "If you need to leave his side for any reason, even if it's just to use the loo, be sure you call for assistance. Wait until someone comes in. Do *not* leave him on his own."

"Oh, don't worry, I won't," Louisa assured the woman. After what had occurred earlier, she wasn't going to take any chances.

She was awakened in the middle of the night by the movements of her husband next to her as he tried to sit up.

"Martin, is everything all right?"

He turned his head quickly towards her. "What are you doing here?" he asked, startled and confused by her presence.

"Martin, it's me ... Louisa. You're at hospital. Do you remember? You were in an accident."

He tried to push the blankets back and pull his feet up, but lacking the strength to do so, he flopped back on to the bed. "I need to pee."

"Remember, you can't get out of bed," she said, tugging the blankets back up over his legs.

Grabbing them away from her, he pushed them back down and attempted to roll to his side. "I *need* to pee!"

Louisa scrambled down and, keeping one eye on him, grabbed the plastic urinal from the lavatory.

She turned the light on beside the bed and handed him the container.

Martin looked at her, wide eyed, as she stood watching him. "Louisa! For God's sake, turn around!"

She planted her feet and folded her arms in front of her. "I'm *not* taking my eyes off you, Martin. Now just ... wee. Or do you need help?"

"Gawd. Never mind, I can wait," he said, handing the urinal back to her.

"Oh Martin, it's not like you've got something down there I haven't already seen before. Maybe I should call a nurse and *she* can watch you." Louisa reached for the call button, but Martin slapped his hand down on it first.

"All right, all right! You can ... watch."

"How 'bout I keep my eyes on the wall behind you?"

"Mm, yes," Martin said, his face flushing.

He finished taking care of the necessities, and she returned the source of his humiliation to the lavatory.

Turning out the light, they settled back in and dozed off quickly.

Louisa was awakened again a couple of hours later by her husband's fingers as they tickled her cheek.

"Everything okay?" she asked.

"You're very beaudiful," he said, his speech sluggish.

"Thank you, Martin."

"Did you know thad I stayed here because of you?"

Louisa propped herself up on an elbow and smoothed out his tousled hair. "After the thing with Mrs. Tishell?"

Martin cocked his head at her. "Hmm?"

"I'm not sure what you mean ... that you stayed because of me."

"After my first week here. I bollocksed things up, so I was going to leave. I was even packing my things in boxes again." He gave her a small smile and put his hand on hers. "Bud I saw you through the window of the school and I ..." He sighed. "Then I was looking across the harbour ... at the school ... at you, and I decided I was going to stay. I decided I was going to marry you someday."

"Oh, Martin." She reached over and cupped his cheek in her hand.

"Would you like to have dinner with me sometime, Louisa?" he asked, eyeing her shyly.

"You're asking me out? On a date?" She tipped her head down and peered up at his rather laddish expression. "Here? In the hospital?"

Martin blinked his eyes at her before his brows pulled together. "Louisa, why would I take you to a hospital on a date?"

"Martin, I think that head of yours is a bit fuzzy. But I kind of like your head a bit fuzzy. Maybe there's something to be said for adverse reactions, hmm?"

"I don' know. Yes—maybe—I don' know." His eyes flitted to the side. "I don' know."

"I think you should go back to sleep."

"Mm, yes."

She planted a light kiss on his nose before settling back in next to him.

They lay quietly for a few moments before Louisa said softly, "Martin?"

"Hmm?"

"If that offer still stands, I *would* very much like to have dinner with you sometime."

Chapter 37

As far as Louisa could tell, Martin remembered nothing of their nocturnal conversations by the time they woke the next morning. Mr. Christianson had given the staff instructions to begin tapering the pain medication that he was receiving, but it remained to be seen whether the reduced dose would alleviate her husband's mood swings and confusion.

The surgeon stopped by the room mid-morning. "I want you to tell someone if your pain increases to a three or higher on the pain scale, Martin. Is that understood?" Ed asked firmly.

Martin mumbled inaudibly, and Louisa shot him a stern look before he said grudgingly, "Yes, fine."

"Good. I'm going to have the PT people come in again today. I've also asked to have an occupational therapist stop by this morning ... prepare you for the challenges you'll be facing once you're home.

"And I know you're anxious to get out of here, but you need to be at least somewhat ambulatory before I can release you." He wagged a finger at his patient's legs. "I don't want any weight bearing activities just yet, but perhaps by the end of the week we'll get you up with a walker. Once you can get yourself in and out of a wheelchair, I'll consider letting you leave."

"So, that's the criteria? Once I'm ambulatory I can go home?"

Louisa could see the eagerness in her husband's eyes. Ed Christianson could see it as well.

"Martin, *don't* overdo with this. You need to be careful or you'll set yourself back. I've already told the physio people they won't need to push you. They'll be watching that you don't go at this too hard."

Ed turned his attention to Louisa. "How's the confusion and irritability this morning? Any better?"

Martin threw his head back. "Good God! I'm sitting right in front of you! *Yes,* the confusion's better today!"

Louisa put her hand on her husband's arm and gave him a nod. "Yes, the confusion does seem to be better today, although there were some muddled moments in the night."

Martin gave her a questioning look. "No there weren't!"

She turned her head towards the surgeon and winced. "Irritability might still be a bit of an issue."

"I'm not muddled *or* irritable," Martin said, jutting out his chin.

Ed held his hand up in front of him. "It's all right, Martin. Try not to worry about it. You're making progress. I'll stop by tomorrow ... remove some of those sutures."

The surgeon tapped his hands on the bedrail before turning to leave, and then stopped in the doorway. "Oh, I spoke with Barrett Newell. He didn't want to interrupt your time with your son yesterday, so he's going to stop by today to check up on you."

The Parsons, Ruth, and James approached in the hallway.

"Morning, Ed," Chris said.

"Morning, Chris." Mr. Christianson stepped aside to allow them into the room before continuing down the hall.

Carole made her way towards Louisa, handing her several story books. "I understand James could use some *appropriate* reading material," she said, shaking her head at Martin.

Chris shrugged his shoulders at his friend before placing his breakfast on the tray table and rolling it in front of him. "Here you go, Mart, eat up."

"Mm, thank you."

Though his weight was still down from where it had been before the accident, Martin had gained two kilos since Carole had been supplementing the meals provided by the hospital, and his appetite seemed to increase daily.

"How are the plans for the changes to the farm progressing, Ruth?" Martin asked, spreading marmalade on his toast.

"Well, we're coming along with getting the contractors lined up. Al's quite particular about these things. And he knows his stuff, especially about plumbing. He's been able to do much of that work himself. You'll have to come out and take a look around when you get out of here," Ruth said as she walked over to gaze out the window.

Chris dropped into a chair and leaned back, folding his hands behind his head. "Have you given any thought to how you'll get around the surgery once you're at home, Mart? I can't see you taking those steps two at a time for a while."

"Mm, Louisa and I discussed it." He glanced over at his wife. "If patients are going over to Wadebridge for the time being, we can use the consulting room as a bedroom temporarily. I'm hopeful that with a bit of hard work I can get things back to normal fairly quickly."

"Martin, don't go overboard. Ed and I were talking about this the other day. You have a tendency to throw yourself into whatever project you happen to have going at the moment, but getting back on your feet is a big project. You won't be able to do this on your own you know."

Ruth waggled her finger at her nephew. "You do realise that you're going to have to learn to accept help from people now, don't you?"

"Yes, I'm aware of that."

The elderly woman took a seat next to the bed. "It's going to be a very steep learning curve given your tendency to shut others out."

Martin clenched his jaw as the lecture continued.

"And you'll need to be gracious about it, or you'll find yourself stranded at the bottom of Roscarrock Hill because no one will want to risk incurring your wrath to offer you assistance."

"Yes, all right! I'm perfectly capable of being civil ... when it's required." He rubbed his palm against the rapidly growing ache in his forehead.

"I'm merely pointing out a few hard truths, Martin. There will be times when you'll not only need to accept help, but you'll need to *ask* for it. That won't be easy for you," Ruth said.

"Are you finished?" he asked, his scowl deepening.

"Oh, I could go on, but I'll stop there."

Martin rolled his eyes before focusing them on the door to his room, mentally willing his guests to leave.

A nurse came in carrying his obligatory bowl of ice cream.

"Well, Christopher, I think we should be going," Carole said. She tapped a fingernail against the tray table and narrowed her eyes at Martin. "You ... eat!"

"Yes, I will!" Martin was beginning to feel the little gathering more of an intervention than a visit.

He looked down at the large bowl in front of him and curled his lip. He had his suspicions that the serving size of the creamy confection was growing daily, but he ate it without much more than a soft grunt.

After the Parsons left the room, Louisa set James on the bed and handed Martin one of the books that Carole had brought with her. The baby immediately scrambled over to him, grabbing on to the edge of the tray table and pulling himself up. The boys weight rolled the table away from the bed, dropping him on to his father's stomach.

A loud and emphatic utterance of words his wife had admonished him to not use in the presence of their son escaped his mouth, and he quickly rolled to his side to protect his abdominal wound from any further assault. Ruth jumped up to tend to her nephew as Louisa picked James up, now distraught by his father's outburst. Martin rocked from side to side as he tried to find an antalgic position. He attempted to pull his knees up to lessen the tension on the surgical site, but his legs refused to respond.

Louisa came around the bed and handed James to Ruth. Martin was pale and perspiring as tears formed in his eyes.

"Should I get a nurse ... or Ed?" she asked.

He shook his head back and forth vigorously. The sharp pain began to abate to an intense ache as a wave of nausea hit him.

"Vomit!" he sputtered.

Louisa grabbed the basin and helped him roll again to his side before his stomach contents were expelled. The resultant muscle spasms intensified the pain, and he released a long groan.

The grimace on his face slowly relaxed, and he closed his eyes, trying to block out the residual throbbing in his abdomen. Louisa wiped the sweat from his face with a wet flannel as his breathing began to return to normal.

"Martin, I really think I should get Ed," she said, watching him nervously.

"No." He gave one more short groan. "I don't want them ... to keep James away because of this."

The boy's wails had now dwindled to whimpers, interspersed with ragged breaths. Louisa took their son from Ruth's arms and comforted him.

"Shh. It's all right, James. See ... your daddy's going to be okay." Louisa crouched down beside the bed, and the baby looked at his father somewhat fearfully before turning to bury his face in his mother's shoulder.

Martin's brow furrowed as he watched his son turn away from him to hide his face. The flash of fear that he saw in James's eyes when he looked at him and the comfort and reassurance that he received from his mother's touch, created a small spark of understanding in Martin.

Chapter 38

Ruth had excused herself to get a cup of tea, leaving Louisa time alone with her husband and son.

"Martin, are you sure you're all right?" she asked as she scrutinised his face for any sign of continuing distress.

"I'm fine; how's James?" He reached for the boy's hand, and Louisa dropped down beside him, setting the child between them.

"I think he was just startled," Louisa said. "James Henry, you need to be more careful; you hurt your daddy!" she said in mock admonishment, giving the boy's belly a gentle poke.

"Louisa! Don't blame James!" Martin wrapped his arm around his son and pulled him close. "It wasn't his fault. I should have been more vigilant."

He brushed his hand across the child's head.

"Martin, I wasn't serious you know," she said, tipping her head down and peering up at him.

"I don't care. Just don't ... don't ..." He hissed out a breath, and Louisa reached over and caressed the back of his neck before kissing his cheek.

The latch on the door clicked, and a diminutive middle-aged woman peeked into the room. "Knock, knock," she singsonged before stepping in from the hall.

"Sorry to interrupt, Dr. Ellingham. I'm Dorothea McVey, one of the staff occupational therapists. Mr. Christianson wanted me to come by and go over some things that need to be addressed before you're discharged."

The woman leaned down, bracing her hands against her knees before greeting the baby. "And who is this fine looking young man?"

"This is our son, James," Louisa said proudly. "And I'm Martin's wife."

"Hello, James." Dorothea reached an arm out to touch the boy, and Martin tightened his hold, looking at the woman uncertainly.

"Have you washed since you touched your last patient?" he asked curtly.

"Martin, I'm sure tha—"

"No, no. That's quite all right, Mrs. Ellingham. Your husband's right to check," she said, walking to the sink and turning on the tap. "Lots of nasty things lurk in hospital rooms, I'm afraid."

Martin pulled in his chin as Louisa gave him an apologetic smile, and he returned his attention to his son.

The therapist went over the many considerations and practicalities that needed to be addressed before Martin's homecoming—skills he would need to hone and changes that would need to be made to the surgery to make his transition from hospital to home workable.

His years spent as a surgeon and repairing clocks had already made the change from being a right-hand dominant individual to using his left hand exclusively, much easier. But the therapist pointed out that many of the simplest tasks were difficult when a patient was restricted to the use of the non-dominant hand—putting on a sock and tying shoes, writing out a cheque, cutting food at the dinner table, and shaving to name a few.

Ruth returned to the room with two cups in her hands. She passed one to her nephew's wife. "Coffee?" she said. "Sounds like you may need it." She gave the younger woman a crooked grin before taking a seat by the window, listening in as

Dorothea went over the adaptations that would need to be made to the Ellingham home.

The injury to Martin's arm meant that it would be a while before he could use crutches to get himself around. Doorways would need to be wide enough to accommodate a wheelchair or a walker, and the small lavatory off the reception room would never allow for that. It also lacked a bathtub or shower.

A ramp would need to be installed so that he could navigate the step up into the kitchen, and the kitchen cupboards would need to be reorganised so that he could access the things he needed when there was no one available to help him.

He would need new clothing that would be easy to get on and off despite the bulky fixators on his limbs, or they would need to find someone who could make modifications to his existing clothing. The considerations and tasks to be completed seemed endless.

Louisa was left with a lengthy list of tips to help her provide for Martin's needs, as well as contact information for people in the Portwenn area who offered the services the Ellinghams would likely require.

When the therapist left the room, Louisa turned to Martin and heaved a heavy sigh. "A lot to do, hmm?"

"I'm not sure this is going to work, Louisa," Martin said, shaking his head. "For one thing, I don't think it's possible to change the lavatory off the reception room. I checked into that after I bought the practice, and I was told that it would compromise the structural integrity of the building to enlarge that room. Even if it were possible, finding someone in the Portwenn area competent enough to do the work is an unlikely scenario, and by the time they finished the job I'd be functioning normally again."

Ruth looked on with her typical flat expression. "If I may be so bold, I do have a possible solution to your problem."

Louisa turned. "I'm sorry, Ruth. We didn't mean to exclude you. Please, go ahead."

"If you recall, I purchased my cottage from Mrs. Honold."

"Yes ...?"

"Mrs. Honold was confined to a wheelchair. My cottage is already handicapped accessible. It would seem logical for you and Martin to move into my cottage for the time being, and I could move into the surgery temporarily."

Martin and Louisa exchanged glances.

"It would be a solution to our problem," Martin said as he mulled over the possibility.

"Oh, Ruth, would you really be willing to do that?" Louisa asked, taking the woman's hand in hers.

"Well, I wouldn't have suggested it otherwise, dear."

One major hurdle had been crossed, but there was still a lot to be done in a short amount of time. Louisa felt a growing excitement mixing with the apprehension that she had been feeling about having Martin home again.

Ruth and Louisa took James to the canteen for lunch, leaving Martin to rest.

He had been dozing, off and on, when Barrett Newell knocked on the door. "Hello, Martin. Sorry, I bet I woke you, didn't I?"

"Mm, I wasn't really sleeping ... just thinking."

Dr. Newell pulled a chair up to the bed and took a seat before picking up a sheet of paper lying on the tray table. "Puzzling over the lunch menu?"

"Hmph. Not much to puzzle over."

The therapist tipped back in his chair. "I hear your son's been in for a visit. How did that go?"

"It's been really ... fine."

"Just fine?"

"No, good really. Very good."

"Ed Christianson mentioned that there had been a mishap yesterday. Care to talk about it?"

Martin winced as one of the recurrent pains he'd been having shot through his left leg. He tipped to the side, trying to shift the weight from the complaining appendage. "I've been having some side effects from the morphine. Ed increased my dosage after yesterday's procedure, and it resulted in some confusion."

"That's not uncommon at higher dosages," the psychiatrist said as he laced his fingers over a knee.

Martin gave a shrug of his shoulders. "My son was visiting. He'd fallen asleep next to me. I nodded off, and when I woke up I was alone in the room. I panicked. I thought my mother had taken him."

"That wouldn't be unexpected given your history and the current circumstances."

"It was *idiotic.* I tried to get out of bed to find him, and I ended up on the floor."

Dr. Newell leaned forward in his chair. "No damage done though, I take it?"

"No ... no, not really."

"That's fortunate. So ... what *had* become of your son?"

Martin rubbed a hand across his face. "My aunt had taken him out of the room when he woke up from his nap. She didn't want him to disturb me. Like I said—idiotic."

"What were your concerns when you thought your mother may have taken James?"

"That *was* my concern," Martin huffed. "She's taken away just about everything I've valued in my life. And if she took James ... I don't want her touching him—hurting him."

"Physically you mean?"

Martin's brows tugged together. "I'm not sure."

"Martin, when your mother wasn't punishing you, were there times when you felt safe in her presence?"

"She hated me. I tried. I made her gifts ... drew pictures ... tried to approach her when she appeared to be more open to it, but she ..." He shook his head.

"Were you fearful around her?"

"Of course, I was! The woman hated me!"

The therapist relaxed back into his chair. "Fear's a very strong emotion ... a crippling, paralysing emotion at times."

Martin took in a deep breath. "Yes."

Some seconds passed before he began to speak again. "I frightened James earlier. I wasn't watching. He tried to pull himself up and fell on top of me. I yelled—not at him, but because of the pain. It scared him.

"I saw the fear in his eyes when he looked at me, and I noticed the reassurance he seemed to get when his mother comforted him. Having that comfort from his mother was ... He was able to recover from the fear over my ... my outburst, because of the comfort he received from his mother."

"Did you have anyone that you could go to for comfort, Martin?"

"My aunt Joan—the aunt I'd spend summers with."

"No one throughout the rest of the year though?"

Martin shook his head and then sat silently for a few moments. "The day my grandfather died there was no one. I wanted to see Joan. I knew that she'd know what to do ... to say to make me feel better.

"The day of the funeral, I'd been told to stay in my room. Looking back on it, I suspect they didn't want anyone asking about my arm. Dad told me to say I'd fallen down the stairs if anyone asked, but they were probably wanting to avoid questions. I'm sure they didn't want people to know what I'd done. I don't know. I've never liked dishonesty. I've never been good at lying, and my parents knew that," Martin said.

His head dropped to the side. "Anyway, I was in my room when people came back to the house after the funeral. I heard

Joan downstairs. I almost ran to her when I heard her voice. I had my hand on the doorknob. But I was too afraid of what my parents would do.

"When I heard people leaving later that afternoon, I watched out my window as she walked to the car with Aunt Ruth. I wanted to pound on the window ... to get her attention.

"I've been thinking about that lately, wondering if things would have been different if I'd disobeyed my parents and gone to Joan."

"That's something we'll never know." Dr. Newell said.

"No. But maybe if I hadn't been such a coward ..."

The psychiatrist leaned forward, resting his elbows on his knees. "Martin, here we are, two adults looking back on the situation with the benefit of hindsight, and *we* don't know which way things would have gone had you run to your aunt. It would be completely unreasonable to expect that a seven-year-old in the midst of that nightmare would be able to make that decision. If you *had* disobeyed your parents, it may have only made a bad situation worse."

Dr. Newell got up and poured two glasses of water, handing one to his patient before returning to his chair.

"Martin, children need to feel secure for normal emotional development to occur. It might be helpful for you to bone up a bit on what you learned in your paediatrics courses in medical school ... on emotional development, particularly during early childhood.

"It might help you to understand why you reacted the way you did when you were alone in that room as your grandfather died. How the incident affected you in the days and months ... years following. I'd be happy to bring some reading material by if you're interested."

"Mm, yes. I think that would be good. Thank you."

"You're welcome." The man got to his feet and headed for the door. "I should let you get some rest. You have my number if you should need me. Feel free to call any time."

Ruth, James, and Louisa returned from lunch shortly after Dr. Newell left. James, overdue for a nap, was irritable. Louisa settled him in next to his father before handing her husband one of the children's books on loan from the Parsons.

"Oh ... no, no, no, no, no. I can't read this to him," Martin said, wrinkling up his nose and pushing the book back towards his wife.

"Well, it's certainly an improvement over yesterday's selection, Martin. And we do need to start introducing the concept to him." Louisa slapped the book back down on the bed. "Now, read."

Martin scowled at his wife and glanced down at his son. James grinned up at him, watching in anticipation as his father breathed out a resigned sigh. He cleared his throat. "An elephant makes a big poop ..."

Chapter 39

Neither father nor son made it through the entire children's story, and they were now sleeping soundly next to Louisa as she tried to focus her attention on her book.

Pushing herself up from the sofa, Ruth stretched her arms. "I'm going for a little walk ... limber up these old joints a bit," she undertoned. "Can I get you a cup of coffee or tea while I'm out, Louisa?"

"Yeah. A cup of tea would be great."

Louisa returned her attention to her story for a short time before her eyes became bleary. She laid her book down on her lap and stretched out her arms, glancing over at her husband. He had woken up and was lying staring at the ceiling.

"You look very serious. Anything you want to talk about?" she asked.

His chest rose and fell slowly. "Dr. Newell was by while you were at lunch."

"Oh?" She sat up a little straighter and tucked her legs under her. "If you're comfortable talking about it, I'd like to hear what you discussed."

"I told him about what happened with James earlier ... how I saw the fear in his face when he looked at me. It calmed him when you held him, though ... comforted him."

Louisa smiled. "Hmm, that's what mother's do best." Her husband's wistful expression made her regret her choice of words. "Martin, I'm sorry. I didn't think before I spoke."

"Mm, it's all right. It just catches me off guard."

"What do you mean?" Louisa asked as she cocked her head at him.

"Things people say ... as if they're stating the obvious. Roger Fenn said something once ... a couple of years ago. The day my mother told me how she felt. He and that Doreen woman had just found out they were expecting twins."

Louisa gave him a soft smile and brushed a hand across his head. "Maureen ... Tacey."

"Mm. He was quite naturally excited about it. He said children were the best thing, ask any parent. Something to that effect. I felt like I'd been punched in the stomach."

Martin shook his head and refocused on the discussion with his therapist. "Dr. Newell asked if I had anyone I could go to for comfort. Obviously, that would have been Joan. She was at the house the day of my grandfather's funeral, but I'd been told to stay in my room."

"You mean you knew she was in the house, just outside your door, but you couldn't go to her?"

"Mm. I watched her from my window as she walked down the sidewalk and drove away. The next time I saw her was the following summer. By then, I think I'd forgotten the entire incident."

Louisa got up on her knees and leaned across their son to embrace and kiss him. "Life *does* owe you so very much, you know."

Martin blew a hiss of air from his nose and shook his head. "No, I *don't* know. Louisa, the more I think about that day, the more confused I get.

"I can understand my actions when I look at the incident through adult eyes ... picture a different seven-year-old boy in my place. But I knew it wasn't right for me to not get help. I knew that I should do something.

"If I look at my actions through my parents' eyes ... especially my father's ... what I did seems unforgivable.

"And if I look at it through my *grandfather's* eyes ..." Martin drew in a ragged breath and wiped his palm over his face. "I was dying. I know how that feels—to feel the blood draining from your body. But I had people working to help me. I've been trying to imagine what ... what it would have been like if those men had just sat and watched me die. What must it have been like for my grandfather, knowing he was dying, knowing I was sitting right beside him, but I wouldn't help him? I could see the disappointment—the anger in his eyes." He winced. "If I look at this through his eyes ..."

"Oh, Martin." Louisa took her husband's hand in hers and held it to her cheek. "Maybe you need to figure out whose eyes you should be looking through ... hmm?"

He glanced at her before turning his gaze back to the ceiling.

Ruth returned to the room a short time later. "Do you feel up to a visitor, Martin?" she asked as she handed Louisa her requested cup of tea.

Martin groaned, "Oh, not Penhale."

"No, it's Al. We have some business to take care of, and he came by to pick me up. Am I going to get an answer, or shall I make the decision for you?"

Martin scowled and fidgeted in the bed, trying to get himself sitting more upright. "*No.* It's fine."

Ruth waved her hand, signalling to her assistant.

Louisa, noting the apprehension in the young man's eyes, welcomed him into the room with a wave of her hand. "Come on in, Al. It's so nice to see you."

"Hullo Louiser ... Doc," Al said, giving them a nod of his head as he crammed his hands into his pockets and pulled up his shoulders. He stood awkwardly, trying not to let his eyes fall on the metallic hardware protruding from the doctor's arm, or the bulky brace supporting it.

"I guess I won't ask you how yer doin', Doc. That probably gets annoying, doesn't it?"

"Mm, yes." Martin ducked his head.

"So ... I see you got yer arm messed up. Ruth says you messed up yer legs, too."

After a long, awkward pause, Louisa stepped in to help her husband out with the impromptu exercise in rudimentary social skills.

"Yes, Al, he broke both legs. I'll leave it up to you, Martin, as to whether you want to play show and tell or not," Louisa said, squeezing her husband's shoulder lightly.

"Louisa, I'm not going to ..." He pulled the blankets up a bit higher.

"No worries, Doc. I don't do so good with that kind'a thing. Got some cuts on yer face that are still healin' too, I see."

"Mm." Martin's gaze shifted to his lap, as he brushed invisible lint from the blankets.

Louisa pulled a chair over next to the bed and gestured to the young man to take a seat. "So, Al, Ruth tells us you have business in Truro. It sounds like things are moving quickly with the changes you're making to the farm."

"Yeah, we gotta lot of work ta do yet, though. You and the doc should come out and see what we've done so far. When yer better, Doc."

"We'd love to do that, Al, wouldn't we Martin?" Louisa nodded at him and raised her eyebrows slightly.

"Mm, yes." Martin shifted, trying to find a more antalgic position. "Al, do you think you might be able to spare some time to help Ruth and Louisa move some things around before I come home?"

"Sure, Doc, whatever ya need. I could get Dad ta help out too, if you like."

"No, no, no, no, no. That's fine, Al. I don't think that'll be necessary." Martin grimaced at the thought of Bert, laid out on their sofa with his back in spasms, unable to leave their house.

James woke and was in need of a nappy change, so Ruth and Al said their goodbyes before the unpleasantries began. Louisa was just finishing with the baby's clean up when Tim Spalding knocked on the door. She excused herself to take the toddler to get a snack.

The therapist began with the usual range of motion exercises that had been done at previous sessions, slowly working to loosen Martin's muscles that continually contracted—the body's defence mechanism for protecting injured tissues.

"I spoke with Mr. Christianson yesterday about getting you ready this week to try out those legs. I'm going to work these muscles a little harder today and add in some resistance exercises. We'll also do some strengthening exercises with your arm."

Martin squeezed his eyes shut and swallowed hard. "Sounds like fun."

The therapist gave him a sympathetic smile. "Then I'm afraid you may be in for a letdown, mate. Tell me though when you feel like you can't tolerate any more."

Tim pushed his patient's limbs much farther than he ever had before, and Martin found himself unable to stifle the groans elicited by the movements. "Could we take a break?" he asked breathlessly.

"Yeah sure, let me get you a glass of water."

"So, what's your son's name?" the therapist asked as the tap squeaked.

"James," Martin snapped. Despite having a generally positive opinion of his physiotherapist, he found the young man's habit of conducting small talk while his patient was in pain, to be quite annoying.

"Is he walking yet?"

"Oh, for God's sake! Can we just get this done without all the contrived chit-chat?"

The therapist had been warned of Martin's tendency towards irritability, but this was the first he had seen it rear its ugly head. He dismissed the less than tactful remark and returned to the work at hand.

"All right, Dr. Ellingham, we're going to do something a little different. You can't do any weight bearing yet but we need to ease you in that direction. I'm going to push on your foot and I want you to try to resist me." The therapist held his patient's left heel in one hand and pushed against the bottom of his foot with the other. "Don't try to push back. Just keep your foot where it's at now. Let me be in control."

The unaccustomed pressure caused intense pain in the bones of Martin's leg, and he let a string of expletives slip from his mouth. The pain continued as Tim worked back and forth, but it became less intense with each manoeuver.

The same procedure was repeated with the opposite leg, and although the fractures in Martin's right leg were not as severe, femoral fractures are inherently painful, and his reaction reverberated down the corridor.

Louisa heard her husband as she was nearing the nurses station, and she hurried towards his room.

"Mrs. Ellingham! Wait, he's with the physiotherapist!" a nurse called to her.

Louisa forced herself to a stop outside the door, holding back tears as she listened to her husband's groans.

It soon grew quiet, and she walked down the hallway, stopping now and then to show James the pictures hanging on the walls. Tim emerged from Martin's room, heading in her direction.

"We just finished up, Mrs. Ellingham. It was an intense session today, so he's going to be pretty uncomfortable. I'll stop at the nurses' station and ask them to get some ice on him ... maybe some extra morphine. But hopefully we can get him upright by the end of the week."

"Thank you. Martin was adamant that he didn't want me here for his physiotherapy." She shifted James as he flopped to the side in an attempt to free himself from his restraints and get to the floor. "I think he probably knew best in this case, didn't he?"

"It would be difficult for you to watch, I'm sure. He's doing very well with it, though. And I'll take good care of him."

"I appreciate that ... very much," she said, giving the young man a weary smile.

Martin was trying to wipe himself down with a wet flannel when Louisa returned to his room. A nurse came in and took over, helping him into dry clothes before packing his limbs in ice.

"You look absolutely shattered Martin," Louisa said as soon as the nurse had left the room. "Are you all right?"

"I'm fine ... just tired."

She brushed her fingers through his sweaty hair. "Maybe James and I should head home ... let you sleep, hmm?"

Martin hated to see them go, but he didn't want them on the road after dark, and he *was* absolutely shattered.

Chapter 40

Louisa woke Monday morning feeling positive about the future. Martin's health was improving more rapidly now, and soon he would be home again.

There was a lot to get organised, but having the use of Ruth's cottage eliminated much of the work that would need to be done. She brought her list of tasks that she needed to complete to work with her, hoping to have some time here and there to make phone calls.

But the best laid plans often go awry. Halfway through the morning the year two teacher became ill and needed to leave. That meant that Louisa had to step in and teach that class. It would have been easier if it had been a class of older children; she could busy them with whatever was in the lesson plan schedule for the day. Teaching the little ones required her to be a bit more creative.

"All right, year two!" she said, clapping her hands together loudly. "Miss Soames can't be here to teach you because, as you know, she's not feeling well. But she has your lessons all ready for you, so we'll work on them together. Please get your science books out." There was a flurry of activity as books and papers were shuffled about in desks.

Louisa waited for the noise to die down before continuing. "Turn in your books to chapter three. Garrett, would you please take the first paragraph?"

The children took turns reading about the musculoskeletal system before their teacher went on to discuss the importance of proper nutrition in maintaining healthy muscles and bones.

"How many of you walked to school today?" Louisa asked. Three fourths of the hands shot up and waved about in the air.

"And what part of our bodies do we use to walk up and down all the big hills in our village?"

More hands were raised and Louisa pointed to a petite blonde girl in the first row. "Anna?"

"Our feet."

"Yes, we use our feet. And our feet are attached to our ...?"

There was a collective shout. "Legs!"

"Yes, and we have bones and muscles in our legs and the rest of our bodies that help us to do many, many things. Some bones and muscles help us to chew our food, some help us to breathe, and some help us to write in our exercise books or to colour beautiful pictures.

"But we have to take care of our bones and muscles, or they don't stay strong. We need nutritious foods, like milk and meat, which have calcium and protein. We also need the vitamins from other foods that help our bodies *use* the calcium and protein."

Louisa saw a hand pop up and she called on the girl. "Becky?"

"Is that what happened to Evan? He didn't eat the right stuff and his bones got weak?" the child asked, pointing to a small boy in the back of the room.

"Well, there are many reasons that bones break and muscles get weak. Evan, can you tell us how you broke your arm?"

The boy looked down at his desk and began to kick his foot back and forth. "I fell," he finally mumbled.

Louisa hesitated as she recalled Martin's conversation with her about a child who had been abused by his father. With all that had happened since that dinner out together, she hadn't made the connection. "Well, that's certainly one way for it to happen, isn't it class?"

A chorus of agreement echoed through the classroom.

"My mum said Dr. Ellingham broke *his* bones because he ran into a lorry," said Lydia Bigelow.

Louisa paused and nodded her head. "A lorry ran into him ... yes. But he's getting better every day, and soon he'll be back at the surgery to take care of you lot when you get sick or hurt. Now, get out your crayons, and I'll give you all a picture of our bones and muscles to colour. When you finish that, you can come up and get a blank sheet of paper from Miss Soames' desk and draw a picture of something that you use your bones and muscles to do. When you're done, bring them up and lay them on the table under the bulletin board. And work *quietly*, please."

Sitting down in the teacher's chair, Louisa busied herself with paperwork while waiting for the children to complete their assignment. Pippa Woodley stopped in a short time later, offering to relieve her of her substitute duties.

"Thanks, Pippa. I'll make it up to you with lunch someday," she said as she hurried out the door.

She rang up the number she'd been given for Cornwall Home Health Aide Services as soon as she got back to her office and scheduled interviews with several different potential candidates.

She was packing her satchel before heading home for the day when there was a knock on her door.

"Pippa, come in! How did it go with year two?"

"Fine, no problems. I just wanted to drop this off," she said as she laid a folded sheet of paper on Louisa's desk. "I found it in with the drawings the kids turned in today ... thought you'd want to pass it along to Dr. Ellingham."

Louisa pulled in her chin. "Oh? Thank you, Pippa. Have a good night."

"Yep, you too. See you in the mornin'."

Louisa opened the crudely folded piece of paper and couldn't help but smile. Yes, she did want to pass it on to Dr. Ellingham.

Martin had gotten very little rest the night before. The morphine had blunted the pain left by yesterday's physiotherapy session, but it had also made him edgy and had muddled his thinking. Ed Christianson had insisted on a nurse being present in his room at all times, which exacerbated his anxiety and irritability.

Sleep had proved elusive, and when he did drift off, his slumber was disrupted frequently by disturbing dreams and nightmares. He woke several times, confused by his surroundings, and he took out his frustrations on whichever unfortunate attendant happened to be in the room. By morning, both patient and hospital staff were relieved to see the light of day ease its way in through the window.

Mr. Christianson stopped in shortly after breakfast to remove Martin's sutures, replacing them with butterfly strips. "Things are looking good, Martin. The scary part's over I think, but now the hard part begins, eh?"

"Mm, yes. Therapy was ... difficult yesterday."

"Well, don't push yourself too hard. I told Tim Spalding to keep an eye on you, but he's not a mind reader. Don't try to hide the pain."

Ed pulled up a chair and took a seat. "How's everything else going ... keeping your spirits up?"

Martin shook his head. "I do fine most of the time, but there are times it gets discouraging."

"This one of those times?"

"Mm. It helps when my family's here, but they won't be back until Friday ... seems like a long way off."

"Hang in there, Martin. With any luck, we'll have you back home soon."

Chris dropped by over his lunch break, bringing with him a cup of espresso from the cafe near the hospital. "I thought you might like a little company," he said.

Martin reached for the control handset and raised the head of the bed.

"How was it to have James and Louisa here for the weekend?" Chris asked as he pulled a chair over and sat down.

"It was good. I think James has grown since I'd last seen him. Having Louisa here at night was ..." A wave of heat flashed through Martin's cheeks. "It was good."

"Yeah, I would imagine," Chris said giving him a roguish grin.

The two men sat silently for some seconds before Chris got up and began to fish around in the box of amusements he had brought in. He pulled out a board and a box filled with chess pieces.

"Care for a game?"

Martin raised his hand in the air apathetically. "Why not."

The chessmen scratched and tapped against the board as the two friends sat without saying a word to one another. Martin finally broke the silence.

"That book you gave me, Chris ... I didn't get a chance to thank you."

Chris allowed his concentration on the game to lapse as he peered up. "You're welcome, Mart. I'm sorry, though, if it upset you for some reason. That wasn't my intent."

Martin shifted his weight to his other hip. "No, no. I realise that. I should, erm ... explain. I ... well, it triggered a memory."

Chris leaned forward on to the bed rail. "Yes?"

Martin tapped one of his bishops against the checkerboard. "You already know about some of it. Do you remember my telling you about what my father said?"

"Yeah."

"That I thought it might be connected to when I broke my arm?"

Chris sat back down and propped his feet up on the bed. "Yeah. So, was there a connection?"

Martin breathed out a heavy sigh. "The book you gave me was the same book my grandfather gave me the day he died. He had a ruptured pulmonary aneurysm while I was alone in my father's study with him. He'd just given me a pocket watch to fix ... and the book," Martin said nodding his head towards the dresser top. "He kept pleading with me to get help, but my parents were having a row in the other room. I was afraid to open the door. So, I sat and watched him die."

Chris grimaced. "Hemoptysis? Massive blood loss?"

"Yeah," Martin said, rubbing his eyes in an effort to alleviate the ache that was intensifying behind them.

Chris blew out a breath of air. "What a gruesome thing for a little kid to witness, Mart. I'm sorry."

"Mm. I'd forgotten all about it for more than forty years, and now I can't get the images out of my head."

"Well, you're the vascular specialist. I don't have to tell you ... there was nothing that could be done. He would have been dead before the ambulance arrived."

Martin shook his head. "Not necessarily. I sat next to him for a long time. I suspect it started as a slow bleed. But I think it's the fact that I did nothing to help the man that I can't seem to deal with. I see his face all the time, Chris; the blood being pumped through his mouth, the fixed stare. I blink my eyes and it's there. I try to go to sleep and it's there. He's staring at me ... pleading for me to do something ... to get help. I could see in his eyes how disappointed he was in me."

Martin turned his head away as he blinked back tears. "I've tried to imagine what it would have been like if the paramedics had done what I did ... just sat and watched me bleed to death.

"And I think about what my grandfather must have thought of me ... how ashamed he must have been of me when I wouldn't help him. I know he was proud of me *before* that day, but he wasn't—"

Chris threw his head back. "You were a little kid Martin. Kids don't think like adults you know. You were in a no-win situation. You had no power over your hideous parents."

"Mm," Martin grunted before returning his attention to the game. He slid his bishop diagonally across the board to capture his opponent's knight. "I do appreciate the book, Chris. The copy my grandfather had given me disappeared. I suspect my father binned it. I never saw it after that day, so I do appreciate it ... very much."

"You're welcome, mate. I'm glad you like it." Chris stood up and gave his friend a small smile before moving his remaining knight forward. "I don't mean any disrespect to you, Martin. I hope you know that, but I can't think of two people I dislike more than your mum and dad."

"Mm, yes." Martin's queen tapped against the board as he moved it to the left.

"It was like they were bound and determined to break you. I mean, Mart, they did every bit as much emotional damage as that bloody lorry did physical damage." Chris stared at the red and black squares on the tray table, shaking his head before a smile spread across his face. "Good thing you're so damn ballsy."

Martin's cheeks grew warm again, and he pulled in his chin. "Are you going to move or not?"

Chris scratched at his head and then slapped his king down before giving his opponent a cocky grin. "Sorry, mate."

Martin shrugged his shoulders and studied the chessboard before glancing over at his friend. He tugged at his ear and then moved his rook to the side. "Checkmate."

Special Preview of "Fragile"—Book Three In The Battling Demons Series

An occupational therapist stopped in Martin's room that afternoon, introducing herself as Katie Gardner.

"I spoke with Tim Spalding," she said. "He worked your legs pretty hard yesterday evidently, so we'll give you a break today, and he can torture them some more tomorrow, hmm?" she said trying, unsuccessfully, to coax a smile from her patient.

The therapist went through several less painful exercises with him, having him touch each of his fingers to his thumb before resting his arm on the table while moving each digit up and down.

She then took out a box filled with items, varied in size and shape, and dumped them out on to the table. Martin's task was to pick them up, one by one, and return them to the box. Nerves had been damaged in the accident, leaving his arm and hand numb, and he found it maddeningly difficult to control his fine motor movements, often dropping the objects before they made it close to their final destination. The therapist had him close his eyes and feel around for the pieces before picking them up.

"I can't do this," he said, embarrassment and anxiety quickly building in him.

"Just keep trying, Dr. Ellingham. This will take time and practice."

Martin could hear the pieces rattling around on the table as he bumped them with his fingers, but he felt as if he was grasping at the air as he inadvertently knocked the items off on to the bed.

He was frustrated by his inability to perform such a simple task. All the pain and stresses of the last weeks, which he had managed to keep fairly well hidden up to this point, were bubbling to the surface. The exercise forced him to face the severity of the injury to his arm as well as the possible long-term consequences, and it terrified him.

It was all released in an explosion of emotion. He swept the objects from the table with his good hand, flinging them forcefully across the room. He then gave the tray table a mighty shove and sent it toppling to the floor.

"Get out! Bugger off and leave me alone! And take your infantile game with you!" he screamed as he pulled at his hair.

Katie could see both rage and fear in her patient's eyes and knew it would be best to leave him be for the moment. "I'll have someone come in after a bit to tidy up and help you with your brace," she said before slipping quietly from the room.

Martin collapsed back on the bed, feeling an immediate sense of shame for his behaviour. He waited until the door closed before fully releasing his emotions in ragged sobs.

Late that evening, Louisa's mobile rang and she pulled it from her pocket. A smile came to her face when she saw her husband's name on the screen. "Hello, Martin," she said breathlessly.

"Hello. Did I catch you at a bad time?"

"No, not at all. I just put James down for the night. How are you?" she asked as she sat down on the bottom step.

"Mm, it was a busy day, so I'm tired."

"A *busy* day? They don't have you seeing patients over there, do they?"

"Hmm?"

"Just a little joke, Martin. Not a very good one, I'm afraid." She brushed a wisp of hair from her eyes and tucked it behind her ear.

"Ah."

"So, what did they do with you today?"

"Ed removed most of my sutures this morning. Those in my left leg need to stay in for another week. And Chris stopped by. He talked me into a game of chess."

Louisa tried to picture the pair sitting together, contemplating their next move. "So ... who won?"

"Does it matter?" Martin asked. He wasn't a competitive person and never liked talking about his accomplishments, no matter how large or small.

"It does to me. I don't know if I could sleep tonight without knowing the final score," she said in jest.

"You don't keep score in chess, Louisa. It's not that kind of a game. You either win or you lose. The object is to—"

"Yes, Martin. I know."

"Ah, you were joking again."

"Mm, hmm. What else did you do today?"

Louisa heard a long sigh at the other end of the line before he began to talk. "An occupational therapist came in and discussed some considerations in regard to the move back home ... er, to Ruth's. Mostly ambulation issues."

Louisa waited anxiously for his next words. She could hear a despondency in his voice. "Martin, what is it? Something's wrong ... did something happen? Have you had another setback?"

"*No.* It's just that ...." He groaned. "I'm sorry, Louisa. I lost my temper with the occupational therapist."

"What do you mean, you lost your temper?" she asked, apprehensively.

"I embarrassed myself ... I threw some things ... yelled at her."

"Did he do something to upset you?"

"She ... it's a she. No, she was quite professional. I ... I .... Well, she dumped all these bits out on my tray table ... blocks, paper clips, pencils ... that sort of thing. She expected me to pick them up with my right hand and put them back in the box! It was so hard to get my fingers to function normally.

"Then she told me to close my eyes and do it and.... I *tried.* I really tried, but I couldn't do it. I couldn't even feel anything. I could feel the table a bit ... against my arm, but nothing with my fingers. I couldn't feel all those little pieces.

"It was so—so humiliating! I kept knocking things off on to the bed, but I wasn't able to pick a bloody thing up!"

Louisa leaned forward, her chin resting in her hand. "I'm sure that was unsettling."

"Unsettling! I've been hoping to have the option of performing surgery again. Now I'm finding myself wondering if I'll be able to practice medicine again! I can't even be a GP if I only have one usable hand. How would I suture cuts, reduce a dislocated shoulder, start an IV?" he sputtered. "What am I going to do if I can't even be a damn GP?"

"Martin, you're just getting started with the therapy. You need to give it time ... give your body time to heal. I can certainly understand why you're upset. This must be frightening for you. It is for me too, you know ... this not knowing the final outcome. But please understand this, Martin. I am only frightened for *you*, for how this will affect *you* ... mentally and physically. All I care about is whether or not you can be happy, and I'm afraid this accident will be the straw that breaks the camel's back!"

"I'm sorry, Louisa. I didn't intend to add to your worries. I didn't mean to do that." Martin was silent for several seconds before adding, "I'll be fine. I'm fine."

He shifted his weight from his right side. "I miss you when you're not here," he said softly. "I miss your warmth. I miss your softness ... your smell, the way you look at me."

Her husband had never expressed his desire for her so openly before, and Louisa didn't know if she should be swooning at his words or fearing for his mental state. "Are you alright, Martin?"

"I'll be fine, Louisa. If we're together, I'll be fine no matter what happens. When you're here I don't worry about this, but when you go back home, I start thinking that ..."

Louisa could hear a heavy sigh on the other end of the line.

"Martin, I promise you that I will *not* leave you. If it would help, I could just stay on the phone with you all day," she said facetiously.

"Mm, that wouldn't be very practical. You wouldn't get any work done. And if you're not getting any work done, you could just as well be here."

A small smile came to her face. "I know, Martin. Seriously, though, would you like me to come and stay with you until you can come home?"

What Martin wanted and what he knew to be sensible were two entirely different things. Louisa needed time to get things organised for his return, both at home and at school.

"No, I think you should stay there. I'm doing better now. It helps to hear your voice."

"Okay, but call me anytime you want to talk. I mean that, Martin. *Anytime.*"

"Mm, you may regret those words. I haven't been sleeping well lately, and I miss you, especially at night." He began to feel his tensions ease.

"I love you, Martin."

"I love you, too."

Don't miss out!

Click the button below and you can sign up to receive emails whenever Kris Morris publishes a new book. There's no charge and no obligation.

Sign Me Up!

https://books2read.com/r/B-A-PAJD-RCSK

BOOKS 2 READ

Connecting independent readers to independent writers.

Also by Kris Morris

Battling Demons
Battling Demons
Fractured
Fragile
Headway
Insights
A Cornwall Christmas

About the Author

Kris Morris was born and raised in a small Iowa town. She spent her childhood barely tolerating school, hand rearing orphaned animals, and squirrel taming. At Iowa State University she studied elementary education. But after discovering a loathing for traditional pedagogy and a love for a certain tall, handsome, Upstate New Yorker, she abandoned the academic life to marry, raise two sons, and become an unconventional piano teacher. When she's not writing, Kris builds boats and marimbas with her husband, who she has captivated for thirty years with her delightful personality, quick wit, and culinary masterpieces. They now reside in Iowa and have replaced their sons with ducks.

Read more at www.ktmorris.com.

Made in United States
North Haven, CT
24 January 2022

15229813R00188